Christopher Fowler, one of Britain's most highly regarded horror writers, is the author of eighteen published books, including the bestselling *Roofworld*, *Rune*, *Spanky*, *Psychoville* and *Disturbia*, as well as numerous screenplays and collections of short stories. He lives and works in London, where he runs The Creative Partnership, a Soho film promotion company.

Also by Christopher Fowler and published by Serpent's Tail

*Personal Demons*

'Gothic stories in a realist vein, a technique that allows Fowler to explore the pathologies of everyday life and remind us that people are much weirder than they're meant to be. Ian McEwan used to mine a similar seam; Fowler does it better' *Arena*

'Throughout this excellent collection there is a real sense of sophisticated Englishness' *SFX*

'A reassuring wallow among wolves, ghost trains and the whole Judeo-Christian brat pack of predestination and sin' *Guardian*

'His most complex and assured collection so far, with compelling plots, emotional resonance, bizarre invention, satires, fantasies, psychological fables and nightmares' *The Edge*

'A superb set of short stories. Just the right shade of black to have considerable appeal. As weird and wonderful as ever' *Bookseller*

'He consistently scores points with his suave, mocking and ultimately inclusive voice. His latest collection of short stories shows he has lost none of his venom' *i-D*

'Bleak as these stories are, they all pay tribute to the resilience and courage of the human spirit' *British Fantasy Society*

'Compulsive – gruesome, gory and great fun' *Time Out*

'Ghoulishly irresistible' *The Times*

# THE DEVIL
# IN ME

◆

## SHORT STORIES
## BY
## CHRISTOPHER FOWLER

Library of Congress Catalog Card Number: 2001087181

A complete catalogue record for this book can
be obtained from the British Library on request

The right of Christopher Fowler to be identified as the author of this
work has been asserted by him in accordance with the Copyright,
Designs and Patents Act 1988

First published in 2001 by Serpent's Tail,
4 Blackstock Mews, London N4 2BT

Website: www.serpentstail.com

Phototypeset in 10pt Sabon by Intype London Ltd
Printed in Great Britain by
Mackays of Chatham plc, Chatham, Kent

10 9 8 7 6 5 4 3 2 1

# CONTENTS

'There's a devil in me
sometimes
that spells danger
I become a stranger
you've never ever seen before.
...This means war.'
David Heneker

# FOREWORD: FLARE GUNS

Welcome to my seventh collection of short stories. Looking back through previous volumes, most notably *Personal Demons*, I'm surprised to see how many tales acted as springboards into novels. It seems an odd way to go about the writing process, firing off little rockets before sending up a flare, but I've grown to like it.

In the early days, I wrote horror stories; they were generally quite simple in structure, and you could soon tell if you'd managed to produce the effect you wanted. The settings were mostly urban, rarely supernatural and often contained an element of black comedy. I expanded certain themes, experimented a bit and ended up here, which is to say somewhere else, in my own peculiar territory. This collection is so far removed from the first as to contain no traditional horror stories at all, although there are many echoes. The genre still appeals immensely to me, but I feel I've pretty much covered the bases, both in terms of what I've read and what I've written.

Horror is often seen as an adolescent roadhouse on the way to more sophisticated forms of entertainment, probably because it starts to appeal at an early age. The young are far from the threat of death, and have suffered no intimations of mortality. They're flexing their imaginations for the first time, opening their minds, exploring the boundaries of speculative fiction in order to explain their own feelings. Each time we read, see or experience something that appeals, we drive another fencepost into the map of the imagination in an effort to discern its topography. I think authors have to meet their readers halfway in this mapping process, which makes writing a craft first, then an art. It doesn't inhibit your ideas, but it does give them a shape.

Among the questions I'm most often asked are 'Do you write under your own name?', which is a polite way of saying 'I've never heard of you', and 'What have you written that I've read?', to which I reply that I'm a writer, not a mind-reader. But I guess I should be thankful that anyone is reading at all, given the fracturing of leisure time that occurs in the average household. Anyone who has wasted several hours trying to find the right software to download something from an obscure website when they were meant to be writing will testify to this. And writing takes time. You have to reduce hours spent drinking or watching television or making phonecalls. When Samuel Beckett was asked what he had given up for his art, he replied; 'I have fairly often not gone to parties.' So much for the struggling artist.

Readers often say they like stories that refuse labels – because the trick is to entertain first, then pose questions. Much SF does this, speculating from within an exotic framework – one thinks of Alfred Bester, Joe Haldeman, J. G. Ballard or Christopher Priest. The books and films we enjoy most touch universal feelings. There's no simple template for a human being; you prove this when you ask someone 'What was the last thing that made you laugh?'

Film is a touchstone for me because it evokes strong instant responses – reading is a more private pleasure – so I find it easier to draw film analogies. Back in 1968, Michael Reeves made a film called *Witchfinder General*. Based on a forgotten historical figure, it was scripted from a very dull book, produced for peanuts, directed through a troubled shoot by a barely-experienced 23-year-old, and starred a hopelessly miscast actor because the backers wanted him to play the lead.

Over thirty years later, the film is still on critics' lists. Why? It is highly atmospheric, with a fatalistic plot and an elegant score, but the devil is in the details. For instance, there's a scene where the heroine agrees to meet Vincent Price in her room in order to spare her father's life. She must seduce the lustful witchfinder, but Price is visibly shocked when she makes herself available, because her actions go against the grain of human nature. The director had thought carefully about that moment – it's not in the script – and directed Price to react accordingly. The film is precise in its effects, as stories should be. It would not have been made today – too marginal, too visceral, too uncommercial – but it was finally acclaimed because it illuminates. Like it or not, there are few better representations of the English countryside on film. It's our loss that Reeves died tragically at the age of twenty-five.

So what is weird yesterday is mainstream tomorrow. Dross is everywhere, gems are hidden. But it's like searching through paperback piles in car boot sales – isn't it always more satisfying to find something of quality after you've had to work for it?

So you can't find James Blish or John Collier or Ian Watson (or a hundred other marvellous authors) in print, but Stephen King's entire output is available in emerging nations. Perhaps that's the point; the canon of creativity repeats itself in endless variation. The learning curve starts again the moment we breed, and as every generation demands its own style, perhaps it is wrong to look back. Still, the John Collier Reader contains fifty unique stories and remains a touchstone volume, but I doubt you can find it in any modern bookstore.

For me one of the greatest pleasures will always be the rooting out of oddities. The first six books I can reach from this keyboard are Ian R. MacLeod's *The Great Wheel*, Brian Moore's *The Great Victorian Collection*, Magnus Mills's *All Quiet on the Orient Express*, Marguerite Yourcenar's *Oriental Tales*, Maurice Richardson's *The Chronicles of the Surrealist Sportsman's Club* and Peter Tinniswood's *The Stirk of Stirk*, and five of them are hard to find. This is not obscurity for obscurity's sake; they are simply good books, epic, haunting, discomfiting, elegant, bizarre, amusing. Typically, Mr MacLeod is an astonishingly talented English writer whose work is rarely published in his home country. I hope these authors prove to be tomorrow's mainstream. I believe that the true picture of anything lies in its barely registered peripheries.

So, if yesterday's weird *is* tomorrow's mainstream, what's the present?

This is the present. Open it.

The English treat London in the same way that they treat their language; with a certain amount of healthy disrespect. We like new words and new buildings, and see no reason why they should not coexist with the old. When I was commissioned to produce a tale for 'Vox 'N' Roll' I decided to write something that would foreground the location rather than the main character. I'm always making lists, and love exploring cities. I limited myself to thirteen sites in one city, as I had with an earlier story called 'Thirteen Places of Interest in Kentish Town'. This is how it worked out.

# AT HOME IN THE PUBS OF OLD LONDON

## THE MUSEUM TAVERN, MUSEUM STREET, BLOOMSBURY

Despite its location diagonally opposite the British Museum, its steady turnover of listless Australian barstaff and its passing appraisal by tourists on quests for the British pub experience (comprising two sips from half a pint of bitter and one Salt 'N' Vinegar flavoured crisp, nibbled and returned to its packet in horror), this drinking establishment retains the authentically seedy bookishness of Bloomsbury because its corners are usually occupied by half-cut proofreaders from nearby publishing houses. I love pubs like this one because so much about them remains constant in a sliding world; the smell of hops, the ebb of background conversation, muted light through coloured glass, china tap handles, mirrored walls, bars of oak and brass. Even the pieces of fake Victoriana, modelled on increasingly obsolete pub ornaments, become objects of curiosity in themselves.

At this time I was working in a comic shop, vending tales of fantastic kingdoms to whey-faced netheads who were incapable of saving a sandwich in a serviette, let alone an alien planet, and it was in this pub that I met Leslie. She was sitting with a group of glum-looking gothic Gormenghast offcuts who were on their way to a book launch at the new-age smells 'n' bells shop around the corner, and she was clearly unenchanted with the idea of joining them for a session of warm Liebfraumilch and crystal-gazing, because as each member of the group drifted off she found an excuse to stay on, and we ended up sitting together by ourselves. As she refolded her jacket a rhinestone pin dropped from the lapel, and I picked it up for her. The badge formed her initials – L. L – which made me think of Superman, because he had a history of falling for women with those initials, but I reminded myself that I was no superman, just a man who liked making friends in pubs. I asked her if she'd had a good Christmas, she said no, I said I hadn't either and we just chatted from there. I told Leslie that I was something of an artist and would love to sketch her, and she tentatively agreed to sit for me at some point in the future.

## THE WORLD'S END, HIGH STREET, CAMDEN TOWN

It's a funny pub, this one, because the interior brickwork makes it look sort of inside out, and there's a steady through-traffic of punters wherever you stand, so you're always in the way. It's not my kind of place, more a network of bars and clubs than a proper boozer. It used to be called the Mother Red Cap, after a witch who lived in Camden. There are still a few of her pals inhabiting the place if black eyeliner, purple lipstick and pointed boots make you a likely candidate for cauldron-stirring. A white stone statue of Britannia protrudes from the first floor of the building opposite, above a shoe shop, but I don't think anyone notices it, just as they don't know about the witch. Yet if you step inside the foyer of the Black Cap, a few doors further down, you can see the witch herself, painted on a tiled wall. It's funny how people miss so much of what's going on around them. I was beginning to think Sophie wouldn't show up, then I became convinced she had, and I had missed her.

Anyway, she finally appeared and we hit it off beautifully. She had tied back her long auburn hair so that it was out of her eyes, and I couldn't stop looking at her. It's never difficult to find new models; women are flattered by the thought of someone admiring their features. She half-smiled all the time, which was disconcerting at first, but after a while I enjoyed it because she looked like she was in on a secret that no-one else shared. I had met her two days earlier in the coffee shop in Bermondsey where she was working, and she had suggested going for a drink, describing our meeting place to me as 'that pub in Camden near the shoe shop'. The one thing Camden has, more than any other place in London, is shoe shops, hundreds of the bastards, so you can understand why I was worried.

It was quite crowded and we had to stand, but after a while Sophie felt tired and wanted to sit down, so we found a corner and wedged ourselves in behind a pile of coats. The relentless music was giving me a headache, so I was eventually forced to take my leave.

## THE KING'S HEAD, UPPER STREET, ISLINGTON

The back of this pub operates a tiny theatre, so the bar suddenly fills up with the gin-and-tonic brigade at seven each evening, but the front room is very nice in a battered, nicotine-scoured way. It continued to operate on the old monetary system of pounds, shillings and pence for years, long after they brought in decimal currency. I'm sure the management just did it to confuse non-regulars who weren't in the habit of being asked to stump up nineteen and elevenpence halfpenny for a libation. Emma was late, having been forced to stay behind at her office, a property company in Essex Road. The choice of territory was mine. Although it was within walking distance of her office she hadn't been here before, and loved hearing this mad trilling coming from a door at the back of the pub. I'd forgotten to explain about the theatre. They were staging a revival of a twenties musical, and there were a lot of songs about croquet and how ghastly foreigners were. I remember Emma as being very pale and thin, with cropped blonde hair; she could easily have passed for a jazz-age flapper. I told her she should have auditioned for the show, but she explained that she was far too fond of a drink to ever remember anything as complicated as a dance step. At the intermission, a girl dressed as a giant sequinned jellyfish popped out to order a gin and French; apparently she had a big number in the second act. We taxed the barman's patience by getting him to make up strange cocktails, and spent most of the evening laughing so loudly they probably heard us on stage. Emma agreed to sit for me at some point in the future, and although there was never a suggestion that our session would develop into anything more, I could tell that it probably would. I was about to kiss her when she suddenly thought something had bitten her, and I was forced to explain that my coat had picked up several fleas from my cat. She went off me after this, and grew silent, so I left.

## THE PINEAPPLE, LEVERTON STREET, KENTISH TOWN

This tucked-away pub can't have changed much in a hundred years, apart from the removal of the wooden partitions that separated the snug from the saloon. A mild spring morning, the Sunday papers spread out before us, an ancient smelly labrador flatulating in front of the fire, a couple of pints of decent bitter and two packets of pork scratchings. Sarah kept reading out snippets from the *News Of The World*, and I did the same with the *Observer*, but mine were more worthy than hers, and therefore not as funny. There was a strange man with an enormous nose sitting near the gents' toilet who kept telling people that they looked Russian. Perhaps he was, too, and needed to find someone from his own country. It's that kind of pub; it makes you think of home.

I noticed that one of Sarah's little habits was rubbing her wrists together when she was thinking. Every woman has some kind of private signature like this. Such a gesture marks her out to a lover, or an old friend. I watched her closely scanning the pages – she had forgotten her glasses – and felt a great inner calm. Only once did she disturb the peace between us by asking if I had been out with many women. I lied, of course, as you do, but the question remained in the back of my head, picking and scratching at my brain, right up until I said goodbye to her. It was warm in the pub and she had grown sleepy; she actually fell asleep at one point, so I decided to quietly leave.

## THE ANCHOR, PARK STREET, SOUTHWARK

It's pleasant here on rainy days. In the summer, tourists visiting the nearby Globe fill up the bars and pack the riverside tables. Did you know that pub signs were originally provided so that the illiterate could locate them? The Anchor was built after the Southwark fire, which in 1676 razed the South Bank just as the Great Fire had attacked the North side ten years earlier. As I entered the pub, I noticed that the tide was unusually high, and the Thames was so dense and pinguid that it looked like a setting jelly. It wasn't a good start to the evening.

I had several pints of strong bitter and grew more talkative as our session progressed. We ate Toad-In-The-Hole, smothered in elastic gravy. I was excited about the idea of Carol and I going out together. I think she was, too, although she warned me that she had some loose ends to tie up, a former boyfriend to get out of her system, and suggested that perhaps we shouldn't rush at things. Out of the blue, she told me to stop watching her so much, as if she was frightened that she couldn't take the scrutiny. But she can. I love seeing the familiar gestures of women, the half-smiles, the rubbing together of their hands, the sudden light in their eyes when they remember something they have to tell you. I can't remember what they say, only how they look. I would never take pictures of them, like some men I've read about. I never look back, you understand. It's too upsetting. Far more important to concentrate on who you're with, and making them happy. I'd like to think I made Carol feel special. She told me she'd never had much luck with men, and I believe it's true that some women just attract the wrong sort. We sat side by side watching the rain on the water, and I felt her head lower gently onto my shoulder, where it remained until I moved – a special moment, and one that I shall always remember.

## THE LAMB & FLAG, ROSE STREET, COVENT GARDEN

You could tell summer was coming because people were drinking on the street, searching for spaces on the windowsills of the pub to balance their beerglasses. This building looks like an old coaching inn, and stands beside an arch over an alleyway, like the Pillars Of Hercules in Greek Street. It's very old, with lots of knotted wood, and I don't suppose there's a straight angle in the place. The smoky bar is awkward to negotiate when you're carrying a drink in either hand – as I so often am!

This evening Kathy asked why I had not invited her to meet any of my friends. I could tell by the look on her face that she was wondering if I thought she wasn't good enough, and so I was forced to admit that I didn't really have any friends to whom I could introduce her. She was more reticent than most of the girls I had met until then, more private. She acted as though there was something on her mind that she didn't want to share with me. When I asked her to specify the problem, she either wouldn't or couldn't. To be honest, I think the problem was me, and that was why it didn't work out between us. Something about my behaviour made her uneasy, right from the start. There was no trust between us, which in itself was unusual, because most women are quick to confide in me. They sense my innate decency, my underlying respect for them. I look at the other drinkers standing around me, and witness the contempt they hold for women. My god, a blind man could feel their disdain. That's probably why I have no mates – I don't like my own sex. I'm ashamed of the whole alpha male syndrome. It only leads to trouble.

I made the effort of asking Kathy if she would sit for me, but knew in advance what the answer would be. She said she would prefer it if we didn't meet again, and yelped in alarm when I brushed against her hip, so I had to beat a hasty retreat.

## THE KING WILLIAM IV, HIGH STREET, HAMPSTEAD

Paula chose this rather paradoxical pub. It's in the middle of Hampstead, therefore traditional and oaky, with a beer garden that was packed on a hot summer night, yet the place caters to a raucous gay clientele. Apparently, Paula's sister brought her here once before, an attractive girl judging from the photograph Paula showed me and such a waste, I feel, when she could be making a man happy. I wondered if, after finishing with Paula, I should give her sister a call, but decided that it would be playing a little too close to home.

We sat in the garden on plastic chairs, beside sickly flowerbeds of nursery-forced plants, but it was pleasant, and the pub had given me an idea. I resolved to try someone of the same gender next time, just to see what a difference it made. I picked up one of the gay newspapers lying in stacks at the back of the pub, and made a note of other venues in central London. I explained my interest in the newspaper by saying that I wanted to learn more about the lifestyles of others. Paula squeezed my hand and said how much she enjoyed being with someone who had a liberal outlook. I told her that my policy was live and let live, which is a laugh for a start. I am often shocked by the wide-eyed belief I inspire in women, and wonder what they see in me that makes them so trusting. When I pressed myself close against her she didn't flinch once under my gaze, and remained staring into my eyes while I drained my beerglass. A special girl, a special evening, for both of us.

## THE ADMIRAL DUNCAN, OLD COMPTON STREET, SOHO

Formerly decorated as a cabin aboard an old naval vessel, with lead-light bay windows and a curved wood ceiling, this venue was revamped to suit the street's new status as a home to the city's homosexuals, and painted a garish purple. It was restored again following the nail-bomb blast that killed and maimed so many of its customers. Owing to the tunnel-like shape of the bar, the explosive force had nowhere to escape but through the glass front, and caused horrific injuries. A monument to the tragedy is inset in the ceiling of the pub, but no atmosphere of tragedy lingers, for the patrons, it seems, have bravely moved on in their lives. In here I met Graham, a small-boned young man with a gentle West Country burr that seemed at odds with his spiky haircut. We became instant drinking pals, buying each other rounds in order to escape the evening heat of the mobbed street beyond. After what had occurred in the pub I found it astonishing that someone could be so incautious as to befriend a total stranger such as myself, but that is the beauty of the English boozer; once you cross the threshold, barriers of race, class and gender can be dropped. Oh, it doesn't happen everywhere, I know, but you're more likely to make a friend in this city than in most others. That's why I find it so useful in fulfilling my needs. However, the experiment with Graham was not a success. Boys don't work for me, no matter how youthful or attractive they appear to be. We were standing in a corner, raising our voices over the incessant thump of the jukebox, when I realised it wasn't working. Graham had drunk so much that he was starting to slide down the wall, but there were several others in the vicinity who were one step away from being paralytic, so he didn't stick out, and I could leave unnoticed.

## THE BLACK FRIAR, QUEEN VICTORIA STREET, BLACKFRIARS

This strange little pub, stranded alone by the roundabout on the North side of the river at Blackfriars, has an Arts and Crafts style interior, complete with friezes, bas-reliefs and mottos running over its arches. Polished black monks traipse about the room, punctuating the place with moral messages. It stands as a memorial to a vanished London, a world of brown trilbys and woollen overcoats, of rooms suffused with pipe smoke and the tang of brilliantine. In the snug bar at the rear I met Danielle, a solidly-built Belgian au pair who looked so lonely, lumpen and forlorn that I could not help but offer her a drink, and she was soon pouring out her troubles in broken English. Her employers wanted her to leave because she was pregnant, and she couldn't afford to go back to Antwerp.

To be honest I wasn't listening to everything she was saying, because someone else had caught my eye. Seated a few stools away was a ginger-haired man who appeared to be following our conversation intently. He was uncomfortably overweight, and undergoing some kind of perspiration crisis. The pub was virtually deserted, most of the customers drinking outside on the pavement, and Danielle was talking loudly, so it was possible that she might have been overheard. I began to wonder if she was lying to me about her problems; if perhaps they were more serious than she made them sound, serious enough for someone to be following her. I know it was selfish, but I didn't want to spend any more time with a girl who was in that kind of trouble, so I told her I needed to use the toilet, then slipped out across the back of the bar.

## THE ANGEL, ROTHERHITHE

Another old riverside inn – I seem to be drawn to them, anxious to trace the city's sluggish artery site by site, as though marking a pathway to the heart. The interesting thing about places like The Angel is how little they change across the decades, because they retain the same bleary swell of customers through all economic climates. Workmen and stockbrokers, estate agents, secretaries, van-drivers and tarts, they just rub along together with flirtatious smiles, laughs, belches and the odd sour word. The best feature of this pub is reached by the side entrance, an old wooden balcony built out over the shoreline, where mud-larks once rooted in the filth for treasure trove, and where you can sit and watch the sun settling between the pillars of Tower Bridge.

As the light faded we become aware of the sky brushing the water, making chilly ripples. Further along the terrace I thought I saw the red-haired man watching, but when I looked again, he had gone. Growing cold, we pulled our coats tighter, then moved inside. Stella was Greek, delicate and attractive, rather too young for me, but I found her so easy to be with that we remained together for the whole evening. Shortly before closing time she told me she should be going home soon because her brother was expecting her. I was just massaging some warmth back into her arms – we were seated by an open window and it had suddenly turned nippy – when she said she felt sick, and went off to the Ladies. After she failed to reappear I went to check on her, just to make sure she was all right. I found her in one of the cubicles, passed out.

## THE SHIP, GREENWICH

The dingy interior of this pub is unremarkable, with bare-board floors and tables cut from blackened barrels, but the exterior is another matter entirely. I can imagine the building, or one very like it, existing on the same site for centuries, at a reach of the river where it is possible to see for miles in either direction. I am moving out toward the mouth of the Thames, being taken by the tide to ever-widening spaces in my search for absolution. There was something grotesquely Victorian about the weeds thrusting out of ancient brickwork, the tumbledown fences and the stink of the mud. It was unusually mild for the time of year, and we sat on the wall with our legs dangling over the water, beers propped at our crotches.

Melanie was loud and common, coarse-featured and thick-legged. She took up room in the world, and didn't mind who knew it. She wore a lot of makeup, and had frothed her hair into a mad dry nest, but I was intrigued by the shape of her mouth, the crimson wetness of her lips, her cynical laugh, her seen-it-all-before eyes. She touched me as though expecting me to walk out on her at any moment, digging nails on my arm, nudging an elbow in my ribs, running fingers up my thigh. Still, I wondered if she would present a challenge, because I felt sure that my offer to sketch her would be rebuffed. She clearly had no interest in art, so I appealed to her earthier side and suggested something of a less salubrious nature.

To my surprise she quoted me a price list, which ruined everything. I swore at her, and pushed her away, disgusted. She, in turn, began calling me every filthy name under the sun, which attracted unwanted attention to both of us. It was then that I saw the ginger-headed man again, standing to the left of me, speaking into his chubby fist.

## THE TRAFALGAR TAVERN, GREENWICH

I ran. Tore myself free of her and ran off along the towpath, through the corrugated iron alley beside the scrap-yard and past the defunct factory smoke-stacks, keeping the river to my right. On past The Yacht, too low-ceilinged and cosy to lose myself inside, to the doors of The Trafalgar, a huge gloomy building of polished brown interiors, as depressing as a church. Inside, the windows of the connecting rooms were dominated by the gleaming grey waters beyond. Nobody moved. Even the bar staff were still. It felt like a funeral parlour. I pushed between elderly drinkers whose movements were as slow as the shifting of tectonic plates, and slipped behind a table where I could turn my seat to face the river. I thought that if I didn't move, I could remain unnoticed. In the left pocket of my jacket I still had my sketchbook. I knew it would be best to get rid of it, but didn't have the heart to throw it away, not after all the work I had done.

When I heard the muttered command behind me, I knew that my sanctuary had been invaded and that it was the beginning of the end. I sat very still as I watched the red-headed man approaching from the corner of my eye, and caught the crackle of radio headsets echoing each other around the room. I slowly raised my head, and for the first time saw how different it all was now. A bare saloon bar filled with tourists, no warmth, no familiarity, no comfort.

When I was young I sat on the step – every pub seemed to have a step – with a bag of crisps and a lemonade, and sometimes I was allowed to sit inside with my Dad, sipping his bitter and listening to his beery laughter, the demands for fresh drinks, the dirty jokes, the outraged giggles of the girls at his table. They would tousle my hair, pinch my skinny arms and tell me that I was adorable. Different pubs, different women, night after night, that was my real home, the home I remember. Different pubs but always the same warmth, the same smells, the same songs, the same women. Everything about them was filled with smoky mysteries and hidden pleasures, even their names, The World Turned Upside Down, The Queen's Head And Artichoke, The Rose And Crown, The Greyhound, The White Hart, all of them had secret meanings.

People go to clubs for a night out now, chrome and steel, neon lights, bottled beers, drum and bass, bouncers with headsets. The bars sport names like The Lounge and The Living Room, hoping to evoke a sense of belonging, but they cater to an alienated world, squandering noise and light on people so blinded by work that their leisure-time must be spent in aggression, screaming at each other, shovelling drugs, pushing for fights. As the red-haired man moved closer, I told myself that all I wanted to do was make people feel at home. Is that so very wrong? My real home was nothing, the memory of a damp council flat with a stinking disconnected fridge and dogshit on the floor. It's the old pubs of London that hold my childhood; the smells, the sounds, the company. There is a moment before the last bell is called when it seems it could all go on forever. It is that moment I try to capture and hold in my palm. I suppose you could call it the land before Time.

## THE LOAD OF HAY, HAVERSTOCK HILL, BELSIZE PARK

The red-haired officer wiped at his pink brow with a Kleenex until the tissue started to come apart. Another winter was approaching, and the night air was bitter. His wife used to make him wear a scarf when he was working late, and it always started him sweating. She had eventually divorced him. He dressed alone now and ate takeaway food in a tiny flat. But he wore the scarf out of habit. He looked in through the window of the pub at the laughing drinkers at the bar, and the girl sitting alone beside the slot-machine. Several of his men were in there celebrating a colleague's birthday, but he didn't feel like facing them tonight.

How the hell had they let him get away? He had drifted from them like bonfire smoke in changing wind. The Trafalgar had too many places where you could hide, he saw that now. His men had been overconfident and undertrained. They hadn't been taught how to handle anyone so devious, or if they had, they had forgotten what they had learned.

He kept one of the clear plastic ampoules in his pocket, just to remind himself of what he had faced that night. New technology had created new hospital injection techniques. You could scratch yourself with the micro-needle and barely feel a thing, if the person wielding it knew how to avoid any major nerve-endings. Then it was simply a matter of squeezing the little bulb, and any liquid contained in the ampoule was delivered through a coat, a dress, a shirt, into the flesh. Most of his victims were drunk at the time, so he had been able to connect into their bloodstreams without them noticing more than a pinprick. A deadly mixture of RoHypnol, Zimovane and some kind of coca-derivative. It numbed and relaxed them, then sent them to sleep. But the sleep deepened and stilled their hearts, as a dreamless caul slipped over their brains, shutting the senses one by one until there was nothing left alive inside.

No motives, no links, just dead strangers in the most public places in the city, watched by roving cameras, filled with witnesses. That was the trouble; you expected to see people getting legless in pubs.

His attention was drawn back to the girl sitting alone. What was she doing there? Didn't she realise the danger? No-one heeded the warnings they issued. There were too many other things to worry about.

He had been on the loose for a year now, and had probably moved on to another city, where he could continue his work without harassment. He would stop as suddenly as he had begun. He'd dropped a sketchbook, but it was filled with hazy pencil drawings of pub interiors, all exactly the same, and told them nothing. The only people who would ever really know him were the victims – and perhaps even they couldn't see behind their killer's eyes. As the urban landscape grew crazier, people's motives were harder to discern. An uprooted population, on the make and on the move. Fast, faster, fastest.

And for the briefest of moments he held the answer in his hand. He saw a glimmer of the truth – a constancy shining like a shaft through all the change, the woman alone in the smoky saloon, smiling and interested, her attention caught by just one man, this intimacy unfolding against a background warmth, the pulling of pints, the blanket of conversation, the huddle of friendship – but then it was gone, all gone, and the terrible sense of unbelonging filled his heart once more.

*I keep a notebook for ideas, as I'm sure most writers do, and rediscovered a suggestion made in one that set a story in the underground system. It can be very confusing finding your way around the London Underground, as anyone switching from the District & Circle to the Northern Line will know. I thought it would be a good place to test someone's mettle, and wondered how much harder it would be if you hated being there and were looking after loads of children.*

# CROCODILE LADY

## 1. FINCHLEY ROAD TO SWISS COTTAGE

*London has the oldest underground railway system in the world. Construction began in 1863 and was completed in 1884. Much later it was electrified, and since then has been periodically modified. A great many of the original stations have been abandoned, renamed or resited. A partial list of these would include Aldwych, British Museum, Brompton Road, York Road, St Mary's, Down Street, Marlborough Road, South Kentish Town, King William Street, North End and City Road. In many cases the maroon-tiled ticket halls remain, and so do the railway platforms. Even now, some of these tunnels are adorned with faded wartime signs and posters. Crusted with dry melanic silt produced by decades of still air, the walls boom softly as trains pass in nearby tunnels, but the stations themselves no longer have access from the streets above, and are only visited by scuttling brown mice. If you look hard, though, you can glimpse the past. For example, the eerie green and cream platform of the old Mark Lane station can be spotted from passing trains to the immediate west of the present Tower Hill Station.*

'You know what gets me through the day? Hatred. I hate the little bastards. Each and every one of them. Most of the time I wish they would all just disappear.' Deborah fixed me with a cool eye. 'Yeah, I know it's not the best attitude for a teacher to have, but when you know them as well as I do . . .'

'I think I do,' I replied.

'Oh? I thought this work was new to you. Being your first day and all.'

'Not new, no.'

'My boyfriend just decided he wants us to have kids. He never liked them before. When he was made redundant he started picking me up from school in the afternoons, and saw them running around my legs in their boots and rainmacs asking endless questions, and suddenly he thought they were cute and wanted to have a baby, just when I was thinking of having my tubes tied. I don't want to bring my work home with me. We still haven't sorted it out. It's going to ruin our relationship. Hey, hey.' Deborah broke off to shout at a boy who was trying to climb over the barrier. 'Get back down there and wait for the man to open the gate.' She turned back to me. 'Christ, I could use a cigarette. Cover for me when we get there. I'll sneak a couple in while they're baiting the monkeys, that's what all the other teachers do.'

Good teachers are like good nurses. They notice things ordinary people miss. Ask a nurse how much wine she has left in her glass and she'll be able to tell you the exact amount, because for her the measurement of liquids is a matter of occupational observation. The same with teachers. I can tell the age of any child to within six months because I've been around them so much. Then I got married, and I wasn't around them anymore.

But old habits die hard. You watch children constantly, even when you think you're not, and the reflex continues to operate even in civilian life. You bump into pupils in the supermarket. 'Hello, Miss, we didn't know you ate food.' They don't quite say that, but you know it's what they're thinking.

If there's one thing I know it's how children think. That was why I noticed there was something wrong at Baker Street. My senses had been caught off guard because of the tunnels. Actually, I sensed something even before then, as early as our arrival at Finchley Road tube station. I should have acted on my instincts.

God knows, I was nervous enough to begin with. It was the first day of my first week back at work after twelve long years, and I hadn't expected to have responsibility thrust at me like this, but the school was understaffed, teachers were off sick and the headmaster needed all the help he could get. The last time I had worked in the education system, the other teachers around me were roughly of the same age. Now I was old enough to be a mother to most of them, and a grandmother to their charges. I wouldn't have returned to Invicta Primary at all if my husband hadn't died. I wasn't surprised when the bank warned me that there would be no money. Peter wasn't exactly a rainy-day hoarder. I needed to earn, and have something to keep my mind occupied. Teaching was the only skill I was sure I still possessed.

Which was how I ended up shepherding twenty seven-to-eight-year-old boys and girls on a trip to the London Zoological Gardens, together with another teacher, Deborah, a girl with a tired young face and a hacking smoker's cough.

I hadn't been happy about handling the excursion on my first day back, especially when I heard that it involved going on the tube. I forced myself not to think about it. There were supposed to be three of us but the other teacher was off with flu, and delaying the trip meant dropping it from the term schedule altogether, so the headmaster had decreed that we should go ahead with the original plan. There was nothing unusual in this; the teaching shortage had reached its zenith and I'd been eagerly accepted back into the school where I'd worked before I was married. They put me on a refresher course, mostly to do with computer literacy, but the basic curriculum hadn't changed much. But things were very different from when I was a pupil myself. For a start, nobody walked to the school any more. Parents didn't think it was safe. I find parents exasperating – all teachers do. They're very protective about some things, and yet utterly blind to other, far more obvious problems. If they found out about the short-staffed outings, everybody would get it in the neck. The parents had been encouraged to vote against having their children driven around in a coach; it wasn't environ-

mentally friendly. It didn't stop them from turning up at the
school gates in people-carriers, though.

Outside the station the sky had lowered into muddy swirls of
cloud, and it was starting to rain. Pupils are affected by the
weather. They're always disruptive and excitable when it's
windy. Rain makes them sluggish and inattentive. (In snow they
go mad and you might as well close the school down.) You get
an eye for the disruptives and outsiders, and I quickly spotted
the ones in this group, straggling along at the rear of the tube
station hall. In classrooms they sit at the back in the corners,
especially on the left-hand side, the sneaky, quiet troublemakers.
They feel safe because you tend to look to the centre of the
class, so they think they're less visible. Kids who sit in the front
row are either going to work very hard or fall in love with you.
But the ones at the rear are the ones to watch, especially when
you're turning back towards the blackboard.

There were four of them, a pair of hunched, whispering girls
as close as Siamese twins, a cheeky ginger-haired noisebox with
his hands in everything, and a skinny, melancholy little boy
wearing his older brother's jacket. This last one had a shaved
head, and the painful-looking nicks in it told me that his hair
was cut at home to save money. He kept his shoulders hunched
and his eyes on the ground at his feet, braced as though he was
half-expecting something to fall on him. A pupil who hasn't
done his homework will automatically look down at the desk
when you ask the class a question about it, so that only the top
of his head is visible (this being based on the 'If I can't see her,
she can't see me' theory). If he is sitting in the back row, however,
he will stare into your eyes with an earnest expression. This boy
never looked up. Downcast eyes can hide a more personal guilt.
Some children are born to be bullied. They seem marked for
bad luck. Usually they have good reason to adopt such defensive
body language. Contrary to what parents think, there's not a
whole lot you can do about it.

'What's his name?' I asked.

'Oh that's Connor, he'll give you no trouble. Never says a

word. I forget he's here sometimes.' *I bet you do*, I thought. *You never notice him because he doesn't want you to.* 'Everybody hold up their right hand,' I called. It's easier to count hands than heads when they're standing up, but still they'll try to trick you. Some kids will hold up both hands, others won't raise any. I had lowered my voice to speak to them; you have to speak an octave lower than your normal register if you want to impose discipline. Squeaky high voices, however loud, don't get results. They're a sign of weakness, indicating potential teacher hysteria. Children can scent deficiencies in teachers like sharks smell blood.

'Miss, I'm left handed.' The ginger boy mimed limb-failure; I mentally transferred him from 'disruptive' to 'class clown'. They're exuberant but harmless, and usually sit in the middle of the back row.

'I want to see everybody's hand, now.' *Sixteen*, and the four at the rear of the ticket hall. 'Keep right under cover, out of the rain. You at the back, tuck in, let those people get past.' *Seventeen*, the clown, *eighteen, nineteen,* the Siamese twins, *twenty,* the sad boy. 'We're going to go through the barrier together in a group, so everybody stay very, very close.' I noticed Deborah studying me as I marshalled the children. There was disapproval in her look. She appeared about to speak, then held herself in check. I'm doing something wrong, I thought, alarmed. But the entry gate was being opened by the station guard, and I had to push the sensation aside.

Getting our charges onto the escalator and making them stand on the right was an art in itself. Timson, the class clown, was determined to prove he could remount the stairs and keep pace with passengers travelling in the opposite direction. An astonishingly pretty little black girl had decided to slide down on the rubber hand-rail.

'We step off at the end,' I warned, 'don't jump, that's how accidents happen.' My voice had rediscovered its sharp old timbre, but now there was less confidence behind it. London had changed while I had been away, and was barely recognisable to me now. There were so many tourists. Even at half-past ten on a wintry Monday morning, Finchley Road tube station was crowded with teenagers in wet nylon coats, hoods and back-packs, some old ladies on a shopping trip, some puzzled Japanese businessmen, a lost-looking man in an old-fashioned navy blue raincoat. Deborah exuded an air of weary lassitude that suggested she wouldn't be too bothered if the kids got carried down to the platform and were swept onto the rails like lemmings going over a cliff.

'Stay away from the edge,' I called, stirring my arms at them. 'Move back against the wall to let people past.' I saw the irritation in commuters' faces as they eyed the bubbling, chat-tering queue. Single Londoners don't like children. 'We're going to be getting on the next train, but we must wait until it has stopped and its doors are open before we move forward. I want you to form a crocodile.'

The children looked up at me blankly. 'A crocodile shape, two, two, two, two, all the way along,' I explained, chopping in their direction with the edges of my palms.

Deborah gave me a wry smile. 'I don't think anyone's ever told them to do that before,' she explained.

'Then how do you get them to stay in lines?' I asked.

'Oh, we don't, they just surge around. They never do what they're told. You can't do anything with them. The trouble with children is they're not, are they? Not children. Just grabby little adults.'

*No*, I thought, *you're so wrong*. But I elected not to speak. I looked back at the children gamely organising themselves into two wobbly columns. 'They're not doing so badly.'

Deborah wasn't interested. She turned away to watch the train arriving. 'Crocodile, crocodile,' the kids were chanting, making snappy-jawed movements to each other. The carriages of the train appeared to be already half-full. I had expected them to be almost empty. As the doors opened, we herded the children forward. I kept my eyes on the pairs at the back, feeding them in between my outstretched arms as though I was guiding unruly sheep into a pen. I tried not to think about the entrance to the tunnel, and the stifling, crushing darkness beyond it.

'Miss, Raj has fallen over.' I looked down to find a minuscule Indian child bouncing up from his knees with a grin on his face. I noted that no damage had been done, then lifted his hands, scuffed them clean and wrapped them around the nearest carriage pole. 'Hang on,' I instructed as the doors closed.

'Miss, how many stops is it?' asked a little girl at my side.

'We go to Swiss Cottage, then St John's Wood, then Baker Street, then we change from the Jubilee line to the Bakerloo line and go one stop to Regent's Park.'

'Miss, is there a real cottage in Swiss Cottage?'

'Miss, are we going to Switzerland?'

'Miss, can you ski in Swiss Cottage?'

'Miss, are we going skiing?'

'We're going skiing! We're going skiing!'

The train pulled away and everyone screamed. For a moment I sympathised with Deborah. I looked out of the window as the platform vanished. When I married Peter we moved out to Amersham, at the end of the Metropolitan line, and stopped coming into central London. Peter was a lecturer. I was due for promotion at the school. In time I could have become the headmistress, but Peter didn't want me to work and that was that, so I had to give up my job and keep house for him. A year later, I discovered that I couldn't have children. Suddenly I began to miss my classroom very badly.

'Miss, make him get off me.' Timson was sitting on top of a girl who had grabbed a seat. Without thinking, I lifted him off by his jacket collar.

'I wouldn't do that if I were you,' said Deborah. 'They'll have you up before the Court of Human Rights for maltreatment. Best not to touch them at all.' She swung to the other side of the central pole and leaned closer. 'How long has it been since you last taught?'

'Twelve years.'

'You've been away a long time.' It sounded suspiciously like a criticism. 'Well, we don't manhandle them anymore. EEC ruling.' Deborah peered out of the window. 'Swiss Cottage coming up, watch out.'

## 2. SWISS COTTAGE TO ST JOHN'S WOOD

*Many projects to build new tube lines were abandoned due to spiralling costs and sheer impracticability. An unfinished station tunnel at South Kensington served as a signalling school in the 1930s, and was later equipped to record delayed-action bombs falling into the Thames which might damage the underwater tube tunnels. The Northern Heights project to extend the Northern Line to Alexandra Palace was halted by the Blitz. After this, the government built a number of deep-level air-raid shelters connected to existing tube stations, several of which were so far underground that they were leased after the war as secure archives. As late as the 1970s many pedestrian tube subways still looked like passageways between bank vaults. Vast riveted doors could be used to seal off tunnels in the event of fire or flood. There was a subterranean acridity in the air. You saw the light rounding the dark bend ahead, heard the pinging of the albescent lines, perhaps glimpsed something long sealed away. Not all of the system has changed. Even now there are tunnels that lead nowhere, and platforms where only ghosts of the past wait for trains placed permanently out of service.*

Trying to make sure that nobody got off when the doors opened would have been easier if the children had been wearing school uniforms, but their casual clothes blended into a morass of bright colours, and I had to rely on Deborah keeping the head-count from her side of the carriage. In my earlier days at Invicta the pupils wore regulation navy blue with a single yellow stripe, and the only symbol of non-conformity you saw – apart from the standard array of faddish haircuts – was the arrangement of their socks, pulled down or the wrong colour, small victories for little rebels.

I avoided thinking about the brick and soil pressing down on us, but was perspiring freely by now. I concentrated on the children, and had counted to fifteen when half a dozen jolly American matrons piled into the car, making it hard to finish the tally. I moved as many of the children as I could to one side, indicating that they should stay in crocodile formation. I instinctively knew that most of them were present, but I couldn't see the sad little boy. 'Connor,' I called, 'make yourself known please.' An elliptical head popped out between two huge tourists. So unsmiling. I wondered if he had a nemesis, someone in the class who was making his life hell. Bullies are often small and aggressive because of their height. They go for the bigger, softer boys to enhance their reputation, and they're often popular with games teachers because of their bravado. There's not much I don't know about bullies. I was married to one for twelve years.

'I've got these new assignment books in my bag,' said Deborah, relooping her hair through her scrunchie and checking her reflection in the glass. 'Some government psychology group wants to test out a theory about how kids look at animals. More bloody paperwork. It's not rocket science, is it, the little sods just see it as a day off and a chance to piss about.'

'You may be right,' I admitted, 'but children are shaped far more by their external environment than anyone cares to admit.'

'How's that, then?'

'They recently carried out an experiment in a New York public school,' I explained, 'placing well-behaved kids and those with a history of disruption in two different teaching areas, one clean and bright, the other poorly lit and untidy. They found that children automatically misbehaved in surroundings of chaos – not just the troubled children but all of them, equally.'

Deborah looked at me oddly, swaying with the movement of the train. Grey cables looped past the windows like stone garlands, or immense spiderwebs. 'You don't miss much, do you? Is that how you knew Connor was hiding behind those women?'

'No, that's just instinct. But I've been reading a bit about behavioural science. It's very interesting.' I didn't tell her that before I was married I had been a teacher for nearly fourteen years. The only thing I didn't know about children was what it was like to have one.

'Well, I'm sorry, I know it's a vocation with some people, but not me. It's just a job. God, I'm dying for a fag.' She hiked her bag further up her shoulder. 'Didn't your old man want you to work, then?'

'Not really. But I would have come back earlier. Only . . .' I felt uncomfortable talking to this young woman in such a crowded place, knowing that I could be overheard.

'Only what?'

'After I'd been at home for a while, I found I had trouble going out.'

'Agoraphobia?'

'Not really. More like a loss of balance. A density of people. Disorienting architecture, shopping malls, exhibition halls, things like that.'

'I thought you didn't look very comfortable back there on the platform. The tubes get so crowded now.'

'With the tube it's different. It's not the crowds, it's the tunnels. The shapes they make. Circles. Spirals. The converging lines. Perhaps I've become allergic to buildings.'

Deborah wasn't listening, she was looking out of the window and unwrapping a piece of gum. Just as well, I thought. I didn't want her to get the impression that I wasn't up to the job. But I could feel the pressure in the air, the scented heat of the passengers, the proximity of the curving walls. An oversensitivity to public surroundings, that was what the doctor called it. I could tell what he was thinking, *oh god, another stir-crazy housewife.* He had started writing out a prescription while I was still telling him how I felt.

'We're coming into Baker Street. Christ, not again. There must have been delays earlier.' Through the windows I could see a solid wall of tourists waiting to board. We slowed to a halt and the doors opened.

## 3. BAKER STREET TO REGENT'S PARK

*The world's first tube railway, the Tower Subway, was opened in 1870, and ran between the banks of the Thames. The car was only ten feet long and five feet wide, and had no windows. This claustrophobic steel cylinder was an early materialisation of a peculiar modern phenomenon; the idea that great discomfort could be endured for the purpose of efficiency, the desire to reach another place with greater speed. An appropriately satanic contraption for a nation of iron, steam and smoke.*

'This is where we change,' called Deborah. 'Right, off, the lot of you.'

'Can you see them all?' I asked.

'Are you kidding? I bet you there's something going on somewhere as well, all these people, some kind of festival.' The adults on the platform were pushing their way into the carriage before we could alight. Suddenly we were being surrounded by red, white and green striped nylon backpacks. Everyone was speaking Italian. Some girls began shrieking with laughter and shoving against each other. Ignoring the accelerating dizziness behind my eyes, I pushed back against the door, ushering children out, checking the interior of the carriage, trying to count heads.

'Deborah, keep them together on the platform, I'll see if there are any more.' I could see she resented being told what to do, but she sullenly herded the class together. The guard looked out and closed the train doors, but I held mine back.

'How many?' I called.

'It's fine, they're all here. Come on, you'll get left behind.'

I pushed my way through the children as Deborah started off toward the Bakerloo line. 'You worry too much,' she called over her shoulder. 'I've done this trip loads of times, it's easy once you're used to it.'

'Wait, I think we should do another head check – ' But she had forged ahead with the children scudding around her, chattering, shouting, alert and alive to everything. I glanced back anxiously, trying to recall all of their faces.

I saw him then, but of course I didn't realise it.

Four minutes before the next train calling at Regent's Park. I moved swiftly around them, corralling and counting. Deborah was bent over, listening to one of the girls. The twins were against the wall, searching for something in their bags. Timson, the class clown, was noisily jumping back and forth, violently swinging his arms. I couldn't find him. Couldn't find Connor. Perhaps he didn't want me to, like he didn't want Deborah to notice.

'Let's see you form a crocodile again,' I said, keeping my voice low and calm.

'Miss, will we see crocodiles at the zoo?'

'Miss, are you the crocodile lady?'

Some of the children at the back moved forward, so I had to start the count over. I knew right then. *Nineteen*. One short. No Connor. 'He's gone,' I said. 'He's gone.'

'He can't have gone,' said Deborah, shoving her hair out of her eyes. She was clearly exasperated with me now. 'He tends to lag behind.'

'I saw him on the train.'

'You mean he didn't get off? You saw everyone off.'

'I thought I did.' It was getting difficult to keep the panic out of my voice. 'There was – something odd.'

'What are you talking about?' She turned around sharply. '*Who* is pulling my bag?' I saw that the children were listening to us. They miss very little, it's just that they often decide not to act on what they see or hear. I thought back, and recalled the old-fashioned navy blue raincoat. *An oversensitivity to everyday surroundings.* He had been following the children since Finchley Road. I had seen him in the crowd, standing slightly too close to them, listening to their laughter, watching out for the lonely ones, the quiet ones. Something had registered in me even then, but I had not acted upon my instincts. I tried to recall the interior of the carriage. Had he been on the train? I couldn't –

'He's probably not lost, just lagging behind.'

'Then where is he?'

'We'll get him back, they don't go missing for long. I promise you, he'll turn up any second. It's quite impossible to lose a small child down here, unfortunately. Imagine if we did. We'd have a bugger of a job covering it up.' Her throaty laugh turned into a cough. 'Have to get all the kids to lie themselves blue in the face, pretend that none of us saw him come to school today.'

'I'm going to look.'

'Oh, for Christ's sake.'

'Suppose something really has happened?'

'Well, what am I supposed to do?'

'Get the children onto the next train. I'll find Connor and bring him back. I'll meet you at the zoo. By the statue of Guy the gorilla.'

'You can't just go off! You said yourself – '

'I have to, I know what to look for.'

'We should go and tell the station guards, get someone in authority.'

'There isn't time.'

'This isn't your decision to make, you know.'

'It's my responsibility.'

'Why did you come back?'

Her question threw me for a second. 'The children.'

'This isn't your world now,' she said furiously. 'You had your turn. Couldn't you let someone else have theirs?'

'I was a damned good teacher.' I studied her eyes, trying to see if she understood. 'I didn't have my turn.'

There was no more time to argue with her. I turned and pushed back through the passengers surging up from the platform. I caught the look of angry confusion on Deborah's face, as though this was something I had concocted deliberately to wreck her schedule. Then I made my way back to the platform.

I was carrying a mobile phone, but down here, of course, it was useless. Connor was bright and suspicious; he wouldn't go quietly without a reason. I tried to imagine what I would do if

I wanted to get a child that wasn't mine out of the station with the minimum of fuss. I'd keep him occupied, find a way to stop him from asking questions. Heavier crowds meant more policing, more station staff, but it would be safer to stay lost among so many warm bodies. He'd either try to leave the station at once, and run the risk of me persuading the guards to keep watch at the escalator exits, or he'd travel to another line and leave by a different station. Suddenly I knew what he intended to do – but not where he intended to do it.

## 4. KING'S CROSS TO EUSTON

*There exists a strange photograph of Hammersmith Grove Road station taken four years after the service there ceased operation. It shows a curving platform of transverse wooden boards, and, facing each other, a pair of ornate deserted waiting rooms. The platform beyond this point fades away into the mist of a winter dusk. There is nothing human in the picture, no sign of life at all. It is as though the station existed at the edge of the world, or at the end of time.*

I tried to remember what I had noticed about Connor. There are things you automatically know just by looking at your pupils. You can tell a lot from the bags they carry. Big sports holdalls mean messy work and disorganisation; the kid is probably carrying his books around all the time instead of keeping them in his locker, either because he doesn't remember his time-table or because he is using the locker to store cigarettes and contraband. A smart briefcase usually indicates an anal pupil with fussy parents. Graffiti and stickers on a knapsack means that someone is trying to be a rebel. Connor had a cheap plastic bag, the kind they sell at high street stores running sales all year round.

I pushed on through the platforms, checking arrival times on the indicator boards, searching the blank faces of passengers, trying not to think about the penumbral tunnels beyond. For a moment I caught sight of the silver rails curving away to the platform's tiled maw, and a fresh wave of nausea overcame me. I forced myself to think about the children.

You can usually trace the person who has graffiti-ed their desk because you have a ready-made sample of their handwriting, and most kids are lousy at disguising their identities. Wooden pencil-boxes get used by quiet creative types. Metal tins with cartoon characters are for extroverts. Children who use psychedelic holders covered in graffiti usually think they're streetwise, but they're not.

You always used to be able to tell the ones who smoked because blazers were made of a peculiar wool-blend that trapped the smell of cigarettes. Now everyone's different. Spots around a child's nose and mouth often indicate a glue-sniffer, but now so many have spots from bad diets, from stress, from neglect. Some children never –

He was standing just a few yards away.

The navy blue raincoat was gabardine, like a fifties school-child's regulation school coat, but in an adult size. Below this were black trousers with creases and turn-ups, freshly polished Oxford toecap shoes. His hair was slicked smartly back, trimmed in classic short-back-and-sides fashion by a traditional barber who had tapered the hair at the nape and used an open razor on the neck. You always notice the haircuts.

He was holding the boy's hand. He turned his head and looked through me, scanning the platform. The air caught in my lungs as he brought his focus back to me, and matched my features in his memory. His deep-set eyes were framed by rimless spectacles that removed any readable emotion from his face. He defiantly held my gaze. We stood frozen on the concourse staring at each other as the other passengers surged around us, and as Connor's head slowly turned to follow his new friend's sightline, I saw that this man was exhilarated by the capture of his quarry, just as I knew that his initial elation would turn by degrees to sadness and then to anger, as deep and dark as the tunnels themselves.

The tension between their hands grew tighter. He began to move away, pulling the boy. I looked for someone to call to, searching faces to find anyone who might help, but found indifference as powerful as any enemy. Dull eyes reflected the platform lights, slack flesh settled on heavy bodies, exuding sour breath, and suddenly man and boy were moving fast, and I was pushing my way through an army of statues as I tried to keep the pair of them in my sight.

I heard the train before I saw it arriving at the end of the pedestrian causeway, the billow of heavy air resonating in the tunnel like a depth charge. I felt the pressure change in my ears and saw them move more quickly now. For a moment I thought he was going to push the boy beneath the wheels, but I knew he had barely begun with Connor yet.

I caught the doors just as they closed. Connor and the man had made it to the next carriage, and were standing between teenage tourists, only becoming visible as the tunnel curved and the carriage swung into view, briefly aligning the windows. We remained in stasis, quarry, hunter and pursuer, as the train thundered on. My heart tightened as the driver applied the brakes and we began to slow down. Ahead, the silver lines twisted sinuously toward King's Cross, and another wall of bodies flashed into view.

As the doors opened, fresh swells of passengers surged from carriage to platform and platform to carriage, shifting and churning so much that I was almost lifted from my feet. I kept my eyes focused on the man and the boy even though it meant stumbling against the human tide. Still he did not run, but moved firmly forward in a brisk walk, never slowing or stopping to look back. The carriage speakers were still barking inanely about delays and escalators. I could find no voice of my own that would rise above them, no power that would impede their escape. Wherever they went, I could only follow.

## 5. EUSTON TO CAMDEN TOWN

*Once, on the other side of that century of devastating change, Oscar Wilde could have taken the tube to the West End. The underground was built before the invention of the telephone, before the invention of the fountain pen. Once, the platform walls were lined with advertisements for Bovril, Emu, Wrights Coal Tar Soap, for the Quantock Sanitary Laundry, Peckham, and the Blue Hall Cinema, Edgware Road, for Virol, Camp Coffee and Lifebouy, for Foster Clark's Soups and Cream Custards, and Eastman's Dyeing & Cleaning. These were replaced by pleas to Make Do And Mend, to remember that Loose Lips Sink Ships, that Walls Have Ears, that Coughs And Sneezes Spread Diseases. Urgent directional markers guided the way to bomb shelters, where huddled families and terrified eyes watched and flinched with each thunderous impact that shook and split the tiles above their heads.*

On through the tunnels and passages, miles of stained cream tiles, over the bridges that linked the lines. I watched the navy blue raincoat shifting from side to side until I could see nothing else, my own fears forgotten, my fury less latent than his, building with the passing crush of lives. Onto another section of the Northern Line, the so-called Misery Line, but now the battered decadence of its maroon rolling stock had been replaced with livery of dull graffiti-scrubbed silver, falsely modern, just ordinary. The maroon trains had matched the outside tiles of the stations, just as the traffic signs of London were once striped black and white. No such style left now, of course, just ugly-ordinary and invisible-ordinary. But he was not ordinary, he wanted something he could not have, something nobody was allowed to take. On through the gradually thinning populace to another standing train, this one waiting with its doors open. But they began to close as we reached them, and we barely made the jump, the three of us, before we were sealed inside.

What had he told the boy to make him believe? It did not

matter what had been said, only that he had seen the child's weakness and known which role he had to play; anxious relative, urgent family friend, trusted guide, helpful teacher. To a child like Connor he could be anything as long as he reassured. Boys like Connor longed to reach up toward a strong clasping hand. They needed to believe.

Out onto the platform, weaving through the climbing passengers, across the concourse at Euston and back down where we had come from, toward another northbound train. We had been travelling on the Edgware branch, but it wasn't where he wanted to go. Could he be anxious to catch a High Barnet train for some reason? By now I had deliberately passed several guards without calling out for help, because I felt sure they would only argue and question and hinder, and in the confusion to explain I would lose the boy forever. My decision was vindicated, because the seconds closed up on us as the High Barnet train slid into the station. By now I had gained pace enough to reach the same carriage, and I stood facing his back, no more than a dozen passengers away. And this time I was foolish enough to call out.

My breathless voice did not carry far. A few people turned to look at me with anxious curiosity. One girl appeared to be on the edge of offering her help, but the man I was pointing to had suddenly vanished from sight, and so had the boy, and suddenly I was just another crazy woman on the tube, screaming paranoia, accusing innocents.

At Camden Town the doors mercifully opened, releasing the nauseous crush that was closing in on me. I stuck out my head and checked along the platform, but they did not alight. I could not see them. What had happened? Could they have pushed through the connecting door and – God help the child – dropped down onto the track below? They had to be on board, and so I had to stay on. The doors closed once more and we pulled away again into the suffocating darkness.

## 6. KENTISH TOWN TO SOUTH KENTISH TOWN

*The tunnels withstood the firestorms above. The tunnels pro-*
*tected. At the heart of the system was the Inner Circle, far from*
*a circle in the Euclidian sense, instead an engineering marvel*
*that navigated the damp earth and ferried its people through*
*the sulphurous tunnels between iron cages, impervious to the*
*world above, immune to harm. Appropriately, the great metal*
*circles that protected workers as they hacked at the clay walls*
*were known as shields. They protected then, and the strength*
*of the system still protects. The tunnels still endure.*

He had dropped down to his knees beside the boy, whispering
his poisons. I had missed him between the bodies of standing,
rocking travellers, but I was ready as the train slowed to a halt
at Kentish Town. I was surprised to see that the platform there
was completely deserted. Suddenly the landscape had cleared.
As he led the boy out I could tell that Connor was now in
distress, pulling against the hand that held him, but it was no
good; his captor had strength and leverage. No more than five
or six other passengers alighted. I called out, but my voice was
lost beneath the rumble and squeal of rolling steel. There were
no guards. Someone must see us on the closed circuit cameras,
I thought, but how would eyes trained for rowdy teenage gangs
see danger here? There was just a child, a man, and a frightened
middle-aged woman.

I glanced back at the platform exit as the train pulled out,
wondering how I could stop him if he tried to push past. When
I looked back, he and Connor had vanished. He was below on
the line, helping the child down, and then they were running,
stumbling into the entrance of the tunnel.

We were about to move beyond the boundaries of the city,
into a territory of shadows and dreams. As I approached the
entrance I saw the silver lines slithering away into amber gloom,
then darkness, and a wave of apprehension flushed through me.
By dangling my legs over the platform and carefully lowering

myself, I managed to slide down into the dust-caked gully. I knew that the tall rail with the ceramic studs was live, and that I would have to stay at the outer edge. I was also sure that the tunnel would reveal alcoves for workers to stand in when trains passed by. In the depth of my fear I was colder and more logical than I had been for years. Perhaps by not calling to the guards, by revealing myself in pursuit, I had in some way brought us here, so that now I was the child's only hope.

The boy was pulling hard against his stiff-legged warden, shouting something upwards, but his voice was distorted by the curving tunnel walls. They slowed to a walk, and I followed. The man was carrying some kind of torch; he had been to this place before, and had prepared himself accordingly. My eyes followed the dipping beam until we reached a division in the tunnel wall. He veered off sharply and began to pick a path through what appeared to be a disused section of the line. Somewhere in the distance a train rattled and reverberated in its concrete causeway. My feet were hurting, and I had scraped the back of my leg on the edge of the platform. I could feel a thin hot trickle of blood behind my knee. The thick brown air smelled of dust and dessication, like the old newspapers you find under floorboards. It pressed against my lungs, so that my breath could only be reached in shallow catches. Ahead, the torch-beam shifted and hopped. He had climbed a platform and pulled the boy up after him.

As I came closer, his beam illuminated a damaged soot-grey sign: SOUTH KENTISH TOWN. The station had been closed for almost eighty years. What remained had been preserved by the dry warm air. The platform walls were still lined to a height of four feet with dark green tiles arranged in column patterns. Every movement Connor made could be heard clearly here. His shoes scuffed on the litter-strewn stone as he tried to yank his hand free. He made small mewling noises, like a hungry cat.

Suddenly the torch-beam illuminated a section of stairway tiled in cream and dark red. They turned into it. I stopped sharply and listened. He had stopped, too. I moved as quickly and quietly as I could to the stairway entrance.

He was waiting for me at the foot of the stairs, his fingers glowing pink over the lens of the upright torch. Connor was by his side, pressed against the wall. It was then I realised that Connor usually wore glasses – you can usually tell the children who do. I imagined they would be like the ones worn by his captor. Because I was suddenly struck by how very alike they looked, as though the man was the boy seen some years later. I knew then that something terrible had happened here before and could so easily happen again, that this damaged creature meant harm because he had been harmed himself, because he was fighting to recapture something pure, and that he knew it could never again be. He wanted his schooldays back but the past was denied to him, and he thought he could recapture the sensations of childhood by taking someone else's.

I would not let the boy have it stolen from him. Innocence is not lost; it is taken.

'You can't have him,' I said, keeping my voice as clear and rational as I could. I had always known how to keep my fear from showing. It is one of the first things you learn as a teacher. He did not move. One hand remained over the torch, the other over the boy's right hand.

'I know you were happy then. But you're not in class any more.' I raised my tone to a punitive level. 'He's not in your year. You belong somewhere different.'

'Whose teacher are you?' He cocked his head on one side to study me, uncurling his fingers from the torch. Light flooded the stairway.

'I might have been yours,' I admitted.

He dropped the boy's hand, and Connor fell to the floor in surprise.

'The past is gone,' I said quietly. 'Lessons are over. I really think you should go now.' For a moment the air was only disturbed by my uneven breath and the sound of water dripping somewhere far above.

He made a small sound, like the one Connor had made earlier, but deeper, more painful. As he approached me I forced myself to stand my ground. It was essential to maintain a sense of authority. I felt sure he was going to hit me, but instead he stopped and studied my face in the beam of the torch, trying to place my features. I have one of those faces; I could be anyone's teacher. Then he lurched out of the stairwell and stumbled away along the platform. With my heart hammering, I held Connor to me until the sound of the man was lost in the labyrinth behind us.

'You're the Crocodile Lady,' said Connor, looking up at me.

'I think I am,' I agreed, wiping a smudge from his forehead.

Unable to face the tunnels again, I climbed the stairs with Connor until we reached a door, and I hammered on it until someone unlocked the damned thing. It was opened by a surprised Asian girl in a towel. We left the building via the basement of the Omega Sauna, Kentish Town Road, which still uses the station's old spiral staircase as part of its design. London has so many secrets.

The police think they know who he is now, but I'm not sure that they'll ever catch him. He's as lost to them as he is to everyone else. Despite his crimes – and they have uncovered quite a few – something inside me felt sorry for him, and sorry for the part he'd lost so violently that it had driven him to take the same from others. The hardest thing to learn is how to be strong.

Everyone calls me the Crocodile Lady.

*This began as a commission for* BIG *magazine, who wanted me to write something set in the world of fashion. I have a friend who is a model, so I asked her about the career's benefits and limitations. Poppy sometimes models in Japan, where she risks voiding her contract if she gets a suntan. I find it difficult to take fashion seriously. My favourite comment on the absurdities of style is in the film* Brazil, *when Katherine Helmond walks into the restaurant wearing a leopardskin shoe on her head.*

# THE LOOK

I never wanted to be a model.

I wanted to be *the* model.

He only picks one for each season. And after he picks her, nothing is ever the same again. He sees a special quality in a girl and draws it out. Then he presents it to the world. If you're picked, everything you do is touched with magic. You don't become a star, you become a legend. Ordinary people are awed by your presence. It's as if you've been marked by the hand of God.

As far back as I could remember, I wanted to be the girl he picked.

I got off to a bad start. I wouldn't concentrate on lessons at school. I didn't study late into the night. I hung out with my girlfriends, discovered boys, fell for their lies, fell out with my parents just before they did the same with each other. I had a best friend, a girl called Ann-Marie who lived across the street. Ann-Marie had a weight problem and wore these disgusting dental correctors, and overwashed her hair until it frizzed up and it looked like she'd stuck her tongue in an electric socket, but she helped me out with my homework, and it made me look good to walk beside her when we were out together. She hung around with me because she was seriously screwed up about her looks, and nobody wanted to be around her. It sounds cruel but the lower her self-esteem fell, the more mine rose.

I come from nothing, just faceless ordinary people. My mother would hate me saying that, but it's true. We lived in a rented flat on the tenth floor of a run-down apartment block in a depressing neighbourhood. I had no brothers or sisters, and my father went away years ago. My mother was never around because she worked all the time. Any humour, any life, any joy she had once been able to summon up had been scuffed away by her angry determination to maintain appearances. Nobody in my family ever had any money, or anything else. But I was aware from an early age that I had something. I had the Look. And I knew it.

Kit Marlowe says there's a moment in everyone's life when they have the right look. It may only last for just a single night. It may last for a season. Once in a rare while, it lasts a whole year. The trick is knowing when it's about to happen, and being ready for it. I was ready.

I was so fucking ready.

I should tell you about Kit Marlowe, as if you don't already know. His first London collection freaked people out because he used a blind girl as his model, and everyone thought she was going to fall off the catwalk, which was really steep, but she didn't because she'd been rehearsing for an entire year. She wore these really high stilettos, and tiny skirts like Japanese Ko-Gals, and hundreds of silver-wire bracelets. He has more than one model but the others always stay masked in black or white muslin so that nothing detracts from the one he has selected to bear the Look for his collection.

He had one model who performed in his show under hypnosis. The clothes she modelled were actually stitched onto her, right through the flesh. Her veil was sewn to her forehead, her blouse held tight by dozens of tiny silver piercings that ran across her breasts. Even her boots were held on by wires that passed through her calves. I read an interview with her afterwards in which she stated that she hadn't felt a thing except total faith in Kit Marlowe. But not all of his designs were that extreme. Many of them were simple and elegant. That was the thing; you never knew the kind of look he would go for next.

Kit Marlowe got kicked out of school, and has no qualifications. He's a natural. He says he learned everything he needs to know from television. He's larger than life. I guess I first heard about him when I was eight or nine, and started collecting photographs of his models. I don't know how old he is. He began young, but he may even be in his thirties by now. He's a guru, a god. He changes the way we look at the world. His clothes aren't meant to be worn by ordinary people, they're there to serve a higher purpose, to inspire us. I used to study the pictures in amazement. I never saw anything he did that didn't surprise me. Some of it was grotesque and outlandish, but often it had this timeless, placeless beauty.

It was Ann-Marie who first pointed out the strange quality he brought to his models. We were sitting in a McDonald's waiting for my father to give us a lift home, studying a magazine filled with pictures from his Paris show, and she showed me how he mixed stuff from different eras and countries, so there'd be like, seventies Indian beadworked cotton and fifties American sneakers and eighties Japanese skirts. But he combines everything with his own style, and in the presentation he'll throw in a wild card, like using a Viennese choir with African drummers and Latino house, the whole sound mixed together by some drum 'n' bass Ibiza DJ, and he'll set the whole event in something like a disused Victorian swimming pool, making all these fashion gurus trek miles out into the middle of nowhere to view his collection.

Once he showed his fashion designs on this video installation in New Jersey, setting monitors all around a morgue, where he ran footage of his clothes dressed on real corpses, teenagers who had died in car crashes. Then his model of the season came out from between the monitors with her masked team, all in blood-spattered surgical gowns, which they tore open to reveal the new season's outfits. It was so cool, dealing with social issues through fashion like that.

Kit Marlowe only designs for women. He says it's all about being extraordinary. He searches out girls who have something unique, and what he searches for completely changes every season. He never uses anyone older than nineteen. He says until that age we behave with a kind of animal instinct that is lost as we grow older. His models come from all over the world. He's used a Russian, a Hungarian, a Tunisian, a Brazilian, a Korean and an American as well as English girls, all of them complete unknowns. He just plucks them out of small towns. They give up their old lives for him, and he gives them new ones. He rechristens them. He gives them immortality.

One model to reveal the Look was a girl he called Acquiver-adah. She was from St. Petersburg, seventeen, a little over six feet tall, very skinny and odd-looking, parchment-white skin with pale blue veins, and she wore mothwing purple gowns in gossamer nylon that showed her body in incredible detail. The Look was instantly copied by chain stores, who messed it up to the point of parody by adding layers of cheap material under-neath. I remember her being interviewed. She said that meeting with Kit Marlowe had brought her violently alive for the first time, and yet the experience was 'like being stroked on the cheek with a butterfly wing'. She looked so ethereal I thought she was going to float away from the camera lens and up into the sun.

Kit has a special look of his own, too, but the details change constantly. Long hair, cropped hair, shades, goatee, facial tattoos, piercings, none of the above. He puts on weight and loses it according to the clothes he chooses for the season. Some likes and dislikes remain throughout his transformations. He likes unusual girls, particularly Eastern Europeans who can't speak English but who express themselves with their bodies. He loves to court controversy because he says it gets people talking about clothes. He's always being linked to gorgeous girls, and he openly admits that he has sex with his models. Kit says that understanding their sexuality helps him to uncover the Look. He likes strong women. He prefers fiercely textured fabrics and colours, silver, crimson, black and green. He laughs a lot and jokes around on camera, except when he's discussing his own creations. Then he's deadly serious. He owns houses all over the world, but lives in France. He's physically big (although he might be short, it's hard to tell) and from some angles he has a heavy chin, except last year when he lost a lot of weight. He hates phonies and hype. He says his designs reflect the inner turbulence of the wearer. He explains how his clothes create chromatic harmonisations of the spirit. I filled an entire book with his sayings, and that was just from last season's interviews. It was Ann-Marie who heard about him coming to our town. He'd shown his collections outside London before, but never as far North as this. I wanted to see the show so badly. Of course it was invitation only, and I had no way of getting my hands on one. But we could at least be somewhere close by.

I was very excited about this. I knew that just to be near him would be to sense the future. Kit Marlowe is always ahead of the game. It's like he's standing on a chair searching the horizon while the rest of us are on the ground looking at each other like a bunch of morons. He never tells the press what the Look is going to be, but he drops hints. There were rumours going around in the style press that he was planning a range of computerised clothing; that he was going to combine microchip circuitry with the most basic fabrics and colours. But nobody really knew what that meant or what he was up to, and if they did they weren't saying.

Sometimes we went clubbing at the weekend. I would dye my hair blond while my Dad's girlfriend was out at work on Friday night, then dye it back before school on Monday. Ann-Marie and I figured that if we couldn't get into the show we could maybe get into his hotel and catch sight of him in the lobby afterwards, but it wasn't as easy as it sounded. He was staying near the station in this converted Victorian church covered with gargoyles, a cool place with headset dudes in floorlength black coats guarding the doors. Ann-Marie was smart, though. She figured we needed escorts otherwise we'd never get into the building, so we bribed these friends of Ann-Marie's brother who were going into the centre of town for the weekend. They sold insurance and wore off-the-peg suits and looked respectable, so we dressed down to match them, only I wore another set of clothes underneath. Ann-Marie couldn't because she was heavy enough already, and wasn't bothered anyway, but I wanted to be noticed. I was ready for it. I had the Look. My time was now.

The show was mid-afternoon and we figured he'd come back and change before going to a party. We had a pretty tight lock on his movements because he gave so many interviews, and loved talking to the press; all you had to do was piece everything together and you had the entire trip plan. This was probably how the guy who killed John Lennon managed it, just by gathering news of his whereabouts and drawing all the timelines together. It's pretty easy to be a stalker if you're single-minded. But I wasn't a stalker. I just wanted to be touched by the hand of God. Kit Marlowe says if you're strong about these things, you can make them happen.

It was one of those days that didn't look as though it would get light at all, and was mistily raining when we reached the hotel. There was a sooty slickness on the streets that seemed left over from the area's coal-mining past, and the traffic was creeping forward through the gloom like a vast funeral procession. We were stuck in a steamed-up Ford with the insurance guys, getting paranoid about the time, and they were fed up with us because we hadn't stopped talking for the last hour.

'He's never going to make it through this,' said Ann-Marie, but the rain was good because we could wear our hoods up, and the doormen wouldn't think we were teenage hookers or street trash. Once we had made it safely into the hotel lobby we ditched the boring insurance guys and they went off to some bar to get drunk. We knew that Kit Marlowe was staying on the seventh floor because he had this superstitious thing about sevens (a fact disclosed in another wonderfully revealing interview) but when we went up there we couldn't tell which suite he'd taken. I thought there would be guards everywhere but there was no security, none at all, and I figured that maybe the hotel didn't know who he was. We couldn't cover both sides of the floor from a single vantage point, so we split up, each taking a cleaner's cupboard. Then we waited in the warm soapy darkness.

Every time I heard the elevator ping I stuck my head out. This went on for ages, until the excitement was so much that I fell asleep. The next thing I knew, Ann-Marie was shaking me and hissing in my ear. I wondered what the hell her problem was, and then what the hell she was wearing.

'I found the maid's uniform on one of the shelves, I thought it would make me look less conspicuous,' she explained.

'Well, it really doesn't, Ann-Marie. Pink's not your colour, and certainly not in glazed nylon with white piping. You look like a marshmallow.'

'Take a look down the corridor.'

'Ohmigod.' A group of people was coming straight towards us. I ducked back in. 'How do I look?'

'Take your coat off. Give it to me.' Ann-Marie held out her arms. I was wearing an ensemble I had invented from cuttings of every Kit Marlowe collection. Obviously I couldn't afford the materials his designers used, so I had come up with equivalents, adding a few extra details like plastic belts and sequins. It was a look that was very ahead of its time, and I knew he'd love it the moment he saw it.

I took a few quick breaths, not too many in case I started to hyperventilate, then stepped out of the cupboard. A man and a woman were talking quietly. They looked like a couple of Kit Marlowe's PR consultants or something. They dressed so immaculately in grey suits, black tees, trainers and identical haircuts that they looked computer-generated. Behind them was Acquiveradah, a drifting wraith in some kind of green silk-hooded arrangement. I had forgotten how long and white her arms and neck were, how strangely she moved. She looked like she'd been deep-frozen and only half thawed. Kit Marlowe was at her side (quite a lot shorter than I expected), dressed in a shiny black kaftan-thing. I could see from here that his buttons were silver crucifixes, and every time he passed under one of the corridor spotlights they shone onto the walls. It was as though he was consecrating the hotel just by walking through it.

I realised at this point that I was standing right in the middle of the passage, blocking their way. I felt Ann-Marie tugging at my sleeve, but I was utterly mesmerised. I tried to hear what they were saying. Acquiveradah sounded angry. She and Kit were speaking hard and low. Something about changing dates, deadlines, signing it, moving it, being in Berlin. Oh, God, Berlin's so damned cold, she was complaining, like it was a big chore going there. And then they stopped.

They stopped because I was standing in their way like a fool, staring with my mouth open.

'What the fuck's going on?' Kit Marlowe himself was speaking, actually speaking. 'Who's this? Did somebody order a singing telegram?' He was talking about me. Time slowed down. My skin prickled as he stepped forward through his PR people.

'Who are you?'

I knew I had to answer. 'I'm – ' But I realised I had made an incredibly stupid mistake. I had concentrated so hard on the Look that I had never invented a name for myself. 'I'm – ' I couldn't think of anything to say. I didn't want to tell him my real name because it's so ordinary, but I couldn't make one up on the spot. Behind him, Acquiveradah started hissing again. Kit held up his hand for silence, and continued to stare.

'You, I like what you're wearing.'

I closed my hanging mouth, not daring to move. This was the moment I had waited all of my life for.

'Tell me something.'

I tried to breathe.

'Do they give you a choice?'

What was he talking about?

'I don't suppose so. Hotels only care about their guests, right? Everyone else gets the universal look. Staff are treated the same anywhere in the world.' He wiped his nose on the back of his hand, and looked to one of the PRs for approval. 'Right? I never thought of that, but it's true, right?' The PRs agreed enthusiastically. 'It's a universal look.'

I could see him. I could hear him. But I couldn't piece together what he was saying. Not until I followed his eyeline and saw that he was talking past me. Talking to Ann-Marie. She was standing behind us near the wall, beside a trolley filled with little bottles of shampoo, conditioner and toilet rolls. She was wearing the maid's uniform, and I saw now how much it suited her. It was perfect, like she worked here. But also, like she was modelling it.

'It's a look,' Kit fucking Marlowe was saying, 'I don't know if it's *the* Look, but it's certainly *a* look. Come here, darling.'

'Kit, for God's sake,' Acquiveradah was saying, but he was reaching out to Ann-Marie and drawing her into his little group. My supposed best friend walked right past me into their spotlight, mesmerised, and I felt my eyes growing hot with tears as the scene wavered. Moments later they were gone, all of them, through a door that had silently opened, swallowed them and closed.

I was numb. Left behind in the empty corridor. I couldn't move. I couldn't go anywhere. Ann-Marie had our return money in her bag.

Then the door opened again, and Acquiveradah backed out. I could hear her making excuses to Kit. (Something about 'from my room' – something like 'in a few minutes'.) I can't remember what she said, but I knew she was telling him lies. She moved awkwardly toward me and placed a cold hand on my shoulder. She was stronger and more purposeful than she looked.

'I have to talk to you, little girl. In here.' She ran a swipe card through the door behind me and pushed me into the room. For a moment I was left standing in the dark while she fumbled for a light switch. In the fierceness of the mirrored neon that flicked on around the suite she looked hard and old, nothing like her photographs. There was something else about her appearance I found odd, a lopsidedness that skewed her features and gave her a permanent stare, like she'd only partially recovered from a stroke. 'Sit down there.' She indicated the edge of the bed. I pushed aside a tray of barely-touched food and some empty champagne bottles, and sat. 'Does your friend really want to model?'

I found my voice. 'I never thought she did.'

'A lot of girls act like that. It's a secret of successful modelling, not looking like you care whether you'll ever do it again. The moment you try too hard it shows. I can take it or leave it, they say. The world's top models spend their entire lives telling everyone they're giving it up next season, it's all bullshit. What they mean is, they're frightened they won't cut it next time. Nobody holds the Look for long. I'll ask you again; does she really want to model?'

I tried to think. 'I guess she does. She wants to be liked.'

'Fine, then we'll leave it. I don't know what will happen. He's been – well, let's say he's not thinking clearly after a show, and he may change his mind, but he may not, and if you see your friend again you should at least be able to tell her what she's in for. Most of them have no idea.' She was talking in riddles, pacing about, trying to light a joint. 'Look at me, I'm a good example. I had no idea what this sort of thing involved.' She pulled up the hem of her hooded top and exposed her pale stomach. 'I was the wrong shape, too wide here. They took out my bottom three ribs on both sides, here see?' Her pearlised fingernails traced a faint ridge of healed stitches, the skin puckered like cloth. 'I had my stomach stapled. Some of my neck removed and pinned back. My cheekbones altered. Arms tucked. Eyes lifted. The graft didn't take at first and my left eye turned septic. It was removed and replaced with moulded plastic. You can't tell, even close up. It photographs the same because I always wear a full contact in the other one to match the texture.' She drew on the joint, glancing anxiously at the door. 'They removed fat from my ass, but I was still growing and my body started shedding it naturally, and I lost what I didn't have, so now it's very painful to sit down. I can feel the tops of my femurs rubbing, ball and socket scraping bone. Oh don't give me that look, fashion always hurts. Christ, they used to tighten the foreheads of Egyptian girls to prevent their skull-plates from knitting. Chinese foot-binding, ever hear of that?' I shook my head. 'And athletes, they give up any semblance of normal life for their careers, it's just what you have to do to get to the top and most people aren't prepared to do it, that's why they remain mediocre. You have to put yourself out, a long way out. It's pretty fucking elementary.'

'I can't imagine that Kit Marlowe would allow that sort of thing to – '

'Exactly, you can't imagine. You don't get it, do you? There is no Kit Marlowe, he's a corporation, a conglomerate, he's jeans and music and vodka and cars and clothing stores, he's not an actual person. There's always a frontman, someone the public can focus on but he's not real. He's played by somebody different nearly every season. I assume most people recognise that in some fundamental way.'

'But the fashions. His vision. The Look.'

'Whoever's in place for this collection just follows the guidelines. "Kit Marlowe" is a finder. This one picked your friend, but she's the third person he's picked in the last two days. They all have to be submitted to a hundred fucking committees before they get any further. The fabrics people never agree with the drinks people, the car people want older role models and everyone hates the music people.'

I had been trying hard not to cry, but now I couldn't stop my eyes from welling over. 'The Look,' I said stupidly. 'He said anyone could . . .'

'It's not about a look, you little idiot, it's about being young. That's all you need to be. Young. Gap-toothed, cross-eyed, bow-legged, brain-damaged, whatever. If you're young you can wear anything, razorblades, pieces of jagged glass, shit-covered rags – and believe me you'll have to do that while they're all experimenting – you'll still look good because you're so incredibly fucking young. And if there's really a look, something that pleases every sponsor, then you're photographed in it and you do a few catwalks. And then it all goes away. Fast. People are like fruit; they don't stay fresh long before everyone knows they're damaged. That's all the Look is. Anyone should be able to figure it out.'

'But what happens after that? Don't the models go to the press and describe how they've been – '

'Been what, exactly? Been given shit-loads of money and fame and set up for life? Nobody makes you sign, honey, it's a choice, pure and simple. You get a contract and you honour your side of the deal, like any other job. The only thing is if any of the surgical stuff goes wrong, I mean badly wrong, you're fucked because they've got good legal people.'

'But the people who interview Kit Marlowe, they must see that he changes – '

'They see what they choose to see. Ask yourself who employs them. Who owns the magazines they write for, the networks they broadcast for. You've got to think bigger, kid.' She looked at her watch. 'Shit, I have to get back. If you see your friend again, you'll have to make the choice. Do you give her a friendly word of warning, or not bother? After all, she looks like she forgot about you pretty quickly.' The sour smile that crossed her face actually cracked her makeup.

'I don't believe any of this,' I heard myself saying angrily. 'You've lost it and you don't want anyone younger to get their turn. You're jealous of her, that's all.'

Acquiveradah sighed and threw the remains of her joint onto a plate of torn-apart fruit. She stood there thinking. A fly crawled around the edge of a champagne flute. 'All right.' She dug into the pocket of her green hooded jacket, brought out another card, and held it up before me. 'Go to room 820, on the next floor. Take a look, but don't touch their skin, you understand? Don't do anything girly, like screaming. Not that I suppose you'll wake them, because by now they'll be so fast asleep that the place could burn down and they wouldn't feel it. Oh, hang on.' She went into the bathroom and came back out with a pair of nail-scissors. 'Use these to get a good look. Then think about your friend. And leave the entry-card in the room when you leave.'

I left the room and ran off along the corridor on wobbly legs. I knew if I got in the lift I would take it straight back down to the ground floor, so I took the stairs instead. I found room 820 easily. The corridor was silent and deserted. I ran the swipe-card through the lock and slowly pushed the door open. I couldn't see anything because the blinds were drawn and the lights were off. Besides, I guessed it was dark outside now. I stood in the little passage by the room's mirrored wardrobes, unable to leave the diamond of light thrown from the corridor. I listened and heard breathing, slow steady breathing, from more than one body. I could smell antiseptic. I tried to recall the room layout from the floor below. The lights had to be somewhere to my right. I reached out my hand and felt along the wall. Several switches were there. I flicked them all on.

The room had two beds, and someone was asleep in each of them. The pale cotton hoods they always wore in the shows were still stretched across their features. They continued to breathe at the same steady pace, and did not seem disturbed by the lights.

I walked over to the nearest one and bent closer. I could vaguely make out her features under the hood, which was held on tight with a plastic drawstring. I remembered the nail-scissors Acquiveradah had given me, and realised what she had intended me to do. I inserted the points just above the fastened collar and began to cut open the hood.

I found myself looking at the girl who had been hypnotised and pierced for the Kit Marlowe collection three seasons ago. The piercings had left terrible scars across her face, raised lumps of flesh as hard as pebbles, as red and sore as tumours. There were fresh crusts of blood around her ears, as though her skin had still not learned to cope with the demands being made upon it. Her teeth had been replaced by perfect white china pegs, neatly driven through gum and bone, but the gums had turned black and receded. I reached out my hand. I just wanted to see that she was real. I touched her cheek and felt the waxy flesh dent beneath my fingertips. When I removed my hand, the indentations remained, as though her skin was infected.

When I saw that she wasn't going to move, I pulled back her lower lip and saw lines of thick black stitches running around the base of her jawline. I could only imagine that after her turn in the spotlight this poor thing had agreed to stay on as one of the backing models, even though her face would never again be seen. Could fame do that, leave you so hungry for more that you would choose to stay, whatever your new situation might be?

I bent over her until our noses almost touched. The opened muslin hood lay around her face, framing it so that she looked like a discarded birthday gift. One of her eyes was closed. Hardly daring to breathe, I lifted the eyelid. There was a large glass marble in the socket, the kind boys used to play with at school.

I couldn't bring myself to look at the other model. Who knew what fresh horrors I might find? I was still thinking about it when the body beneath my hand moved and sat up. I think I screamed. I know I left that antiseptic-reeking room and shot out into the corridor as though I was running across hot coals. I was more confused than frightened. When I saw that Miss Three-Seasons-Ago wasn't coming after me, I tried to gather my thoughts. I wanted to help Ann-Marie but I badly wanted to leave, and the indecision froze me. At last I decided to try and find the way back. I went to the stairs and ran down to the floor where I had last seen her. The corridor was so silent and empty I could have been inside an Egyptian tomb. I found the door that Kit and his team had closed on me. It was still shut. I stopped in front of it, staring stupidly at the gilded number, willing it to open, praying that it would open.

And then it did.

The PR pair came out. The woman looked at me and smiled. 'I guess you're waiting for your little friend,' she said, as if talking to a stupid child. 'She can't see you right now. She's busy.'

'What are you doing to her?'

'Don't worry, she's enjoying herself. Now, I think you'd better go on home.'

'I can't. She's got my money.'

The woman sighed and pulled a wad of notes from inside her jacket. 'Take this and just go away, okay?' She pushed a roll of bills into my hand. Behind her, the hotel door shifted open slightly, and I caught a glimpse of the room inside. It was very brightly lit. Ann-Marie had no clothes on. She was sitting in a chair looking very fat and white, and there was something sticking out of her, protruding from between her legs. It looked like a long steel tube with a red rubber bulb on one end. She was smiling and looking up at the ceiling, then suddenly her whole body began to shake. Somebody kicked the door shut with a bang.

I closed my fist over the money and ran, out into the night and the rain.

The rest of the evening was awful. I had to hitch home, and this creepy lorry-driver kept staring at my tits and making suggestions. I think he got the wrong idea because of the way I was dressed. Ann-Marie lived with her drunk mother and her stupid stoner brother. I called at their house, but no-one was at home. They were never at home. Anyway, they weren't expecting her back for another day.

I talked to Ann-Marie's mother later, and she showed me the letter, about how her little girl was dropping out of school because she had a modelling contract and was moving to London to become a star. Her family, such as it was, certainly didn't seem too bothered. They were pleased she was going to bring in some money. I guess my own happiness for Ann-Marie had something to do with being glad that I wasn't in her place. She was missed in class for a couple of weeks, and that's about all. She wasn't the kind of person you noticed, whereas I was. Maybe that was why she'd been chosen.

Anyway, when the next season's collection was announced, I received an invitation. The thing was printed on a sheet of pressed steel that nearly slashed the tops off my fingers when I opened the envelope. By this time I was planning to leave home and start media studies at the local college. I went down to London and located the venue, a disused synagogue somewhere behind Fleet Street. Once again, it was raining. I'd decided to play it safe and wear plain black jeans and a tee shirt. To tell the truth, I was growing out of dressing like a Kit Marlowe wannabe, but I was still eager to find out how Ann-Marie had fared in her new career. We were served fancy cocktails in a burnished iron antechamber, then ushered into the main salon.

A few wall-lights glowed dimly. Only the deep crimson outline of the catwalk could be discerned in the gloom. As we took our seats, the room was abuzz with anticipation. A single spotlight illuminated a plump young man standing motionless at the foot of the runway.

Kit Marlowe surveyed his dominion with satisfaction. He waited for everyone to settle, lightly patted the back of his waxed hair, and beamed. 'Ladies and gentlemen,' said a voice emanating from the speakers around us as Kit moved his lips, 'I'd like to thank you for coming out from the West End in such foul weather, and I hope you'll find your efforts well rewarded. Welcome to my collection. This year the Look honours someone very special, someone we all know but never fully acknowledge. This Kit Marlowe season, ladies and gentlemen, is dedicated to the ordinary working girl. She is all around us, she is in all of us, a part of the machinery that fills our lives. She is the spark that ignites and powers the engines of society. She is Andromeda, and this is her Look.'

We realised that the figure speaking before us was an anima-tronic mannequin. As the overhead voice pulsed away into silence, it collapsed into the floor, and brilliant red walls of laser light rolled up to create a virtual room in space.

Along the catwalk and stepping into this lowering box of fractal colour came a figure that could not be recognised as Ann-Marie. She looked like every girl you ever saw serving behind a counter or a trolley, like all of them yet none of them.

Her outfit was that of a streamlined, futuristic servant, but as the electronic soundtrack grew in pitch and volume something happened to the clothes she was wearing. They changed shape, refolding and refitting into different patterns on her body, empowering her, transforming her from slave to dominatrix. I later discovered that every item modelled in the show was manipulated by computer programs, interacting with silicon implants in the fabrics that tightened threads and changed tones. Kit Marlowe had invented digital fashion. The entire room burst into spontaneous applause.

Behind Ann-Marie moved two eighties-throwback robot girls, their heads encased in shiny foil-like fabrics. I wondered if one of them was a mutilated, ageing Acquiveradah. Lights dazzled fiercely and faded. The sonic landscape created a vision of primitive mechanisation tamed and transformed by the all-powerful electron. When I looked again, Ann-Marie had changed into a different outfit. She performed all her changes onstage, dipping within the spinning vectors of hard light, aided by the microcircuitry in her clothes. Or rather, *their* clothes, the creations that had resulted from the findings of so many secret focus groups, research and development teams, marketing and merchandising meetings. What 'Kit Marlowe' had succeeded in doing was gaining access to the birth-point of the creative process.

As the show reached its zenith the room erupted, and stayed in a state of perpetual arousal through the hammering climactic flourishes of the performance. I'd like to think that the audience applause was spontaneous, but even that was doubtful.

I saw her after the show. My ticket admitted me to a party for special buyers. I queued for the cloakroom, queued for the VIP lounge, queued to pay my respects to the new star. Waited until she was standing with only one or two people, and moved in on her. I couldn't bring myself to call her 'Andromeda', nor could I call her Ann-Marie because she wasn't the Ann-Marie I knew any more. There was something different about her eyes. She had little markings carved into the actual ball of each eye, as though the pupils had been scored with a scalpel and filled with coloured ink.

'Eye tattoos,' she explained when I asked. 'They're going to be big.'

Her eyelashes had been shaved off and her mouth artificially widened somehow, the lips collagen-implanted and reshaped. She still had heavy breasts, but now she had a waist. And great legs. I had never seen her legs before tonight. She was wearing a body-stocking constructed in the kind of coarse material you saw on African native women, but the fabric glowed in faint cadences, like the pulse of someone between dreams and wakefulness.

'How does it do that?' I asked.

'The material has microscopic mirroring on one facet of the thread. It twists slightly to the rhythm of my heartbeat,' she explained.

'Jesus, couldn't it electrocute you?'

'The voltage is lower than that required to run the average pacemaker. Don't worry, I'm better than fine.' She spoke as if she had learned her reply from a script, and I guess she had. I looked down at her hands. She had no fingernails. There were just puckers of ragged flesh where her nails had been.

'I'm glad you could come. It means a lot. I wondered if you'd ever forgive me.'

'I'm not sure I have. Your mum says you never write any more.'

'I don't know what I'd say to her. I send money, of course. She wouldn't approve if I told her half of what happens around here. I mean, it's great and everything, but – '

'But what? Can we have a drink together?'

Ann-Marie looked around guiltily. 'I'd love to have a drink, but I'm not allowed. The first few weeks were rough, but I feel a lot more centred now. You wouldn't believe the eating and exercise regime.'

The Ann-Marie I knew would never have used a word like 'centred'. I was hungry for answers. I wanted to know what went on behind the hotel doors. I went to touch her and she flinched. 'All models have to work out,' I told her, 'but there's more to it than that, isn't there?'

She gave me her patented blank look. Her eyes went so unfocused she could have been watching a plane land.

'Come on, Ann-Marie, I *know*.'

'Well, I admit,' she said softly, 'there's a downside, a real downside. I wish we could talk more. I miss you.'

'I just want to know if you're happy,' I asked. 'Tell me you made the right choice.'

'I don't know. They took out a length of my gut. Stripped my veins and tried to recolour them. They tried out some piercings at the top of my legs and attached them to the flesh on the backs of my arms, but it wasn't a good look. If I eat the wrong things I start bleeding inside. They tried little mirrors instead of my fingernails but my system rejected them. They were going to run fine neon wires under my skin to light me up, but their doctor said it would be too dangerous for me to move around with so much electric cable in me. I won't tell you what they wanted to do to me down below. There are other things going on that you wouldn't – '

Suddenly a tiny LED on her collar blinked, just once, so briefly that I later wondered if I imagined it. Ann-Marie's face paled. The fine wire collar around her neck automatically tightened, cutting into her skin, closing off her throat and the carotoid artery in her neck. A vein throbbed angrily at her temple. Liquid began to pool in the bay of her mouth. The bodysuit closed more tightly around her as its circuitry came alive. She could barely find the air to speak. A second later the spasm ended, and the collar released itself to its preset diameter.

'I have to go now,' she whispered hoarsely, her eyes searching my face as if trying to memorise my features for some future recollection. She turned away, stiffly walking back to her keepers. I figured she was miked up, and wondered if that was the first time they had been called upon to jerk her lead. But for now, Ann-Marie was gone. Andromeda returned to her celestial enclosure of light, away from the mundane world, into the mists of mythology.

I understood then what she had surrendered to keep the Look.

The terrible truth is, I would still have changed places with her for a taste of that life, just for a chance to be someone, to look down upon dreary mortals from the height of godhood. I would have done anything – I would still do anything – to get a second chance. To have Kit Marlowe look at me and smile knowingly. To let his people experiment with my body until they were happy no matter how much it hurt, and I would smile back at them through the stitches and the blood and the endless tearing pain. I would surrender everything.

Because nothing can ever take away the power of the Look. To be adored is to become divine. All your life is worth its finest moment. And when at last you fall from grace, you still have eternity to remind you of that time.

*Sometimes, the best bits of books or sitcoms are the parts near the beginning where nothing much happens. I like these quiet moments because characters still have room to breathe before becoming subject to the constrictions of the plot. Simon Nye always gave Gary and Tony a bit of dialogue on the sofa in 'Men Behaving Badly'. The scriptwriters Galton and Simpson excelled at timewasting in 'Steptoe And Son', but their masterpiece is 'A Sunday Afternoon At Home', which they wrote for Tony Hancock. Absolutely nothing happens for half an hour; the episode is a small miracle of economy and timing. I wanted to write a novel in a similarly minimalist style, and may do someday. Until then, this tale, written for* The Second Time Out Book of London Stories, *must suffice.*

# RAINY DAY BOYS

There aren't many moments in life when you can point and say with certainty that something got decided, but this is about one of those moments. It involved a friendship, a city and a death. Davis and I were the friends. London was the city. And the death – well, that was probably the part that got things decided.

It was a wet Sunday afternoon in November, the kind of day that never gets light or dries out. The sky was low and sulphurous, an evil-tempered shade of sienna that had everyone running to find cover. King's Cross was bathed in the sort of light you see in old paintings of a biblical nature, where hapless mortals take up a tiny fraction of the canvas and jagged lightning cleaves the heavens. On such a day the area's residents look dirty and depressed, as though they've been deserted by their gods and left to die. Even the pigeons, huddled on damaged stumps in the eaves of St. Pancras, looked suicidal. King's Cross is for transients; it isn't a spot to stop. It isn't for saying 'Oh, let's have a cup of coffee and wander about for a while.' In this part of town you keep on the move if you know what's good for you. Not a refreshing place. It's incapable of regenerating itself, let alone anyone who visits it.

And yet.

I always think that London looks best on a day of rain. The houses and streets slink back into proportion. Traffic diminishes, pavements reflect, structures of glass and steel dull down in shame so that neglected stone buildings can emerge from the gloom like safe harbours.

London in the rain.

Trees and hedges drip. Rich greens and browns predominate. The Thames flattens. Railway arches exude a strange childhood smell, like old cinemas. Coffee bar windows steam over. Bookstores and rummagy junk shops beckon. Interior lives are illuminated from the streets. It's a time for thinking and dreaming. A time when I usually attempt to clean my flat.

I had been trying to reach the streaks of dirt smeared along the top window in the lounge with a tomato cane, on the end of which was tied a Windolene-soaked J-Cloth. I thought the rain would help to keep the cloth wet. The frame was stuck because its sash-cords had seized up, and it had been painted over about a hundred and fifty times. When I raised the bottom pane it covered the one above, rendering cleaning impossible. I had broken three canes so far, my jeans were soaked and the window remained dirty. The thought of tackling the job from the outside on a dry day up a ladder never crossed my mind. I didn't possess the capacity for that kind of deductive reasoning.

I lived on the second floor of a council block off York Way, a part of King's Cross so architecturally decimated by railways, roads and canals that Camden council, having destroyed everything of interest that the Blitz hadn't removed (including one of London's most loved landmarks, the Euston Portico), was clutching at straws by decreeing the area's gas holders to be of aesthetic merit. In a city where Knightsbridge airing-cupboards were selling for half a million, King's Cross was still pretty cheap. To survive in the area I had to breathe in the shuddering filth from a million gridlocked vehicles. I had to tack my way along canal towpaths between tramps who sang at the sky, while the bloated bodies of river rats bobbed past in a miasma of polystyrene pellets. I had to regularly pull my wallet back from the palsied hands of inept pickpockets. I had to skirt the grey-faced junkies who built their nests outside McDonald's like big bedraggled pigeons, and remember to walk on the other side of the road during gang confrontations (rival factions of school-children divided by territory, ethnicity and haircuts). Then I had to barter access rights to my flat with two local whores who brought new meaning to the term 'oldest profession'.

I wasn't much safer at home, either; my next-door neighbour regularly got drunk and threw items of furniture over the balcony in fits of self-loathing. The people in the flat below (five shifty-looking young men in tracksuit bottoms and jackets with grey cotton hoods) were, I suspected, not a family unit but drug dealers; they received visits around the clock from people who never stayed longer than five minutes. And the danger didn't end there, because Battle Bridge House was built so close to the railway lines, there was always the possibility that the front carriages of the 17:45 to Barnsley might jump the signals, flinging commuters in all directions, and end up embedded in my bedroom wall.

When you think about an area in architectural detail, certain images spring to mind. Holland Park has sedate redbrick villas, Lisson Grove has leafy LCC forecourts, St. John's Wood has plexiglass balconies, but all I see when I think of King's Cross is a sturdy drain-fed weed pushing its way through brickwork halfway up a wet tunnel wall. The only things that live here do so because they're hardy.

Despite all this, I liked King's Cross. Too much of the city had been colonised by decaf-latte television producers dropping their homunculi off at school in Sahara Land-Cruisers. Fulham, Putney and Hampstead had long since become no-go areas, but now the disease was so widespread that even Deptford probably had a Starbucks. Every Saturday morning I walked down to the paper shop, under the dripping railway arches, past the Beverly Hills Hair Salon (which had about as much to do with Beverly Hills as Sid James), past the sad plaque marking the spot where a fifteen-year-old boy had been brutally stabbed to death, past stupefied clubbers returning home from Bagley's Warehouse and Northern lads in thin summer jackets looking for B&B accommodation, past all kinds of life, seeing everything but taking care to touch as little as possible. I don't interfere. I'm too much of a dreamer. I don't like to see things as they really are.

I was a few days away from turning thirty. From the age of five until my hormones kicked in I had been a child actor, starring mostly in commercials, the son of a single stage mother. I'd attended Anna Scher's drama school in Islington, and had been accepted by RADA, to end up, after a lengthy period of unemployment, in the stage version of Disney's *Beauty And The Beast*. Annoyed by the fact that I had undergone years of tortuous classical training in order to play a dancing spoon in Tottenham Court Road, I had ignored my fellow performers' cries of 'at least it's work' and violated my contract, drifting away from the acting profession altogether. I was now employed by a replacement car-part company under one of the area's many arches. In my spare time I was trying to write The Screenplay, but I'd been stuck on page seven for about two years. On my days off I sat on my stool by the window in my flat, half-heartedly waiting for a big break and a perfect partner to come along, but meanwhile I sold exhaust pipes and dated a girl who had first come to my attention soaping the aerial of my boss's van in the Chicago Car Wash two doors down.

On this particularly sodden Sunday afternoon I abandoned my window-cleaning exercise to sit with my elbows on damp jeans staring out at the rain, hypnotised by my own inactivity. I was vaguely thinking about my script when I became aware of a buzzing noise.

'Thanks a lot, Jake. It's chucking it down out there, didn't you hear me ringing?' Davis stamped his feet on the mat and shook water everywhere. The little hair he had left was plastered to his head. He gave me a beady look. 'Lend a hand with this.' He dragged a tall, heavy-looking cardboard box in through the door and thumped it down. Something inside clanged dully.

I went over to the box and poked it with the toe of my trainer. 'The bell's packed up. Where are your keys?'

'You want to get that fixed, I'm soaked. In my other jacket.'

'There's a towel somewhere. What's in the box?'

'Look at the state of this place. If you don't mind me saying so, you are living in the most disgusting area in the whole of London.'

'I like King's Cross. And I do mind you saying so. I believe in psychic geography. It's a place of great mystery.'

'The only mystery is why you stay here.'

'You wouldn't understand.' I cleared a patch of condensation on the window. 'Did you know the whole area used to be called Battle Bridge, after the road that crossed over the River Fleet? It was where Boadicea fought against Paulinus. The Roman generals rode on elephants up Goods Way.'

'Yeah, I know, she turned into a hare and escaped, we did it at school. There's nothing mystical about it, just a load of bollocks to cover up the fact that the English lost.'

'It doesn't matter whether it happened exactly like that,' I replied hotly, 'it's the significance of the events occurring on this ground that's important. It affects everything. There are cen-turies of conflict and deception all around us. Thieves and murderers used to lie in wait for their victims – '

'They still do,' Davis retorted.

' – and as Boadicea was buried just up the road, they decided to reduce the area's notoriety by changing its name to Boadicea's Cross, which became St. George's Cross, then King's Cross.' I warmed to the subject. It was a bit of a hobby with me. 'After the Great Fire of London, it was the only place where Neapolitan cress grew. It was picked by the Pinder of Wakefield himself. Then George IV marked the junction of its six roads with a huge octagonal building of white stone that housed a pub, a police station and a camera obscura. The dustheaps of Victorian London grew here, and pigs fed on mountains of horse bones. The Russians bought the dustheaps to rebuild Moscow after the French invasion. The Pandemonium Company bought the flattened cinder-ground for their theatre, the Royal Clarence, and it became a practice-spot for acrobats and clowns. Later they opened a healing spring near the smallpox hospital called St. Chad's Well, and people came from all over the country to drink the waters and promenade in the gardens. See, it's all paradox; warriors and clowns, pestilence and healing waters, kings and cut-throats, cities and bone-mounds. Typical London. Every time you think you see it, it slips away from you. It's a view of the world from an acute angle. The picture keeps changing . . .'

I could feel Davis staring at me. 'Thanks very much for the lecture. You know what I think? You're going round the twist. You want to stop thinking so hard and get out more. Breathe some fresh air. Get yourself sorted. Have a tidy up for a start.'

I glanced back at the crinkled piles of comics and the dirty crockery stacked on top of the gas fire. 'I know where everything is.'

'Then you must have psychic powers. You could get a job with the Egyptian government, locating antiquities. We'll have to clear a space.' He pulled the top of the box toward me.

'What's in it?'

'Birthday present. Happy thirty.'

Davis was thirty-four, and liked to give me the benefit of his advice, even though most of it was inaccurate or useless. He was always perfectly groomed, and even at the weekends dressed as though he was just about to go out to dinner. His clothes looked as though they had never been worn before, unlike mine, which looked like they had been worn by several people at once.

Davis and I were friends in that odd urban way in which people find themselves drifting into the circle of each other's company for no particular reason. We certainly didn't have much in common. Looking back, it was a relationship that allowed our weaknesses to flourish in a faintly disastrous symbiosis. Davis was a surly bundle of complaints and grudges. His attitude stemmed from the fact that he was a dot.com workaholic who had uniquely managed to lose his company money at a time when everyone else appeared to grow rich. He trusted no-one and was desperate to succeed, but the more desperately he tried, the less he succeeded. He had never forgiven himself for being bamboozled out of an IT business partnership, and he had never absolved his girlfriend Erica for leaving him just as he was about to suggest getting engaged, which shows how little he understood her. An aura of bitterness radiated from him like flu-germs.

Davis was staying at my place while his own apartment was being redecorated. He wasn't thrilled about the arrangement but it was convenient for his office, which was situated in a feature-less block behind Liverpool Street Station. His own flat was a pristine loft conversion in Primrose Hill, where the streets had a pre-war look that reminded me of the locations for old Ealing films, except that the pubs were full of coke-addled television executives on mobile phones instead of beery cockneys with Woodbines behind their ears.

Davis's flat was filled with state-of-the-art technology. He could communicate instantly with anyone in the world, but the only calls he ever received were from computer companies updating him about software or people trying to sell him dormer windows. He chased after girls who didn't even bother to pretend liking him, and had virtually no friends. In the days after Erica upped stumps and returned to the Disillusioned Single Women's pavilion, we would sprawl in Davis's creepily immacu-late lounge and multi-task our leisure time, rolling post-pub joints, downloading smut from the internet, thrashing Playst-ation race-cars and staring at trailer-trash TV shows about stupid fat people driving the wrong way up Miami freeways.

Since Davis had moved in with me, we had refined this process of mental ossification to include sitting all night nursing pints in the Hoop And Grapes, and having the kind of peculiar conver-sations you only bother with when you're truly bored. After three weeks passed drifting in this state of mutual dysfunction, we realised that we were getting on each other's nerves, and something had to give.

'I suppose you want to see inside,' said Davis. He dropped the other end of the box on the floor and pulled out a number of chromium-plated rods. 'It's a home gym.'

'For me? I don't need a gym.'

'Of course you do. You're falling to bits. You walk down to

the shop when you're out of snouts, and that's about it. "Twenty Kensitas and a Daily Mirror, please." Stop on the landing to get your breath back. That's not exercise. You'll have your first heart attack before you're forty.'

'I don't think they make Kensitas any more.' I wandered into the kitchen to find the kettle. 'If you're going to stay here you could do some washing up occasionally.'

'You want to be fit like me, mate. I go to the gym four times a week. Nearly kill myself. Veins standing out in my temples, heart hammering, dizzy spells. Does me the world of good. Eight hundred quid a year it costs me. You'll save a bloody fortune.'

'I don't go now, so I'm already saving a fortune. Just think of all the things I don't do, and add up all the money I'm saving. No sky-diving, no polo, no water-skiing, no trying to book tables at The Ivy, there's loads saved right there.'

'We can put this up in half an hour. I've got the brackets. Ten minutes a day and you'll be as perky as a cat in a sack. Birds'll be falling over you with their tongues hanging out.'

'That's an attractive image.'

'Trust me, the only way you'll get more pussy is to go for gender reassignment.'

It was useless to argue. Davis was already emptying various bolts and hinges out of the box. I filled two Cornish pottery mugs with tea and sat cross-legged on the floor. 'You know how to put this together, then?'

'It can't be hard, can it?'

'No instruction book. Knocked off, is it?'

'It belonged to someone at work. He doesn't need it any more. He's in a coma.'

In addition to the brackets there were cables, pulleys and two red plastic cushions mounted on squares of plywood. 'Butterfly press,' Davis explained, 'needs to go against a load-bearing wall. You got a hammer-drill?'

'I've got a hand-drill.'

'That's no good, we need a Black & Decker. Can't you borrow one?'

So, against my better judgement, I went next door to ask Mr Gorridge. My neighbour was a retired teacher and a solitary drinker. I sublet my flat from him, and owed him quite a bit of back-rent, but he never made a fuss about it. He resembled his old school nickname, Porridge, with masses of frizzy grey hair and kaftany brown clothes that appeared to be fashioned from knitted rope. He had African masks and crocheted mandalas hanging in his kitchen window, taught yoga at an adult education college, and spent his evenings getting pissed to old Hawkwind albums. He only ever had one visitor, his daughter Holly, a smart-looking financial services consultant in her late twenties, although it beat me how she could allow her father to live in such a dump. Gorridge was pleasant enough and kept his distance, which was fine with me. There were three main types of resident in our building: people who were infringing the law in some way, and who kept to themselves so much that you wouldn't know if they were dead or if they had been arrested, families whose appalling public rows held the entire block in thrall, and loners who you occasionally saw creeping up staircases with plastic bags full of bottles. I had Gorridge down in the latter category.

For once, when he opened the door he wasn't paralytic, but his frizzy hair was flat on one side and sticking up on the other, so he must have been sleeping. He left me on the step while he went to get his drill. Something inside smelled awful. I peered around the front door. His hall floor was covered in linoleum. I hadn't seen lino in years. It was exactly the shade you get when you mix every plasticene colour together. The lights were hung with those huge dusty paper globes that were once the staple fixture of every student flat in London.

'You will let me have it back, won't you?' he called, dragging miles of tangled flex into the hall. 'You can come in and have a drink if you like.'

'I won't stop, thanks.' I caught myself feeling sorry for him, and made a mental note to be more friendly at some point in the future, just not this century.

It took over two hours just to assemble the butterfly press and its counterweights. 'This is a support wall,' explained Davis, knocking on the plaster, 'you want to put a hole here.' He drew a cross with a felt-tip pen about three feet from the floor, 'and here.' He put his ear against the wall and tapped it with his index finger. 'Okay, give me the drill. We can get this fitted together and working in no time, then go over the Hoop And Grapes for a pint.'

But we weren't destined to reach the pub.

I realised that we didn't have any drill bits. The logical thing would have been to go next door and ask Gorridge if he had any, but by then Davis had come up with an alternative plan. He said we should knock a nail into the wall, extract it, then screw the first of the bolts into the hole we had made. I rooted through the paltry contents of my tool box, and came up with a single six-inch masonry nail and a pathetically small hammer.

'What's that for, cracking toffee?' he scoffed. 'Haven't you got anything bigger?'

'Hang on a minute.' I came back from the hall with a sledge-hammer the workmen had left behind when they'd demolished one of the concrete staircases in the building's courtyard.

'Christ on a bike. Just don't miss.' Davis gingerly held the nail over its cross. I drew the sledgehammer back as far as I could, then swung it down. There was an explosion of filthy plaster as it smashed a hole clean through the wall to my neighbour's flat. In the ensuing silence I stared at the splintered crater as plaster dust settled in my hair. Davis appeared unconcerned. He pressed his face against the hole and tried to see inside. 'That wasn't a supporting wall. It's been subdivided.' He dug out a Kleenex and blew his nose. 'So much for co-operative housing. It's another Ronan Point. I wonder where the nail went.'

I knew Gorridge would be knocking on my door at any minute. He had complained several times in the past when Davis had cranked up my CD player in order to hear some obscure stereo effect on one of his Orbital albums. I decided to get the jump on Gorridge by apologising first, so I left Davis complaining about the poor quality of my walls and ventured across the balcony. I hadn't decided what I was going to say, but after trying the doorbell a few times and receiving no answer, I figured he must have gone out. I was about to walk away when I noticed that his front door was ajar.

I stepped into the hall. The horrible smell that had assailed me earlier intensified. On my right was the kitchen, where something gurgled in a pot on the cooker. The lounge lay directly in front of me. I reached the doorway and saw a tablelamp on its side, the shade broken, the bulb lighting one corner of the room. Nuggets of glass crunched in the carpet. I had an ominous feeling that we had caused something bad to happen.

Gorridge was lying in the gloom with his face buried in a putty-coloured sofa. The cushions beneath him were soaked red. He had fallen forward on his knees, apparently from a position beside the hole we had made in the wall, and my six-inch nail was sticking out of the back of his head. I could see the gleaming end of it poking through his hair. I only looked at him for a second, but I knew the sight would stay with me for a lifetime. Panic crowded in and I galloped back to Davis, fighting to catch my breath.

'You'd better come and see,' I managed. Before he could ask questions, I grabbed his arm and pulled him outside. Checking that there was no-one else on the balcony, I re-entered Gorridge's flat with Davis in tow.

'God, what's that awful smell?' asked Davis. 'What's he doing, boiling a cat?' He headed off into the kitchen and checked the saucepan on the cooker. 'This has gone dry. Looks like sock casserole. Lucky it didn't catch fire. Why hasn't he turned it off?'

By way of an answer, I pulled Davis toward the Lounge Of Death.

'Blimey, so that's where the nail went. What a mess.'

'Is that all you can say?' I screamed.

'I need a fag.' He pulled out a cigarette and lit it from the lighter on Gorridge's coffee table.

'We've killed him!' I yelled. 'He was a yoga instructor!'

'What the hell's that got to do with it?'

'He did yoga. He sits against the wall with his legs folded and meditates. Meditates with his head against the wall.'

'Well, he reached Nirvana this time.' Davis leaned in for a closer look and exhaled.

'Don't blow smoke over him!'

'Why not, he's dead, isn't he?'

I was incandescent with panic. 'You've left your fingerprints on the lighter. And on the table. And – everywhere.'

'Yeah, but who cares? I mean, you're the one who killed him.'

'What?' I shrieked.

'You were holding the hammer, mate.'

'It was an accident. You know that.' I thrust an accusing finger at Davis. 'You told me it was a support wall. Everything you ever tell me is wrong. What are we going to do? We can't just leave him here.'

'I'm not going to drag him down the corridor wrapped in a carpet, if that's what you mean.'

'We'll have to call the police.'

'Forget it. I'm not being beaten into a confession by a bunch of uniformed monkeys. Think what it would do to my career. And you – you've got a motive. You owe him money.'

He had a point. Gorridge's daughter apparently took care of his finances; the old teacher had once confided to me that he was hopeless with money. Which meant that there was a Living Gorridge who knew about my debt.

'Wait a minute, his front door was ajar. Someone else could have crept in, killed him and left.'

'And they shifted the blame to you by inserting your nail into his head. Bit unlikely, don't you think?'

The smell from the kitchen and the oppressiveness of Gorridge's lounge was making me feel sick. 'I have to get out of here,' I swallowed, moving back into the hall. I was about to go onto the balcony when I heard the boys from the flat below coming up the stairwell. 'Shit, we can't let them see us.' I grabbed

Davis and pushed him back. Once they had bounced past we crept out of the flat, just as Gorridge's neighbour Mrs Lynch opened her front door.

'Oh hello, Jake, how are you?' she asked, pulling her rainhood tightly around her perm.

'Fine thank you,' I mumbled.

'Someone reported my Sean for keeping pets in his bedroom,' she explained, as if in response to an enquiry on my part. 'I let them out of their cages. He's ever so upset, but it seemed the kindest thing to do. Now I'm worried that they might breed, so don't be alarmed if you see anything running about. They'll probably get eaten by something from the canal. Have you been to see Mr Gorridge? Is he all right?' She tried to look back through the door that I was hastily pulling shut behind me. 'Only there was a crash earlier and I thought he might have fallen over.'

'No, he's fine,' I lied, 'never better, fantastic in fact.'

'Perhaps I should look in and see if he wants anything from the shops. Save him going out in this awful weather, with his legs.'

'No, he's got everything he needs, I've just checked, weeks of shopping in, he doesn't need to go out for ages if he doesn't want to, he's feeling a bit whacked and having a lie-down – ' Davis jabbed me in the ribs, and I snapped my mouth shut.

'Well.' She looked at both of us indecisively, then looked at Gorridge's closed front door. 'So. I'd better be getting on.'

'Great,' I hissed at Davis as we hustled back into my hall, 'she can place me in my neighbour's flat at the time of his death, and you pulled the front door shut so we can't get back in and wipe our prints, wonderful.'

'I don't know why you're obsessing about fingerprints. Your nail is sticking out of the back of his head.'

'I shouldn't be worrying at all, should I? I've got nothing to hide. I should just tell the truth, say that it was an unfortunate accident. I can't be held responsible, surely?'

'Surely.' He mimicked my pronunciation. 'No wonder you've

never been able to hold down a real job. People would walk all over you.'

'Acting was a real job,' I said indignantly.

'Acting is not a job, it's just showing off. It's for people who can't grow up.'

'It's a respectable adult profession.'

'Oh yeah? You were a spoon.'

'A *dancing* spoon. I stepped in for Mark a couple of times when he was off sick.'

'And what was he?'

'A candlestick.'

'The résumé just keeps getting better, doesn't it? You could have played the contents of an entire kitchen drawer and you still wouldn't have found any employment other than a car exhaust shop.'

'I like where I work. And I'm writing a screenplay.'

'Oh yes, the famous *screenplay*. How is that coming along, by the way?'

'It's not at the moment.'

'Stalled again? It can't be writer's block, because you haven't actually written anything yet, have you?'

I was tempted to point out a few of the glitches in Davis's career, the bankrupted mobile phone company, the on-line services nobody wanted, the lousy investments, the failed entrepreneurial bids, but what was the point? I headed for the kitchen.

'Now what are you doing?'

'I'm going to put the kettle on. I need a cup of tea. I have to concentrate my mind.'

We stood in the kitchen waiting for the contents of the teapot to brew, watching the rain stream down the window, the trains drawing into the station below, the umbrellas of commuters opening like sinister black flowers.

'He might lie there undiscovered for days,' Davis pointed out.

'No, his daughter comes around...' I was chewing my thumbnail, and had made it bleed.

'When?'

My stomach twisted. 'Um, Sundays.'

'Today? What time?'

I looked at the kitchen clock. 'In about half an hour.'

'Then we have to get the body out before she finds it and calls the police.'

'How? I shut the front door.'

'The hole.' David darted back into the lounge. 'Maybe we can pull him through the hole you made in the wall.'

'Will you stop saying I made the hole? I didn't want a sodding home gym in the first place.'

The shattered centre of the crater in the lounge wall was only about an inch across, and when I tried to peer through it I couldn't see anything. It would mean tearing down a sizeable chunk of the room.

'You want to hit it really hard with the sledgehammer. You want to – '

'Will you stop saying I want to all the time? I don't want to do any of it.'

'You want to go to jail?'

'No. But the hammer.' I studied it anxiously. 'The neighbours will complain about the noise.'

'They'll complain a lot more if they find out you murdered him. "He was a quiet bloke, always kept to himself, didn't seem like a nutter." That's what they'll say when they're interviewed on the news.'

'You think this is my fault for living here. Like it couldn't happen in Primrose Hill.'

'You're right it couldn't, because my neighbours aren't vile old hippies.'

'No, they're advertising executives who park their mountain tanks in handicapped spaces while they're making dinner reservations at fucking Granita.'

'I don't know what you've got against the middle classes,' said Davis. 'I've never seen this bitter side of you before.'

I tried to stay calm. 'I hope he didn't feel anything. If he was meditating, his mind was probably on a different plane. I wonder what was going through his head.'

'Your six-inch nail.'

'That's it, I'm going out for some air,' I said. 'If you touch my wall, I'll kill you.'

I found a raincoat and opened the front door, but got no further than the balcony. A black Mercedes Kompressor had pulled into one of the parking spaces below. It was the car Holly drove. She was early. I ducked back into the hall.

'Now what?'

'His daughter's here.'

'Well, you'll have to go downstairs and stop her from coming up.'

'I can't do that.'

'You've got to send her away, Jake. You want to go to jail?'

'Stop saying that.'

'Then stop her.'

He shoved me out onto the balcony, and after a moment of hopping about in indecision I ran to the stairwell. Hearing Holly slam her car door and bip-bip the alarm, I stuck my head over the staircase wall. She was as sleek and beautiful as her car, dressed in a charcoal grey business suit and a white blouse, blonde hair tied back, a slimline leather briefcase in one hand. I looked like I'd been in some kind of explosion. I didn't have the authority to impede her progress. If she'd seen me in the street she would probably have given me 50p. I ran back and knocked on my front door. Davis eventually answered and peered around it as if expecting Jehovah's witnesses. 'What is it now?'

'I can't talk to her.'

'Oh, for God's sake. One simple thing. How can you let a woman intimidate you?'

'Fine, if you're so good with women, you do it.'

'I don't even live here.'

This was costing us time. Holly had reached the top of the stairwell.

'She's coming, she's coming, let me in.' I shoved against the door. Davis shoved back.

'You stay out there and send her away.'

'This is my flat!'

'No, it's *his* flat, and you owed him money and you killed him by driving a six-inch nail into his skull so you'd better stall his daughter, otherwise she'll find the body and call the police and they'll dance on your face with their stupid boots until you tell them everything, and I'll lose my job and the precious scrap of dignity I've been able to muster in the last ten years, and you'll be sent to Holloway and the convicts will find out you were a spoon and they'll gang-rape you, all because you can't remember how to strike up a conversation with a bird.'

'Hang on, Holloway's a women's prison.'

'Brixton, then.'

I pushed hard against the door, whacking Davis back against the wall. 'Davis, I've had it with you always telling me what to do. Let her find the body. I'll make a clean breast of it because it's the decent thing – the moral thing – and if they ask me how come I was hammering nails into the wall I'll tell them the truth, that it was your bright idea in the first place – '

I heard a key turn in the lock next door and realised we were too late to do anything. Davis was seething, leaping about in anger and hissing like a pressure cooker. 'You *fuckwit!*' he fizzed. He hurled himself back into the lounge and threw his hands over his ears. 'Any second now she's going to start screaming the place down!'

And we waited. We hovered near the hole, listening without daring to hear, but there was nothing, no sound at all.

'What's going on?' Davis whispered after several minutes had elapsed.

'I don't know, she must have seen him by now.' I crept away toward the kitchen.

'Where are you going?' Davis hissed.

'I didn't finish my tea.'

'Bloody hell, how can you think of tea at a time like this,

your freedom is about to come to an end. It'll be cold by now, make a fresh one.'

'Freedom's an illusion,' I told him, looking for my Cornish pottery mug. 'I tell people I'm an actor but I'm not, I sell car exhausts. I say I'm writing a screenplay but I've written nothing at all, and even if I did it would probably be utter rubbish. You tell everyone you're a financial director but you work in a phone centre making cold-calls, you think you're charming but people hate you even before they've met you. It's all a load of self-deluding bollocks because everyone wants to look as successful as – that.' I pointed out of my window at the billboard opposite. The poster hoarding showed Christian Bale in *American Psycho*.

'Then what do you really want to do?' asked Davis.

'I'd like to work in the Museum of London, just as a guard or something, just to be near the exhibits. I've read millions of books. I know tons of history. But I only remember the things that interest me. That's why I kept forgetting the words to "Be Our Guest".'

'You haven't even got the qualifications to be a museum guard, mate. Look at the way you live, in this collapsing dump of a flat – '

'It wasn't in a state of collapse before you arrived. But even if it was, I'd like it because that's the beauty of living here, we can all do what we like, and the difference between you and me is that I'm basically content to be like this, and you're not.'

'What, happy with your lot, are you?'

'Er, yes,' I faltered.

'Content to shag that dog who works in the car wash?'

'Yes, and she's not a dog, she's great, she's a dish, and she's gonna run away with this spoon.'

'Go on then, enjoy your crappy little life.'

'Thanks, I will. It twists you up inside to see people having fun, doesn't it?'

'You're about to be done for murder, I hardly think it qualifies as fun.'

If Davis and I had been married, we would have gone on like

this for the next thirty years before one of us died. By now twenty minutes had passed since Holly had entered her father's flat.

'Listen.'

I heard Gorridge's front door open and close. Davis ran back into the passage and tried to see through the fluted glass of the hall window. 'She's going back out. What's the deal here?'

'Maybe she called the rozzers and she's going to meet them downstairs.'

'Do you see any police?'

I ducked into the front room and pulled back the curtains, but she had already passed by. We gave her a minute to reach the stairwell, shot back out onto the balcony and looked over the wall. Holly was dragging a black binliner across the car park. She unlocked the Mercedes, hauled the bag into the boot and then drove off. Silence fell once more, broken only by the patter of flooded gutters.

'Right,' said Davis, 'I've had enough of this. I'm going through the wall.'

He used the handle of the sledgehammer to prise off a three-foot panel of plasterboard. Beyond this was a narrow gap filled with mouse droppings, then the wall of the next flat. 'You can go first, seeing as you caused this.' He cracked the panel back on the far side, and shoved me through. I snagged my sweater on the damaged wooden struts, and tore my way through into Gorridge's lounge.

'Well?' called Davis, 'how is he?'

'I don't know,' I replied.

'For God's sake. How does he look?'

'It's hard to tell.'

'What do you mean?'

'He's not here.'

'What do you mean, not here?'

'Gone.'

'Yes, I understand the words, I just don't see how he could have gone.'

'Come through and see for yourself.'

'Not in these strides. Go around and open the door.'

Gorridge's body had disappeared, the table lamp had been placed upright and the stained cushions had been removed from the sofa. Holly had apparently hidden her father's corpse and covered up for us – but why?

'She took the cushions out in the binliner, but what the hell did she do with the body? She couldn't have taken it out of the flat.'

We searched the place room by room. We checked under the bed and inside the airing cupboard. Davis even emptied out Gorridge's hoover bag hunting for clues. Everywhere we looked we found Rioja bottles and underpants, but no Gorridge.

'There's nowhere else she could have put him,' said Davis. 'Unless she slipped out with him earlier and you didn't hear her.'

'I don't think she just "slipped out" carrying her dead father. What, you think she managed to manhandle him down to the rubbish chute?'

'Oh my God.'

We dashed out onto the balcony and yanked open the chute, but couldn't see anything.

'Try the floor below,' Davis suggested. Taking the stairs two at a time, I swung around the bend in the staircase and crashed straight into Holly Gorridge.

'Well, you're in a hurry,' she said, righting herself and pushing her hair behind her ears. I had never seen her close up. Big green eyes, cheeky smile, astonishingly attractive. A future life together flashed before my eyes; courtship, engagement, betrothal, procreation, maturity, dotage, this domestic fantasy only disrupted by the knowledge that Holly would probably not be keen on marrying her father's assassin.

'Have you got my money?' she asked cheerfully.

I tried to look puzzled and innocent. 'What do you mean?'

'You owe my father three months' rent.'

She had a nerve to start going after her old man's outstanding debtors before his body was even cold, but perhaps that was how she managed to keep a good job in the city.

'Um, I can pop around with it in the morning. Will he be in?'

'No, he won't.'

'What about the day after tomorrow?'

'He won't be there then, either. You can give the money to me.'

She's playing it very cool, I thought. She carried a sense of inner strength. Outer strength, too, if she could clear up the Lounge of Death and stash Gorridge somewhere in just under twenty minutes.

'You can give me a cheque if you like.'

'I can do that,' I countered. 'Shall I make it out to your father?'

'No, make it out to me.'

It suddenly crossed my mind that she might not be above a little blackmail. 'If I do, can I ask you something, just out of scientific curiosity?'

Holly tilted her head to one side and, for the first time, smiled at me a little. 'All right then. Go ahead and ask.'

'What did you do with the old man?'

When I returned to my flat, I found Davis sitting on the stool by the rainy window with his head in his hands. He looked sheepish and miserable. 'I'm sorry I left you to deal with Gorridge's daughter. I just couldn't do it. I knew I'd seen her somewhere before. She drinks in a bar in Primrose Hill. I tried to pick her up once and she just gave me a look.'

'What kind of look?'

'The worst kind. What did she tell you?'

'Oh, not much. I think it was my fault.'

'What do you mean?'

'I got it all wrong. I mean, I didn't see what I thought I saw. You know how things look – '

'What the *shagging fuck* are you talking about?'

'Gorridge was drunk. He'd dropped his bottle of Rioja and passed out on the couch. He was already face down when my nail shot through the wall and lodged in his hair. Holly roused her old man and sent him off to her place while she cleared up the mess.'

'You mean the yoga and everything? We put ourselves through all that for nothing?'

'There was no harm done. Except to the wall.'

'Well, it defeats me.' He slumped down on the stool and stared gloomily into the goods yards. 'I just can't get to grips with things.'

'What things?' I asked.

'Oh, fuck it, everything. All of this.' His fingers marked a forlorn trail on the glass. 'When I was a kid we lived in the suburbs, near Orpington. I never remember it raining, but now it rains all the time. Nothing ever used to change. No-one went anywhere. No-one did anything more than tend their gardens and go to the seaside in the summer. I *suppose* it was boring. Now I'm stuck here and everything changes all the time. You should see the people I have to work with. They look about eleven years old. They seem to cope all right. Well, I admit defeat. I can't get a fucking handle on it.'

'I wouldn't worry. Not many people can.'

'Then why doesn't it bother you?'

'I guess I like where I live, Davis. Nothing stops here for very long. Railways, roads, rivers, people whizzing back and forth, buildings spring up and get knocked down. You can be among all this and still not making any difference to the world. You can go unnoticed, like a blur on an old photograph. That's okay, I don't need to make my mark, I just want to be happy.'

Davis rested his forehead against the window and sighed. 'Maybe I should move home. Perhaps going back is the only way I'll count for something.'

A feeling of melancholy settled over us. I was sorry that Davis felt so driven to succeed, and sad because I knew we had moved too far apart to remain friends. 'I'll put the kettle on.' I patted him awkwardly on the back.

'It's already boiled once. I was waiting for you.' Davis rose from the stool and brightened up a bit. 'Have we got any biscuits?'

We walked down to the Hoop and Grapes, but weren't in the mood to stay for long. On the way back we stopped in Liverpool Road and watched something shifting beneath the lamp light. It was a small animal of some kind, creeping out from under a rain-beaten bush. At first I thought it must be a cat. Then it hopped onto the glistening pavement.

'The rats around here are certainly getting bigger.'

'No, it's a rabbit,' said Davis, amazed. 'Right here in town.'

'Mrs Lynch said she had to get rid of her son's pets,' I reminded him. 'She was worried they might breed.'

'Maybe it's a hare.' Davis smiled ruefully. 'Maybe it's Boadicea.'

'That's the spirit.' I smiled back.

'I think I'm going to go home, Jake. I'll come by for my stuff.'

'Sure thing, Davis. Whenever you like.'

'I wonder if it'll ever stop raining.'

'Oh, I suppose so.'

We solemnly shook hands and walked off in opposite directions. When I got back to the flat, I turned on my computer and set to work.

I completely forgot to give Gorridge his cheque. He came by a few evenings later to complain about the damage we had done to the wall, but I'd remembered to buy some Rioja, so he left a happy man.

I didn't see too much of Davis after that, but I sometimes thought about him and wondered vaguely what he was up to.

Even at night, you can hear everything moving on.

*The crime writer and editor Maxim Jacubowski asked me to write a story connected in some way to the internet. I'm a big net user and it seemed an easy brief until I came to write it. The problem is that the seductive technology of the net leads you away from creating the effects you desire. It has spawned its own set of clichés; the victim and the user, the codes and aliases, the dark underbelly that's just a click away. It's rather a sedentary occupation, and the terminology dates fast. What if you wanted to tell a traditional story that could only happen using new technology?*

# THE BEACON

Mr Canvey lived on a wild Cornish clifftop where the trees could barely stand, and where the hedgerows were hobbled by the pounding gales that blasted up from the sea. His tough little box of a house was one of only four left in a village that had been shrinking for a hundred years. You could still see the flint foundations of the old churchyard, the post office and the schoolhouse, left like tidemarks around the remaining homes.

For five months of the year it was too inclement to venture far from the house, so Mr Canvey watched the world from his window, what he could see of it, which chiefly consisted of the sea from the lounge and kitchen windows, and from the sitting room, the back of the derelict church. In high summer a few tourist cars passed, and bickering seagulls alighted on the head-stones, but all in all it was a lonely existence, one that required you to keep a tight grip on life lest it tore itself free and blew away into wildness. Everything clung on to the land. Even the orange lichen that bedded into the roof tiles had to be removed with a chisel. In a less severe climate the spirit could rise and drift in warm air currents, but here it dug in its heels and refused to budge. The land bred a certain type of person; self-sufficient, kind but suspicious of generosity in others, dry and hard as stone.

Mr Canvey was of this stock, but lonelier and somewhat gentler, although he attempted to dismiss these newly recognised feelings. He had moved here from Truro after the end of his marriage. Now he led a very ordered life. The drawing of the curtains at dusk, the turning of the key in the mantelpiece clock, the lighting of the gas fire, Chopin or Handel in the CD player, a favourite old book from the shelf in the lounge. He was fifty-three, but he felt much older. Men often do when they think they have reached the end of being useful. Mr Canvey had lived, to a degree; he had travelled and worked and fallen in love. He had fathered a child, lost it and lost his wife as well. He had seen his fortunes wax and wane, survived accidents and illnesses. And although dissatisfaction sometimes gnawed at him, he had come to accept his lot, and to appreciate his time on earth. As he watched the restless sea from his window, he was aware that he had been forgotten.

An asthmatic condition had forced Mr Canvey into early retirement, and as his isolation grew he decided, if not exactly to break out of his shell, then to crack it open a little.

Just before Christmas, on a morning bogged in browns and greys, and capped with a slippery silver sky, he drove into Truro to buy himself a computer. If the adverts were to be believed, the internet would expand his shrunken world. Mr Canvey did not consider himself to be resistant to change, but his lack of experience with technology made him feel prehistoric compared to people he watched on television, navigating their way around the electronic universe with fleet fingers. He was capable of setting his video recorder and tuning his satellite stations. He understood the basic principles of computing. He liked the idea of having the world at his fingertips. He'd made a note of the model he wanted, and the software he would like to go with it. He had carefully compared prices, then made his purchase.

Later in the week, a young technician arrived at the house. He wore black overalls with the name of the store on the back and his own name – Danny – stitched in gold thread over his heart. He quickly set about unpacking the equipment. Then he installed various items of software and registered his new customer as the user.

Men of Mr Canvey's age had, supposedly, seen more changes in their lives than anyone who had ever lived. Post-war rationing, the rebuilding of bombed cities, the loss of empire, the end of monarchy, the collapse of the class system, the disintegration of the family, raised living standards, lowered sexual inhibitions, space travel, mass transit, and electronic communication, which shrank the world from something vast, alien and mysterious down to a more manageable size. Now here was something completely new. A world within a world, he thought, as he waited for the technician to finish.

It was becoming dark. He drew the lounge curtains and turned on the television, but was bored by what he saw. The channels were filled with the obsessions of youth. Sex, cars, clothes, music; girls becoming aroused by haircare products, boys stroking their chins as they compared triple-blade shaving to piloting jet fighters. The dream market, spending power coupled with inexperience. Pity today's youth, he thought. Lambs being readied for slaughter. *Tanquam ovis*.

Mr Canvey sat back in his chair as Christmas commercials blurred before him. In a world where there's less and less to discover, you have to be contented with small pleasures, he thought. In the next room, the technician tapped away at the keyboard. Outside, the wind flounced against the hedgerows.

'Nearly finished. I'll explain the set-up to you.'

The technician pulled up a second chair and sat Mr Canvey down beside him. He ran through the basic procedures, but forgot that his customer had never used a computer in his life, and went too quickly to be fully understood. Mr Canvey attempted to keep up, but it seemed that few concessions were made for neophytes. The stream of information finally washed over him, and he knew that he would have to resort to the manual for help. He made the technician a cup of tea, and they sat dunking biscuits as little coloured boxes scrolled across the screen.

'Man, I hate Christmas. See, I hardly ever take a drink, don't like the taste of beer, an' it bores the arse off me watching my friends get drunk, and I'm always the designated driver, so I just hate the whole thing.'

'You should try tea with a shot of whisky in it. I often have one at the end of the day, if I'm feeling good about something.'

He looks a little like my Tony, thought Mr Canvey. When he reclines his head in that fashion. 'So, what do you do instead?' he asked.

'Spend most of my time on the net.'

'Doing what, exactly?'

'The usual. Lookin' at websites, sendin' messages, stuff like that. Stuff you'll be doin' soon.'

'Have you always done this kind of work?'

'No. I've been a postman and a poet.' The technician chuckled. 'In some ways this isn't so different.'

'But now you teach.'

'I suppose so. I've got a natural aptitude for it, see. I learn fast.'

'Do you ever get anyone who can't learn?'

'How do you mean?' Danny barely heard the question as he reached forward to tap the keyboard. He had the distracted air of someone taking a phonecall while trying to watch a television programme.

'Your company runs management training classes, doesn't it? Are there ever any people who simply fail to understand how it all works?'

'Oh, yeah.'

'Then what do you do?'

'We have a special programme for them. It's a kind of electronic colouring book. Stops them from looking stupid in the eyes of their colleagues. They sit quietly at their desks foolin' around until it's time to go home, then they rush back to their wives to tell them they learned how to use a computer. Sad, really. A child of four can grasp the basics.'

It's easy for you, thought Mr Canvey. People of my age have had to grow up alongside the system's development. Manual typewriters, IBM Electrics, Golfballs, dot-matrix sixteen-letter screens and BBC Wordstar, probably the least user-friendly software ever invented. In the early eighties we were still punching telex messages out on long strips of tape. The changes we've had to go through. He enviously watched the young man's fingertips feathering the keys.

'This is just the start. Things are going to get a lot smarter. In Germany they've got litter bins that order your groceries. Fridges that tell you when you're eating too much. Soon you'll be able to touch and smell and taste stuff right here at your keyboard.'

'Good heavens. I can't even type with more than two fingers.'

'In a few days you'll be typing as fast as me,' said the technician unconvincingly, but not unkindly.

'You remind me of my son.'

'He good with a computer?'

'Do you know, I – ' Mr Canvey raised his knuckle to his mouth. 'I have no idea! I simply don't know. I don't know if he ever used a computer. Isn't that terrible? A man should know something like that about his own son.'

'Most people use them at work these days.'

'I don't think Tony – in Africa, you see, there was no – well, they barely had electricity. He wrote me letters. That's how I know. Sometimes the conditions were appalling, sometimes diseases travelled in their tyre tracks, they weren't to know.' He saw the puzzled look on the technician's face and tried to explain. 'The health organisations sent trucks with medical supplies from village to village, but it was after the rains, and the bilharzia travelled in the tracks their vehicles left behind. Instead of eradicating the disease, they accidentally caused it to spread.'

Danny looked uneasy. He was happier working at a keyboard than hearing about someone's personal troubles.

'What I mean to say,' explained Mr Canvey, 'is that my son passed away two years ago. Sometimes you get to know more about them after they've gone than when they're here. It's terrible to lose a child, when you would have gone in their place. If I'd known – if we'd talked.' He suddenly realised that he was discomfiting his guest and tried to change the subject, but it wouldn't go away. He didn't get the chance to speak with many people beyond passing the time of day.

He missed his wife, he told the technician, but mostly he missed his son. Never a day passed when he didn't think of Tony. The boy's peculiar view of the world had coloured his behaviour so much that he had hardly ever made total sense to his parents.

'The questions he used to ask me. "Dad, why is it that the first place you always want to touch on a cat is the only place it can't properly wash?" "Dad, what would chairs look like if your legs bent the other way?" How do you answer a child like that?' Mr Canvey poured more tea for his guest. 'Tony spent his entire childhood asking me awkward questions and never getting decent answers. My wife and I both worked, I was always too busy to help him. And what for? A few promotions in a job I didn't like. Meanwhile, Tony, well, let's just say that we didn't see eye to eye . . .'

As Tony grew older, his questions had become the symptom of a broader dissatisfaction with the world. How could his father work for a company that loaned millions to bankrupt countries at rates they could never afford to pay back? They argued all the time. Finally, the boy had left early one morning, propping a letter of explanation on the mantelpiece. He had walked away from his home, his job, his country, to go and work for a voluntary health aid service in a place hardly anyone had heard of. Mr Canvey, wanting him to be happy, had let him go. Three years later his son had died in the field, sickened and destroyed in less than two days by a virulent strain of amoebic dysentery. He was twenty-six.

'I really have to go,' said Danny, pushing back his cup.

'Yes, of course, how rude of me, going on. I'm sorry to have kept you.'

Mr Canvey saw the technician to the door, and promised to call if the computer's manual defeated him.

To his surprise, however, he proved to be rather good at using his word-processing package, his games software and his e-mail.

It was the internet he had trouble with. It made less sense because it seemed to be driven by people of alien intelligence to his own. Perhaps, like the technician, they were all simply younger and faster.

But he felt it was something beyond that. The more he experimented with it, the more the internet seemed a world of unnecessary information and unwanted destinations, of blind alleys and one-way cyberstreets where the fantasies of the friendless and the polemics of the mentally agitated were more intimidating than wandering the night slums of post-war Britain. As for the rest, those sites which weren't driven by the need to sell seemed to exist purely to feed the egos of their creators.

Mr Canvey was not without imagination; he could appreciate the system's uses, and had also heard the tales of its dark side; the reports of women who had formed electronic relationships with their future attackers, some going willingly to their protracted deaths, the men who had been exposed as paedophiles after foolishly downloading lurid jpegs, the lonely males who spent twenty hours a week on the net challenging each other to jousts and duels in medieval virtual villages, living idiot-lives in fantasy worlds, the viruses, the 'sticky' websites that clung to hapless users and could not be eradicated, the live sex-change operations filmed in California for private-view appointments by net voyeurs. The dancing cartoon animals, for God's sake.

He mainly comprehended electronic matters on a personal level. To him, e-commerce was ultimately reliant upon a postman shoving a rare book through a letterbox six weeks after it had been ordered. He had no need for internet purchases, invisible friends, singing hamsters, webcam sex-booths, special offers he did not want or messages he could not be bothered to answer. He knew that sitting hunched at a desk staring at a screen was a poor substitute for walking in parkland after a spring rain, that fantasy and reality would always remain separate, no matter how many scientists tried to convince him otherwise.

And yet it drew him, because it was the future.

The faster-than-thought hotwire of connections, the neural net connecting millions of different minds, the sheer possibilities overpowered him. 'Surfing' was an inaccurate description – it was more like bobbing about on an electronic ocean, being pulled back and forth by warring currents. It seemed to him that the sargasso of information could do with a few beacons, shining lights that meant something more to the user than just another futile directional arrow.

A few days later, Mr Canvey walked past his old office in Truro. He did not miss working there; his colleagues had been pretty colourless individuals. It didn't pay to have too much personality in banking. Mr Canvey drove back through the tortured hedgerows to his village. After his son's death, Mr Canvey's wife had divorced him and married someone happier. His life seemed to have emptied out. He went home, turned on the computer and looked up a website he had been meaning to visit, a site for model railway enthusiasts. He thought he might find some carriages for his collection, but the site had not been updated in ages. It was virtually derelict, and most of the hot-links led nowhere. They had been capped off, like the bricked-up streets of the village. He shoved the mouse aside and went to make a cup of tea.

What annoyed him was the disparity of the world. Somewhere out there litter bins were sending messages to each other, and children were drinking from infected rivers. People talked about the hypocrisy of the Victorians. How could they dare, when everything around them was so routinely tainted?

He knew he was behaving like his son. The more he used his computer to tap into the world, the more he found himself thinking like the boy he had not understood. He found single-page websites that were little more than desperate pleas for provisions; food and clothing being bartered in the electronic ether. He found insanely elaborate interactive sites dedicated to minor characters in television soap operas. And he found the site of the health aid agency his son had worked for. It had the longest website address he had ever seen, consisting of nine separate sections.

The site took ages to download, and seemed chaotically organised. It was separated into five main parts. **Who We Are. What We Do. Where We Work. How You Can Help. Diary Of A Hungry Planet.** The last section was a log kept by various members of staff in different locations, of their daily problems, the deprivations. You clicked on a country, then an area, and followed different paths. Mr Canvey clicked on Africa, then Somalia. He read about the unstable political situation there, about the UN aid workers taken hostage at the Balidogie airport. He read about the bandits and clans, and the guerrilla kidnappings. He read a file on chloroquine-resistant malaria, about the plasmodium parasites that female mosquitos left in your blood system, about the guinea worms, the typhus, the dengue fever, cutaneous and visceral leishmaniasis, meningitis, rabies, schistosomiasis and the Tumbu fly, which eats human flesh and burrows its way under your skin to lay its eggs. He read about the collapse of the state-run health system, and how there was one doctor for every five thousand people before young men like Tony volunteered to run makeshift hospitals.

He bookmarked the site, but could not bring himself to return to it, because it brought the horrors of the outside world into his village, because it brought the death of his son back into his life.

He called Danny at the computer shop, once to discuss setting print margins so that the type didn't come out sideways on the page, once because he couldn't work out how to change to a different search engine, but he was really trying to find out what young people like Danny were all about. He never stayed long on the line, never asked too many personal questions. Sometimes a young girl answered. She sounded bored and replied with quotes from an instruction manual, but when he asked her for answers which couldn't be found in the book she came to life, and tried to respond as truthfully as she could, sometimes going off and asking a colleague for additional advice.

It was just after Christmas. A watery sun hung low in the sky, barely bothering to illuminate the landscape. Mr Canvey had been playing a game on his computer which involved the three-dimensional construction of a Bavarian castle from jigsaw-like pieces. The pastime was just as boring as hunting through the pieces of a regular jigsaw, more so, because at least you had tactile sensation with a regular jigsaw.

He felt his eyes growing tired, and stopped to make some tea. He stood by the window, blowing across the top of his mug, watching the soft grey waves in fading light, looking for the beam from the unmanned lighthouse that blinked beyond the headland, but instead his eye was drawn to the bright square of the screen reflected in his window. He returned to his chair and pulled down the menu of his bookmarked sites, then summoned up the Somalian health organisation pages. There was something he remembered seeing; seeing but not seeing.

The site had not been updated for quite a long while. He ran the cursor to the end of the fifth section, where the diary entries were kept, and studied the roster of contributor names. Anthony Canvey was listed at the end, along with several other staffers from his base.

He shifted the cursor over his son's name and double-clicked. The lettering flashed from blue to red. The screen blanked, then a fresh page scrolled down and he found himself looking at a photograph of his son. Beneath the picture was a brief career résumé, a list of Tony's field interests, the things he liked and disliked about his job, and beneath this a further link; a message-board.

He slid the mouse and double-clicked, barely daring to breathe.

*A Message From Anthony Canvey:*
*Hi Dad I wondered how long it would take you to find me*
He stared at the message. When had this been written? How long before his son's illness? Had it been sitting here all this time, just waiting for him to stumble across it? With trembling

fingers he raised his hands over the keyboard and typed a reply, not knowing what else to do.

**Tony, I just learned about using this. I didn't know about this.**

*I left this for you Dad You were always interested in gadgets I knew you'd figure out how to use it eventually*

**I don't understand. How can you answer me?**

*I have to use a laptop to enter my medical supply requisition forms I dont like using it cant sort out the punctuation never my strong point but you know that*

**Tony –**

He realised that what he typed was not affecting the message from his son. It was coming in like a pulse from a beacon, waiting to be seen by anyone who was lost. It couldn't answer him; it could only beam out.

*They have probably told you about the situation here by now many of us are sick there is an dysentery epidemic it is difficult to get fresh water because our filters are always breaking down*

**Can you hear me? Can you read this?**

*And so much of our equipment has been stolen we have to barter it back Things do not look good we are having to deal with the Mogadishu rebels in order to keep our supply routes open yesterday a girl here in the base died very suddenly I think what I want to say is sorry*

**You don't have to say sorry,** he could not stop himself from typing.

*Sorry for disappointing you sorry for worrying you I have to do this its what I am*

**You don't have to say this.**

*I want you to understand*

**I understand.**

*understand*

**I understand**

*If I don't come home*

**I understand**

*Don't be sad*

**I'm not sad.**

*I'll be here this will always be here think of this as a light in the dark*

There was no more. The message-board file stayed open with its message displayed on-screen, complete and uninterrupted, an envelope in a dead-letter office that had finally been unsealed and read. Mr Canvey found himself reluctant to close it in case it could never be retrieved again, but he decided to print out the message. Then he closed the computer down for the night. He carefully folded up the printed sheet and locked it in the mahogany box where he kept his important papers. Finally, he made himself a cup of tea and stood at the window, watching the crimson pinprick of the beacon glimmering through the night mist out on the sea.

'I wish you'd come to bed.' Fran sleepily pushed against the pillow. 'It's late.'

'It'll just take me a couple of minutes to shut everything up,' he called from the next room. 'I don't want to leave a path anyone can follow.'

'I don't know why you had to do it. It's – unethical or some-thing. Like tampering with the mail. Probably a criminal offence. You shouldn't go upsetting people.'

'He picked up the message. There's no harm done. Nobody will bother tracing it.' Danny closed the pattern of connections and logged off, smiling as the text scrolled down to nothing, leaving just the URL. 'You know, it took me a while to place the bloke. He was in the year above me, but I remember him well. He was famous for hacking into the local bank and leaving a virus.'

'You used to do stuff like that, too.'

'Yeah, well. We all grew up a bit. This is the kind of thing he would have sent. I'm just making the connection.' Danny looked back at the top of the screen and erased the part of the address that read: */indexafr/externe/eastcent/somalia/acanvey.* That was the thing with a lot of the old message-board systems. Nobody knew if you were ever who you said you were, not unless you chose to leave your email address. 'I'm going to have a cup of tea with a shot of whisky in it. Do you want one?'

'Go on, then.' Fran pulled the pillow up behind her and switched on the bedside light.

'It's not like you to drink.'

'I think someone else out there is having one,' said Danny. As he opened the bottle, he looked out of the kitchen window in the direction of the beacon, and although he could not see it, he knew it was there.

*This began as something else entirely, a look at suburban towns where trouble seems to brew at bus-stops as the pubs shut. It was an idea that didn't work because I had no real reason for the character's anger, so I set it to one side for possible use at a later date. Then I received an e-mail requesting a story – to tell you who commissioned it would detract from the subject – and was suddenly provided with the cause and effect of the tale.*

# COME ON THEN, IF YOU THINK YOU'RE HARD ENOUGH

3 . . . 2 . . . 1 . . .

Happy New . . .

Sometimes your life revises itself in a single heartbeat. Certainly, I believe there are moments of decision that you remember all your life. It only took that midnight second for the past to flood my senses, and for me to truly see myself. It triggered two key memories, one of Frank violently attacking me, and one which was something quite the opposite. In that moment I recalled who I had once been. I remembered every detail of the night. I could even hear what I was thinking.

Those silly bitches who insisted on herding their children a quarter of a mile across flat tarmac to school in four-wheel-drive jeeps deserved to have their tyres punctured, I thought, as I shoved my penknife deep into another rubber wall.

It was New Year's Eve, and the three of us had blazed a trail of destruction down Ferris Road, doing the jeeps, keying the sides of BMWs, trashing the new-age-candles-and-embroidered-herbal-sachet shop on the corner, noisily hurling a dustbin through its plate-glass window and kicking some panels out of the front door, but our rowdiness petered out after Russell failed to get the Vauxhall started and we all began arguing about how we would get home. It was starting to snow.

Frank 'The Bank' Matthews said he knew how to hotwire a

vehicle, but clearly had no idea because he was only able to gain entry to a Nissan by kicking out the passenger window, and then couldn't find the bonnet catch. I was tired of smashing things up; I knew our behaviour was born of boredom, but back then I had no idea how to structure an evening that did not involve slamming around with Frank and Russell. None of us had girlfriends or money, and we weren't likely to get hold of either in each other's company. Absence of sex led to frustration, lack of respect led to violence; it didn't take a genius to figure out why we were stuck with each other, but no-one had warned me how fucking boring it would become. I was the leader because intellectually I ran rings around the rest, I'd read books about leadership from Machiavelli to Hitler, I knew that most people were gagging for someone else to make up their minds for them. But eventually I couldn't help thinking that the other two were holding me back.

Russell was pretty stupid, probably because he'd stopped bothering with school the year his parents split up after a series of ugly assaults on one another. He now lived with an uncle who spoiled him because he was afraid of him. Frank was cheeky but a bit psycho; he'd tainted his childhood early on, shooting sparrows with his grandad's airgun, then graduating to the neighbourhood cats. It was something to do with wanting attention. His mother, catatonic with disappointment, watched television in her dressing gown day and night with the volume up and the lounge blinds drawn. His father was still inside for dealing drugs that ultimately found their way back to his own children. Everyone seemed to be covered in tattoos, home-made ones, drunk-for-a-dare ones, been-inside ones. I remember there was a girl on our street who had the name of her boyfriend tattooed on her backside, but she misspelled the word Brian, getting the 'a' and the 'i' in the wrong order, and when everyone took the piss out of her (making the obvious joke) she tried to remove it by pouring burning lighter fluid over her arse, which put her in the hospital. I hated where I lived. I was ignored at home. I needed acolytes like a plant needs sun and water, I wanted to see my cleverness reflected in the eyes of others, and I'd been forced to settle for idolisation from the most dysfunctional duo in the neighbourhood.

We slashed the roof of a soft-top Honda and found some money in the glove box, enough to buy a bottle of mystery-brand vodka, and drank it to keep out the cold, but Russell and Frank began drunkenly fighting about some character on a TV show, and Russell cut Frank's hand with my pen-knife. Frank chased Russell and me through the deserted backstreets, across a four-lane road shouldered with corrugated steel barriers and down under the railway arches until we had to stop, gasping and rasping, with our hands on our knees. That was when we realised we had run into a really bad part of town.

Some guys in leather jackets and grey cotton hoods were swapping packets of smack in the damp darkness beneath a bridge, and dead-eyed us with a Wot-You-Fuckin-Lookin-At? as we passed. Suddenly I didn't feel like so much of a leader. I was out of familiar territory but the others were still following me, and to turn around now would be the act of a coward, so we kept on walking. Boarded-up shops, burned-out cars, industrial units blasted with so much graffiti they looked like alien artifacts. Junkies, dealers, dossers, trouble everywhere you looked, not that you dared to look.

Except that Frank was looking now, and one of the dealers was answering him back in a fierce low voice, and Frank was drunkenly playing the big man but it wasn't washing, it was just making things worse, so suddenly we were all running again, being chased this time, off under the arches and around onto wasteground where Russell slipped over in a puddle and got left behind, and me and Frank were forced to vault into a yellow skip inside the shadow of the archway, dropping noisily onto off-cuts of MDF and sacks of restaurant rubbish, and hiding there until our pursuers had given up the chase.

'We had to stay there for a whole hour in enemy territory, stuck in this skip, shitting ourselves in case they found us,' Frank laughed uneasily as he drained the bottle into Russell's glass. It was far past midnight on New Year's Eve. Everyone who had been drunk was sobering up, and the Indian restaurant was starting to empty out. 'Froze our bollocks off. Meanwhile this one had pissed off home. We were only – how old, Russell?'

'I dunno, fifteen I guess.' Russell slipped his arm around the back of Emma's seat. 'Always in trouble, we were. The other one, Malcolm, he was a really smart bloke, don't know what happened to him.'

'He had a fucking rough time,' said Frank. 'You know he was always nicking cars? He twocked one that belonged to a mate of his dad's, thing was the judge would have let him off but he was carrying a lot of gear and they sent him down, but while he was away, right, he got into a fight with some geezer and ended up with a punctured lung. Nearly didn't make it back out.'

'I've heard this one before,' muttered Emma, who was stupified with boredom. When men were like this, she ceased to exist.

'Do what, love?'

'I said can we change the subject?' Emma wanted them to get the bill so they could leave. Hearing about her boyfriend's adolescent glory days over the remains of a prawn biriani was not her idea of seeing the New Year in with a bang. She had wanted to take something and go to a club and let the beats pump through her until it felt like she was alone inside a giant heart. Instead she had left it to Russell to buy the tickets in advance, and he had forgotten to do so.

Russell and Frank had sat next to each other for years in school, and were still hanging out together. In outward appearance, at least, they had changed. Four years had passed since then, and it had taken that long for Russell to lose his puppy-fat, growing lean and gormless in the process. When his uncle died and left him some money, everyone expected him to spunk it all on something stupid, but he hadn't. He had used it as a downpayment on a house, because he had become the father of

Emma's child, although not on purpose, and was turning out to be a vaguely responsible parent, and the last thing she needed was him being influenced by his stupid former classmates.

Frank had grown heavy and tougher in the passing years, and had got himself a job at Kwikfit, replacing car exhausts. He looked angry all the time. He made Emma feel uncomfortable.

Russell and Frank, together again. They told themselves they weren't who they once were. They were smarter now, more savvy, more sophisticated. They talked about the past as if it had been exciting, but they both knew it had been shit. They talked about it as if it was enough to keep them together forever in friendship.

'Don't look now, but I know the two blokes sitting behind you,' I said. Paul, who was seated opposite me, immediately made a point of staring up at them. The waiter thought he was being beckoned, and came over. He looked as washed-out as the type on the menu, which was floppy from overhandling and sticky from a thousand curries.

'I said don't look, didn't I? So what's the first thing you go and do?'

'The whole restaurant can hear them,' said Paul. 'Who are they?'

'I used to go to school with them. The big one paying the bill is Frank "The Bank" Matthews. They called him that because he was always breaking and entering. The other one is Russell Parnell. We went everywhere together, got into a lot of trouble.' The waiter was still beside us, and in order to get rid of him we ordered too quickly, too much food.

'They were a right pair of bastards, but we had some laughs. I ended up in some serious shit because of them.'

'Well, you're out of it now. And if you decide to get out of here, it can only keep getting better. You'll never have to come back to this town again if you don't want to.' Paul was from London, and was trying to persuade me to move back with him, but I was in two minds about the whole idea. In a week's time we could be living together in his council flat in Stoke New-ington, he said. Not much of a place to look at, nothing fancy, but it would be a fresh start.

To me London was the devil I didn't know. I had always thought of the city as a mysterious, rather sinister playground that only existed for clubbing on Saturday nights, off the edge of our local maps and far beyond the lonely motorway lights that bordered our town. Okay, where we lived was more boring than the surface of the moon, but at least you could predict the shape of the terrain.

'You could go over and say hello to them if you want.'

'I don't want. It sounds like they're reminiscing about the good old days.'

'Or you could send 'em a glass of champagne. After all, you might never have to see them again.'

'No,' I decided, 'I'd have to talk to them, and it would be far too embarrassing.'

'Why? They don't know you're a poof, do they? They'll think you're out with a mate.'

I pretended to examine the menu. 'We were the hardest kids on our part of the estate, everybody was scared of us.'

'So?'

'Blokes like that sense something.'

'You mean they'll suss me. How?'

'Well. Your hair.'

'This cut is fashionable in London.'

'Which makes it far ahead of its time in the Midlands. You know what they say about British time zones; when it's 2 a.m. in London it's 1985 in Cardiff. And look at what you're wearing.'

Paul looked down at his T-shirt. 'Yeah, what? It's the most expensive item of clothing this shithole has seen in a while, I can tell you.'

'Exactly. It's a straight venue. Their idea of smart clothes in here is Tommy Hilfiger.'

'I thought everyone wore Calvin Klein now. I thought that was what democracy was for. Besides, I'm not embarrassed about wanting to smell of CK1 rather than – ' he cast around for a comparison, 'well – Denim and sweat. I mean Denim the aftershave, not the fabric. You're ashamed of yourself.'

'I'm not ashamed. I just don't want to go out of my way to get weird fucking looks, all right?'

'Right. Before we go out tomorrow evening perhaps you could check me for outward signs of faggotry. I'll try to walk as if I'm riding a horse and keep my voice in a deep register, will that help?'

'You know what I mean,' I said, exasperated.

'Anyway, I think your dilemma is about to be resolved.' Paul made a pointing gesture behind his hand. 'I can see them in the mirror. They're leaving, and they've got to walk right past this table.'

I looked up in time to see Frank bearing down on me. I tried not to catch his eye, but of course I did.

'Malcolm? Blimey, we were just talking about you, mate. How are you?'

'Er, good.' I tried to stand up but my chair was jammed against the wall behind. As Frank was joined by Russell and his girlfriend, I was forced to slide out from the table, leaving Paul still seated. 'This is a mate of mine, Paul.'

'Enchanté,' said Paul. I could have killed him.

'Bloody hell,' Russell boomed at Frank as he arrived, 'it's got a bit gay in here all of a sudden. Hello Malcolm, who's your friend?'

'My name is Paul,' said Paul, waving a limp hand across the table, 'care to join us?'

'No, mate, no,' said Russell, suddenly awkward. He slipped his arm around Emma for protection. Paul isn't usually camp, he just gets that way around excessively straight men. As defence mechanisms go, it isn't very effective.

Frank leaned over and tapped the menu. 'We just had a brilliant curry,' he said, for want of something better to say.

'Yeah, a real bum-burner, although you'd probably quite enjoy that,' said Russell, releasing a little snigger.

'Is this going to take very long, the gay jokes thing?' asked Paul. 'Because we're *desperately* hungry and waiting to eat.'

'Look, mate, if you're gonna do a Julian Clary, can you piss off and do it where I can't fucking see you?' asked Frank. 'Go and give somebody a blowjob, we'll call you back if we need you.' I could see that Frank had tried to be pleasant for about twenty seconds, seen that it wouldn't work, and given up on the idea.

'And where would you like me to perform this act?' asked Paul, rising to the bait.

'How about in a skip on a snowy night?' I suggested. It just came out. I really hadn't meant it to sound the way it did, I'd just wanted Frank to leave us alone.

Frank's face paled as he realised what I'd said, then went paler when he saw that Russell realised what was being suggested.

'You didn't.' Russell made a snorting noise. 'With him?' He pointed at me.

'I don't know what you're talking about.'

'You – and him,' said Russell stupidly. Emma let out a weird squeal of laughter, then put her hand over her mouth.

'I don't know what you're fucking talking about.'

Frank started to walk back to his table, but I could hear Russell saying something, and I knew that this was the piece of information he'd been waiting for, the one he needed to give him the edge over Frank, and that now he knew, he would never let it go. Suddenly Frank turned and came charging back to the table, and punched me full in the face. I felt my nose break, saw blood squirt from my nostrils, and stumbled backwards as Paul got the next punch in. The table went over. Cutlery and wine-glasses clattered and smashed. We managed to pull ourselves apart before the long-suffering waiters were forced to act. I grabbed a napkin and held it over my bloody nose, and we burst out of the restaurant with our hearts pounding.

As we walked quickly away, Paul tried to look at the damage done to my face, but I pushed him off me because I wanted to talk, to tell him what had happened on that snowy night.

'It was the night we got out of our territory, and we got into a bit of trouble.' I stopped to hawk and spit a gobbet of blood into the gutter. My nose was stinging like hell. 'We lost Russell, and just the two of us were left, Frank and me, and we had to hide in a skip. I remember it was snowing hard by then and we were frightened, on a real high. I had fallen on my back on some wood, and Frank was kneeling above me, ice-white with cold. Suddenly he pulled my hands inside his jeans, and I realised he had heat coming from him, heat from a tense centre. He pushed my mouth down onto him, then he pulled up my shirt and came all over my chest. It was sort of exciting.'

'So Frank "The Bank" Matthews lost his deposit. You must have been picking splinters out of your arse for a fortnight. I guess you chose the wrong time to revive a fond childhood memory. He's still worried about looking hard.'

'He has nothing to worry about,' I smiled back with crimson teeth. 'He was hard enough then to last a lifetime.'

Perhaps Frank had a reason for always acting hard. Whenever I'd thought back to that snowy night in the skip, I'd automatically assumed that it was a once-only deal for him, a teenage thing, a confluence of time and place and circumstance created by racing pulses and raging hormones. Then in the restaurant I had seen the panic in his eyes, and suddenly I knew that it wasn't once only, that Frank was just like me, and that I had come to within a heartbeat of doing what he did, getting left behind in that sad little town where nothing ever happened and nothing could happen, because you had been cemented into place by your own lies, and would always remain trapped in a corner by your own fear, the fear of being yourself, the fear of being alive.

I felt sorry for Frank then, because I knew that he would always be hardest on himself. Not for doing the wrong thing on one night – but for not doing the right thing on all those other nights. In the moment that I saw all this, I chose to go, and not look back.

One life. One heartbeat.
3 . . . 2 . . . 1 . . .
Happy New Life.

*I did not get to visit East Germany before the end of partition. By the time I went, to attend the Berlin Film Festival, there was relatively little sign that it had ever occurred, and I was struck by the idea of how fast our world can change. I've always been fascinated by the idea of home and what it means. Home to the English is a powerful and private thing. It's partly because of our island status and the unpredictable weather, but there's something else at work, a deeper and altogether more perverse relationship between us and the place where we feel most comfortable. I don't think this story will be my last on the subject.*

# THE TORCH GOES OUT

'If we could all sit quietly in a room and relax, the whole of society would collapse' – Tim Lott

Every Saturday morning, Raymond Hunter pruned his roses whether they needed it or not. The flowers were a variety named after a forgotten actress, one of the Rank starlets whose protuberant busts had decorated third-rate comedies in the 1960s. Her name briefly returned to prominence after she was found murdered in her bed two years ago. Mr Hunter had been annoyed to discover that the actress was still alive, only to be told that she was now dead. Effectively, the newspaper had resuscitated her in his memory solely for the purpose of killing her off again. She had been murdered for a handful of notes and some paste jewellery.

So many people were being attacked in their own homes these days that it wasn't something you wanted to think about. The whole point of taking the *Daily Mail*, thought Raymond as he angrily jabbed at the rose stems, was to read about the exposure of deviant behaviour so that the fragile status quo of counties like Kent could be maintained. The paper was meant to calibrate suburban indignation, not destroy cherished childhood memories. He took careful aim at the branch below the bud and nipped it with his secateurs. A bulb of sap swelled and fell like a drop of blood. Ritual was a key to survival, he knew. The two states were strongly linked.

'Sidney Tafler,' he said aloud. 'There was another one.'

'Another what, dear?'

'Recognisable face. You watch any film made in the fifties and he's in it. Usually a black-market chap selling nylons.' He peered suspiciously into a rose and pulled some petals off. 'Sid James, another wide-boy. Harry Fowler, barrow-boy. Terry Thomas, cad. Irene Handl, charlady. Liz Fraser, girl in coffee bar. They all had faces you knew. Going to the pictures was like being at home.'

'I suppose so,' agreed Mary.

'Michael Ripper, lift-man or pub landlord. Joyce Grenfell, hockey teacher.'

'I think you've made your point, Raymond.' Mary Hunter stood at the back door with tea served in a gilt-edged cup. Such crockery had originally been gilded to reflect the rhythmic shimmering of candles, but there was no candlelight now, only the harsh whiteness of timer-lights left on for security. Candles meant electrical failure, and darkness meant danger. 'There'll be nothing left of those if you don't stop hacking away. Can't you find something else to do? The interior light in the garage needs replacing.'

'I haven't got the right bulb. It's a bayonet.' Another dying stem dropped from his blade. The sky was high and painfully blue, the garden a crisp bright green.

'Then we'll go to the store and buy one.' The faintest air of desperation was detectable in her voice.

'I'm not sure I'll have time to do it today. I still have to clean out the pond. Get algae in the pump and you'll soon know what's what.'

Mary set the teacup down on the wall that connected their property with the Devonshires next door. The Devonshires never went out. They had all their purchases delivered, and stared unflinchingly from behind their curtains until the deliverer had closed the garden gate behind him.

'According to the paper there was a breach in the wall near Bexleyheath last night,' Mary informed him. 'Two men got through, but they were arrested before they could do any damage.'

Raymond stepped back and sized up the remaining buds on his rose bush. 'I wouldn't believe everything you read in the papers. That wall is reinforced concrete with cast iron doors that can only be opened by a certified government swipecard. It's over one hundred feet high and covered with electrified razor-wire at the top. And then there are the sentry boxes.'

'They're nearly all unmanned now.'

'They have sensors that pick up any movement bigger than a moth and relay it straight to the security services. You worry too much.'

Mary studied the unkempt sky with a look of disapproval. 'You hear stories. Remember what happened to the Coopers. You expect that sort of thing in Botswana, but not here. In their own front garden. In broad daylight. Anyone could have seen. With Sabatier knives, if you please. I've got one in the kitchen. And their lovely home set on fire.'

'That was ages ago. Security is tighter now.' Raymond made his way to the shed and began pulling at the flex of the power mower.

'The grass doesn't need cutting again. You did it on Wednesday.'

'I missed a bit.' He busied himself with untangling the cable, then disconnecting the grass box and cleaning it.

On most Saturday mornings, Wellington Gardens was alive with the sound of power mowers. The great controversy about diamond patterns versus alternating-direction stripes had been settled in favour of a more freeform approach to lawn trimming. Saturday afternoons were spent performing household chores, clearing the leaves from gutters, shining windows and testing alarm systems. Sunday mornings were reserved for car, boat and caravan-polishing. Despite all this activity, very few of the residents spoke to one another beyond an occasional acknowledgement of the atmospheric conditions.

Wellington Gardens was the main road into Victoria Grove. It gave way to Waterloo Terrace, which led to Balaclava Crescent, which ran into Sebastopol Avenue. Alma. Inkerman.

Kimberley. Ladysmith. Mafeking. The roads fanned lazily through the suburban countryside. They could have been named after roses or birds, but someone in the council had chosen battles. Nothing recent, though; these wars were long ago, and softened by years of forgetfulness. The warm air of wealth drifted across broad pavements lined with alders and hornbeams, sifting into the newer streets that were planted with cherry trees. The houses all followed a comfortingly similar style, double fronted with white bay windows, porches and alarm boxes, green sharp-cornered hedges, perfectly circular lily ponds and secure off-street parking, a redbrick Eden that remained unchanged from its architectural drawings, repeated geometries of red, green and white. Perhaps there were fewer people on the streets, but that was to be expected. An open-air environment was not as controllable as one's own property, and therefore less safe. 'An Englishman's home is his castle,' Raymond was fond of reminding his wife, 'especially if he electrifies it.' The Hunters were being more houseproud than usual because their daughter Janet was getting married in a fortnight's time, and the wedding reception was to be held in a Union Jack-striped marquee at the end of their garden. The Devonshires had been invited, but only out of politeness. Their agoraphobia would not allow them to venture across the property boundary.

Wellington Gardens. John Betjeman must have written about such places. The housewives who crossed the neighbourhood were sturdy and determined. Their daughters, clean-cut and willowy, sunbathed in back gardens while their fathers pottered in sheds and found things to solder. The young men drove off after dawn and reappeared at dusk, returning from work in company cars, their jackets hanging in the back. Berkshire, Oxfordshire, Marlborough and Bath. Sussex, Wessex, Hereford and York. Broadstairs, Hastings, Sittingbourne and Ramsgate. Everything neat. Everything green. Everything tidy. Everything safe.

Everyone scared.

*

'We've missed someone off the list,' said Mary the next morning, just as the maid was setting out three-minute boiled eggs on their breakfast table. 'Janet rang me last night to ask why he hadn't been invited.'

Raymond folded back his *Mail On Sunday* and set it to one side. 'Who's that?' he asked.

'Ralph.'

'Ralph?' He stared through the conservatory windows for a moment. 'Ralph the *guard*?'

'They've known each other since they were children. They used to go fishing at Green Ponds together. She was quite insistent on the phone. I thought I'd better ask you before I did anything.'

'I don't think it's a good idea to remind our guests of what's – you know.' Raymond removed the top from his boiled egg with a knife and inspected the interior suspiciously. 'On the other side. Don't misunderstand me. He's a very nice man – '

'Everybody in the neighbourhood knows him, and they all like him.'

'I know they do.'

'It's not as if he'd be attending in uniform.'

'But for God's sake, he's up on the wall. I dread to think what he sees every day, every night. The madness, the violence, the mindless cruelties. It must rub off on a man, even a decent one.'

'Ralph's never shown the slightest sign that it has. He performs a necessary job of work. It's like doctors or firemen. He has a strong sense of propriety. He looks clean and dresses smartly. I can't imagine he'd start telling the guests about what goes on in the Inner City, if that's what you're worried about.'

'I don't know. It's meant to be the happiest day of Janet's life. She shouldn't have any worries. We're supposed to protect her.'

'And Ralph protects us. It's the least we can do. It's – Christian.' The word rested uneasily between them.

'He might not want to come. Might feel ill at ease.' Raymond opened his newspaper once more and read a headline: 'Generation Game Star Found Stabbed To Death'.

'There's one way to find out.'

That ended the matter.

Ralph sat in the guardroom with his boots up against the glass, watching the unchanging chaos below. Someone had set fire to an abandoned car, and smoke was pouring across the crowded market-place. People were pushing and shoving through the dense oily clouds, clutching their faces, their eyes streaming. Sirens scaled the distance, but the police could not break through the blockade of makeshift market stalls. In the centre of the square a woman was screaming and screaming. Blood ran down her face, and slim spindles of glass jutted from her right forearm like porcupine quills.

'I love it up here in the summer,' said Ralph. 'It's so peaceful.'

'Double glazing, mate.' Cameron rested his elbows on the window ledge and focused his binoculars on the woman below. 'She's quite pretty. I like women who make a lot of noise. Think we should go down and give her a hand?'

Often the Inner London police and ambulance brigades failed to turn up. Their services were overstretched and undermanned. The main incidents of rioting and looting occurred around the tenement blocks most closely situated to the wall. In the hot summer months, petty squabbles turned into wars. Everyone took sides, and there was much to argue about. The drains, the gas pipes and the electricity pylons all ended at the wall. As the temperature rose, each utility failed in turn, sparking furious complaints and divisions of loyalties. In winter the situation was just as bad, but reaction was muted by the chill frosts that crusted the unheated apartment buildings.

'I was watching the birds, up there.' Ralph tapped his finger on the glass, pointing to the electronic sentry box further along the wall. Its roof had rusted and fallen in, and some bedraggled pigeons had made a nest inside it. 'They're building a home. What's going on down there is too far away to bother them. Everything looks calmer from a distance.' He set down the binoculars and tilted his chair back. 'Janet Hunter's getting married.'

'Blimey. You been invited?'

'Nope. Not a chance in hell that'll happen. Her old man has hated me ever since I caught him in his shed leafing through jazz mags.'

'You did go out with her, though, didn't you?'

'That was years ago. We just fooled around a little.' He tried to sound casual, as though it didn't matter. 'It never turned into anything. She was too – I don't know. Highly strung.'

'That's because they're all closet hysterics.' Cameron swivelled his chair to face the north side of the wall. 'Look at those neat little lawns and gravelled drives. It only takes one small thing to go wrong and they all start pissing themselves.'

Ralph joined him, pressing his forehead on the tinted glass to look down. 'Yeah, but I like the way it looks.'

'You must do, man, you live down there on the Kent side.'

'I've done my duty tour in Inner London. Fucking chaos, mate. Jay comes in at night smeared with blood and shit. She's meant to wear these gloves but she says she can't feel anything through them. She's never supposed to do more than sixteen hours straight but sometimes she does thirty. Our shifts overlap and I don't see her for weeks. I can smell her on the bedsheets, like a ghost. We leave each other notes on the table. That's all.'

'She could give it up.'

'It's not something you give up. People look to her for help.'

'So, they look to us for protection.'

Ralph's gaze shifted from the clinical green-and-white order of Victoria Grove to the crazed fire-brown urgency of the Inner London streets. 'Yeah,' he agreed, 'but they're not the same people.'

Ralph took the stairs down from the tower because the elevator was broken again. It was only the Inner City side that ever got damaged, never the Outer. No graffiti there, nobody pissing in the lift or shagging up against the wall. They had tried every lock they could think of to keep the Inner City lift closed to intruders. They didn't bother to close the outer one at all. They didn't need to. Nobody broke the law. They didn't dare.

'That's democracy in action for you,' he told Cameron. 'You make your choice. Outside, suburban perfection, all right, a bit boring, a bit Swiss, but safe apart from the odd lapse of manners. Coppers on the beat, CCTV, police helicopters, spotlights, searchlights, alarms and sirens. Then you've got your Inner City chaos, a bit lawless, a bit scary, filth, crazies, public transport that never works, good chance of getting stabbed on a Saturday night but great parties.'

'If it was a proper democracy,' said Cameron, 'you'd be able to pass backwards and forwards through the wall without applying in writing for a book of tickets six to eight weeks in advance.'

'No, mate. If they could do that, both sides would contaminate each other. You'd get drug-related crimes and murders in Outer and, oh I don't know, Benetton and Gap in Inner. No-one would be happy.'

'Nobody's happy now,' said Cameron gloomily.

'Bollocks, go and ask Janet Hunter's dad if he's happy. He only has to look at a lawnmower and he gets a hard-on. You're always going to get someone who isn't pleased with what they've got.'

'So you're pleased with what you've got.'

'Sure,' he said uncertainly. 'Fucking delirious with joy, me.'

Ralph always read his mail in the tower because it gave him something to do. He kept a laptop on the desk nearest the window and worked on an art program, reconfiguring photographs he had taken while Cameron read out articles from magazines. They knew the peak times for trouble, and only watched carefully during those flashpoint hours. Even then, their responsibility was limited. Neither was authorised to leave the post. If they saw something happening – usually on the Inner City side – they could call the appropriate service and request a priority attendance that ranged between a One Point Five, which simply diverted the next passing police patrol, to a One Point One, which was an immediate request for help in a life-threatening situation. Although Ralph knew that they were little more than glorified night-watchmen, he was aware that Outer residents treated them with deference and respect, whereas Inner City folk treated them more like traffic wardens, dunces who existed merely to be abused and periodically assaulted. It was no surprise that both Cameron and Ralph chose to live outside of the wall, and preferred the suburban lifestyle, even though the government documents they had been required to sign insisted on their impartiality. Of course, Ralph lived so close to the actual wall that it made no odds. Property was cheaper there, the sense of disturbance greater, the manicured calm of the estates far less orderly.

'I've been invited,' said Ralph, turning over the stiff white card. 'Engravers Gothic, look at that.'

'What?' Cameron tore himself away from an article about porno actresses in *FHM*.

'What are you talking about?'

'Typeface, very cool, picked out in gold. Janet's wedding. She's put me on the list. She wants me there. Wants – me – there.' He tapped the invitation against his teeth.

Cameron dropped the magazine. 'Pisses you off, doesn't it?'

'It's not too late.' He held the invitation by the corner and tipped it to the light as if searching for her fingerprints.

'What, to tell her you've been mooning over her for years? When is it?'

'Two weeks' time.'

'Do you know who she's marrying?'

'No. Why?'

'Nothing. Just that if you want to get back in the running it might be easier to have him knocked off than to ask her to change her mind and consider you as a life partner.'

'You could be right there,' Ralph agreed. He studied the card again. 'Reception to be held in the home of Mrs Mary Hunter & Mr Raymond Hunter. I think I'll go and see her.'

'You see her every night.'

'I don't mean through binoculars, I mean see her. Maybe I should take her a present. I wonder what would be an acceptable gift.'

'I thought she didn't like you anymore,' said Cameron, spotting a commotion below and leaning forward to monitor it. 'I think that mad old shopkeeper's getting robbed again.'

'Flowers. Something traditional. Roses maybe. She used to love roses. Want me to call a One Two?'

'Better make that a Three. His window just got pushed in. There's half a dozen blokes piling in there. Roses are a bit soft.'

'You don't know what you're on about, Janet loves flowers.' Ralph tapped the office keyboard and tapped out the police alarm code. SERVER BUSY flashed up. The system was old and overloaded. Ralph watched the screen and sighed. 'I think I'm going to marry her.'

Jay was asleep on the terrace in her paper jumpsuit. He didn't like to wake her, but wanted her to eat something before setting off on another shift. She blearily eyed the bowl of soup before accepting it. 'Did you cook this?'

'I opened the packet.' He smiled. 'Put it on High for three minutes, let it stand, stirred out the frozen bits, put it back on for another two minutes. Complicated stuff.'

'So I can see.' She pushed her hair behind her ears and took a sip. 'Flavour clue?'

'Vegetable and something. Might be chicken.'

She shrugged, sipped some more. 'God, it was weird today. Todd and Annie didn't show up so we had half a crew. Some woman had set fire to a mattress and thrown it over her balcony. Protesting about the cut in her benefit payments. The mattress landed on a pram someone had left at the bottom of the stairs. Tiny little boy in it, too small to be left alone. We managed to pull him out, thought the job was finished. He had a few minor blisters and wasn't coughing, so I guessed there hadn't been much smoke inhalation.' She cupped the soup bowl in her hands. 'I got him into the ambulance and was checking his chest when he suddenly started wheezing. There was nothing blocking the passage of air to his lungs and my first thought was, you know, delayed reaction to being smothered. I turned around to reach for an oxygen cowl and when I turned back he was dead. Not turning blue, not gasping, just – dead. Christ knows what the mattress had been soaked in, some kind of poisonous liquid, either that or it had been doused with flea-powder, something very fine and fibrous that could have passed directly from his lungs into his bloodstream. Septicaemic reaction, bang. Mother nowhere to be found, woman who threw out the mattress screaming her head off. Usual bloody mess.'

'Drink your soup.'

'Mmm.' She looked up. At least her eyes smiled. 'So how was your day?'

'Oh, very exciting. Phonecall from an old man in Sebastopol Terrace, convinced that someone from Inner London is flying over his property in a Microlite, photographing him. I told him it was probably a bird. He didn't believe me. Says he's going to write to his MP.'

'I didn't think people did that anymore.' The smile spread to her lips now. 'Even if someone from the city could get their hands on a Microlite, why would they do it?'

'Oh, I don't know, plan some kind of robbery, swoop out of the sky and nick his gardening tools. I have no idea what was going through his mind. Paranoia. We get a lot of calls like that.'

'You can't blame the older ones. They grew up in a country without walls. Now their property is bordered by concrete barriers. They feel guilty just for owning stuff. There's nothing like a security system to make you feel unsafe.' She checked her watch. 'I've got to go in a minute.'

'Be nice to eat together one day.'

'You could have heated some soup.'

'You know what I mean.'

She studied his eyes. 'Yes, I know what you mean, Ralph, but now's not the time for that conversation.'

'It never is,' said Ralph.

Mary Hunter checked through the mail and held up a single sheet of folded paper. 'Ralph has accepted. You said he wouldn't.'

Raymond lowered his newspaper a fraction and peered over it. 'I didn't say that, I just wondered if it was appropriate.' From outside came the whine of a milkfloat, the chinking of bottles in the drive.

'His mother used to live in the next street.' She dropped the letter back on the table, catching sight of herself in the mirror behind Raymond's head. She was looking tired. Not sleeping well. It occurred to her that these days she was vaguely worried all the time, about nothing and everything. 'I really don't see the problem.'

'He lives right by the wall. He must be able to hear them at night. I don't know how he can stand it.'

'Those flats were cheap. It was probably all he could afford. His mother left debts when she died. I rather liked her. There was a gentility about her even though – ' She stopped herself.

Raymond looked over his glasses. 'Even though what?'

'Nothing.'

'No, go on, you were going to say it.'

'Well, she was from the other side originally. The husband was from Southwark, I believe, and she was Wapping. Although there was a sister in Faversham.'

'And that makes a difference, does it?'

'Well, one has one's roots, after all.'

'I'm not so bothered about roots, it's where we're going that concerns me. Which appears to be to Hell in a handbasket. I don't care whether they all stab each other to death, the druggies, the immigrants, the queers, the loonies, so long as they leave my family out of it.'

Mary Hunter studied the top of her husband's head. She knew that he wouldn't look up to meet her eyes. He was losing his sense of compassion. Surely he hadn't always been this angry? She tried to remember what he was like when they married, before they moved to Wellington Close, but could only recall the stiff poses of wedding photographs. Ralph was a decent man. A brave man. She assumed it took bravery to keep watch on the wall. At least he saw both sides of the picture. He had opinions, made judgement calls, took chances. Janet could have done a lot worse than go out with him. In fact she had done worse. The groom-to-be was a bore. Douglas was so smug, so organised. It tired her to listen to him explain his financial plans for her daughter's future security. Janet didn't seem to notice that the man she was marrying was incredibly dull. There was a time when she would have laughed at someone like that. Now she was preparing to spend her life with him.

'Ray?'

'Mmm?'

'Do you ever – '

Raymond lowered his paper again. This time there was a trace of theatricality in the gesture that suggested annoyance. 'What?'

'Do you think we should serve champagne before the canapés?'

Ralph dug into the pocket of his overalls, found an uncrunchy Kleenex and blew his nose. Looked into the tissue and saw powdery grey mucus, a trace of blood. Someone was burning a mound of stagnant rubbish. Always something burning on the Inner London side, especially south of the river. You never found a patch of grass – or concrete, for that matter – that didn't have makeshift tents, bonfires or burnt-out cars on it. The walls of the tenements were covered in layers of greasy soot. So many of the old shops were boarded up now. Their owners were tired of being robbed for a few coins. Even the metal shutters they lowered at night had been kicked in, hammered right through in places. Presumably people were living in the empty buildings, although how they survived without daylight, water or electricity was a mystery. You saw their children sitting on the street corners, playing in the sidestreets, glancing at you with suspicion. Little kids like miniature adults, out long past midnight. Jay had shown him the marks on their arms, the lingering scars of rat bites. The rats only attacked small, sickly children, leaving them with scars and nightmares.

Ralph often speculated about the population of Inner London. How big was it now? With so many transients it was hard to get accurate figures. But no matter how bad it got, Cameron was keen to remind him, it could only be worse in the North. Manchester was to get its own wall soon, Dover's was already up and Newcastle's had just been completed. He stopped in the doorway of a shop, surprised to find it still in operation. A few dusty dummies stood in the window, modelling clothes so dated that he couldn't imagine anyone wanting to buy them, ever. Inside he could see an old man seated in the centre of the brown linoleum-covered floor, his hands on his knees, staring off into space, possibly listening to the radio. He was wearing the kind of clothes he sold, trousers almost coming up to the middle of his chest, polished shoes of a style they hadn't made in decades, with perforated patterns around the toecaps. He wondered how on earth the old man survived, why he bothered to stay open in an area where no-one had come to shop in years.

Ralph checked his watch, found a cigarette and lit it. The suits in the window were draped in twists of red tinsel, part of a Christmas display that had never been dismantled. Christmas. He looked down at the littered pavement and shook his head. That was something he and other former Londoners rarely celebrated. It never felt like Christmas in the city anymore, and he did not enjoy the elaborate and faintly bogus displays of ritual that the Kent-dwellers were fond of performing in their homes. The pine trees, the ribboned gifts, the formal shows of exchange, like something from a charming childhood picturebook.

'Hello, you.' He raised his eyes to see Jay walking toward him, smiling about something. 'You're on time.'

'You make it sound like a rarity. We got off early. Somebody nicked our back tyres while we were answering an emergency call. Can't imagine why, they were completely bald.'

'Nice. I thought they only went for the drugs.'

'I think they've finally realised we don't keep anything decent on board. Where do you want to go?'

'Out of here. Somewhere with clean white tablecloths. Look.' He pointed at the old man in the suit shop. 'One of your outpatients?'

'He should be if he's still open here.' She pinched the sleeve of his overalls. 'They won't let you into a restaurant dressed like that.'

'It doesn't have to be anything fancy, just as long as – '

' – it's on the other side, I know. You're never going to convince me this way.'

She linked her arm in his. Ralph had taken her up into the watchtower once. She had always been aware of the contrast between the city and its suburbs – who could not be, looking down at the wall that ran all the way around it? But seeing both sides at once had shocked her. She coped with her job on the streets of the city because it was simply what she saw at ground level each day when she went to work. The ambulance collected her from the forecourt of her apartment, and stopped at the gate to pick up Annie and Todd. What she glimpsed on the Kent side as the gate opened to admit the other crew members into Inner London was just part of the daily journey, like stopping in a commuter train and vaguely noticing the station. But Ralph's attitude to his job as a border guard mystified her. Everyone she knew lived across the wall in Kent, but suffered their share of liberal guilt about it. Not Ralph. He seemed utterly untouched by what he saw when he mounted his sentry box. She wondered if guards ever suffered breakdowns, brought about by their schizophrenic vision of the world. There weren't many left now; computerised alarm systems had proven to be far more accurate, but they were expensive. She knew that he wanted her to move across and live with him, that he worried for her safety, but it never crossed his mind to suggest moving into her noisy little apartment. Perhaps the idea was so appalling to him that he never countenanced it.

'Tell me something.' She took the cigarette from between his fingers and drew on it. 'What do you really think about when you're up there on the wall?'

'I don't think about it.'

'But you must.'

'It's a necessary evil. Things should never have been allowed to reach this state, but they did. There have to be limits, and we have to make the best of it.'

They had reached the gate. He pulled the government identification card from the loop of chain around his shoulder and ran it through the wall-scanner, then punched in his pin number and returned the card to its secure pocket. They waited in the holding pen while the slatted steel shutter rose. The lifting machinery made a noise like an amplified cement mixer filled with rocks. It was hardly surprising that the property bordering the other side of the wall remained cheap to rent.

The shutter stalled a couple of feet above their heads, and they walked through into Kent. The change in their surroundings was immediate and total; a broad avenue hemmed with squares of neatly trimmed grass, flowering cherry trees, safety and calm. The further they walked from the wall, the more manicured everything became. After the dense street life of Inner London, Victoria Grove appeared as uninhabited as the surface of the moon. The residents led interior lives in the calm harbours of their homes.

They found an Italian spaghetti-and-meatballs place with red chequered tablecloths, chianti bottles and a sniffy maître'd who watched their table as if expecting them to steal the cutlery. Jay thought they would make it through the whole evening without the subject coming up, but over dessert Ralph made his customary suggestion.

'It just seems crazy you keeping two sets of clothes, rushing backward and forward between two places. My place is big enough for you to have your own room. It's not as if you'd be losing your independence or anything.'

'It's not about independence,' said Jay quietly. 'I can't live on the wrong side of the wall.'

'There's no right or wrong side.'

'That's not true and you know it.' She replaced her fork on the plate, no longer hungry.

'You drag politics into everything, Jay. At some point you have to consider your own happiness above other people's.'

'I do, it's just that I have strong feelings about this. And I don't understand how you don't.'

He reached over and speared the remaining piece of apple pie on her plate. 'Well, I don't.'

'But how can you do what you do, see what you see, and not care?'

'Look around you. Do you see anyone else in this restaurant beating themselves up about having better lives?'

'Are you so sure they do?'

'Of course I'm sure. Jesus, they behave like civilised people. They're not dropping burning mattresses on babies, they're not trying to set fire to each other.'

'Maybe you're right.' Jay pushed her chair back and threw her napkin onto the table. 'It seems to me you've got the perfect job, Ralph. Sitting on the damned fence.'

'Your mother called about the caterers again. Something to do with sideplates.'

'Mmm?' Janet Hunter opened an eye and looked across at her fiancé. His moustache was beginning to annoy her. It was always so neat, never a hair out of place, like something that had been stuck on with spirit gum. She wanted to examine it more closely, but feared he would catch her looking.

Their loungers were set in a warm corner of the garden, absorbing the last of the afternoon sun. The sky was a deep

August blue, and even now it held the spore of a cool, clear autumn. Bees hummed and bumbled around the flowers. The lawn sprinkler lazily flopped from side to side, sending droplets onto fallen pink petals as opulent as jewels.

'You're not listening. You know, I was wondering if your father had thought any more about my offer.'

'Please, Douglas, don't start that again. So many companies have lost fortunes lately, and you know he prefers to invest in tangible assets – '

'I keep trying to explain that these *are* tangible. A relatively small loan can potentially yield a regular low-risk income of, say – '

'The sun will have gone in, soon, and I'm tired. Let me relax. We'll talk about it over dinner.' Except we won't, she thought, because I'll find a way of avoiding the subject tonight, and tomorrow, and the day after that. She knew her mother wondered why she was marrying him. The words 'security' and 'stability' jumped to mind, but her reasons were more confused. Yes, he was the predictable choice, the distance runner. But he seemed less bitter than most, and he was safe. These days, all she really wanted was to feel safe. So few things were constant anymore. To some it was a repellent notion, marrying a man to protect you, but it was what she needed, if only to protect her from herself.

'The restaurant,' he persisted.

'I thought you said it was a fast-food chain.'

'It is, I just prefer to think of them as restaurants. Nothing has taken the place of McDonald's. After they were closed down in the West End and those so-called eco-warriors went off to protest about something else, no-one else stepped in. We can get Inner London permits and put them up in every street. I have friends who can – '

'It might have escaped your attention, Douglas, but inner city people haven't got any money. Otherwise they'd live somewhere nicer.'

'That's rubbish and you know it. They all seem to have cable television and mobile phones. They prefer to spend their money on lottery cards than feed their own children.'

'I can't think about this now,' she murmured. 'It bothers me.'

Some days she crossed the town and climbed the hill nearest the wall, just to frighten herself. If the wind was in the right direction you could actually hear them, the sirens, the shouts, the tidal swirl of chaos. It's a dam, she thought, placed there to keep the terror at bay, and dams can be breached. She imagined the great gate opening and that nightmare world pouring in, swamping their ordered lives. She knew she would never be comfortable until it happened. When you knew that something was possible, it was annoying not to have it occur.

Years ago on a summer's day just like today, she and Ralph had climbed the hill in pouring rain. Soaked to the skin, they looked down on the world. The wall only existed in selected boroughs then. It had not been joined all the way along. Ralph watched the workmen sheltering beneath the scaffolding, and calmly informed her that he had taken a job with the border patrol. It was as though he had betrayed her in some way, and yet here he was years later, still one of them, living on the right side, the decent side. Technically, it was the outside, but no-one could afford to think of it like that. That rainswept day on the hill she knew she would never be with him, because he wasn't safe. Some inner darkness drove him to take a job where he would always be confronted with the terrible true heart of their world.

'Ralph . . .' She suddenly realised that she had spoken his name aloud.

'Oh, yes? What about him?'

' – I invited him. Not to the ceremony, just the reception.'

'Your father told me.' Douglas fidgeted into the angled light. 'I do wish you'd discussed it with me first.'

She wondered when he had started holding separate conversations with her father.

'Why?' she asked, 'would you have said no? I'm not a child. Why does nobody want me to make my own decisions?'

'We're just trying to protect you, that's all.'

'But you don't approve of me inviting him.'

'I didn't say I didn't want you to, I just think we should have talked it over.'

'I don't see what there is to discuss. Either we do, which I'd like, or we don't, which I presume you'd prefer.'

Douglas peered over the top of his sunglasses at her. 'Sometimes, darling, I see a stubborn streak in you that reminds me of your mother.'

'You're only saying that to annoy me,' she replied. 'I'm going in. I grew up with Ralph. He understands me. And he's coming to the wedding.' She snapped back her head in his direction. 'And for God's sake stop calling me Darling.'

'I would have thought it was obvious,' said Jay, looking for somewhere to extinguish her cigarette. 'You have absolutely nothing in common with them.'

'You're jealous, that's it.' He shook his head in mock disbelief. 'She's getting married, for God's sake. She's hardly going to take a crack at me for old times' sake on her wedding day.'

'I'm not jealous. I just don't think it's very – healthy.' She folded her arms across her chest. 'It's cold in here. Don't you have a heater?' They were in the tower. It had just turned midnight. He wasn't supposed to bring anyone up here after eight in the evening. It was a security risk. Everyone who took the job did it, though. Cameron brought women here after dark, and made love to them while the ambulance lights flared on buildings far below.

'It's odd how the apartments in the Inner City all have their lights on, and the houses of the Outside are all dark.'

'Inner residents go to bed much later. They sit up talking, interfere with each other's lives, bring out the beers, get into arguments, stab each other to death. The outer residents make their cocoa, put on their pyjamas and go to bed like decent human beings.'

'Except at the weekends,' Jay pointed out. 'Then they all pour over into central London to buy drugs, get paralytically pissed and find someone to beat up if they can't get laid. I should know. I have to stitch them back together in the small hours of the morning.' The problem was that all the best clubs were in the centre of the city. The licensing laws were ignored, the music was deafening and the police were usually rushing somewhere else. It was a party town. Local councils prevented anything similar from appearing in the suburbs. 'You get gangs of them in penguin suits coming up from Croydon and Orpington, looking for people to shoot at. You must be able to see them from your window.'

'Oh, yeah, sometimes it gets so nasty out there that we have to close the shutters. The rest of the time we take bets on whether you guys will reach the victims in time.'

'If I thought you were serious, I'm not sure we'd be together.'

He put his arms around her. 'I've never been serious.'

'Maybe that's your trouble.' She touched his arms. 'Don't pull away. I'm trying to tell you something. I don't understand you, Ralph. You told me once that you've seen men die down there, right by the tower. You see people fighting all the time. Riots, rapes, everything's at a distance. You're never inside it.'

'Who'd want to be?' he asked, genuinely puzzled.

'Someone who wants to feel alive.'

'I can feel my life without risking it every day. I'm not you. I don't feel the need to test myself all the time.'

'That's not fair.' It was her turn to pull free and face him. 'What exactly is the point of you and Cameron being up here?'

'We watch, we report back. Sometimes the police turn up in time, sometimes they don't. Sometimes it would have been better if they'd stayed away.'

'Couldn't it be done by CCTV?'

'They'd still need teams to watch the monitors. Direct eye contact is better. So many questions.'

'I'm sorry. You know I love you. I just wish . . .'

'Come back here.' He rested his chin on her shoulder. Somewhere far below, a man was shouting in the street. 'Why do you always want to change things that are beyond your control?'

'Because I don't believe they are. If we all thought they were, wouldn't we just give up?'

'No. I don't think so.' For the first time she sensed uncertainty in his voice. In the dark cabin of the unlit tower, they looked down on the restless world.

'If you and Jay split up, can you put in a word for me?' asked Cameron, lowering his binoculars.

'Are you familiar with the nuances in the phrase Go Fuck Yourself? I'm making a cup of tea, do you want one? Anyway, you don't need a girlfriend.'

'Yeah, I'll have a cup. See if there are any doughnuts left. Why don't I?'

'I know what you watch through those.'

'Don't know what you mean, mate.'

'The brothel behind Waterloo Station. They don't close their curtains. I've seen you.'

'Just checking for misdemeanors, that's all.'

'Right.'

'Are you going to give her a present?'

'I was thinking about that. Janet's special. She's a tricky one to buy for.'

'But you've thought of something.'

'Perhaps.'

The band was playing a medley of Gilbert & Sullivan hits, songs of honour and duty that made no sense in a world where the meaning of such concepts had been irrevocably altered. The sun-smitten lawn was filled with guests, mostly neighbours from Victoria Grove, families Janet had grown up with, faces as familiar as those of her own uncles and aunts. The Devonshires were a no-show, but occasionally bobbed up at their kitchen window like a pair of meerkats. A small girl had pricked her thumb on Raymond's denuded rose bushes, and crimson drops

were staining her white party dress as she screamed, waiting to
be cossetted by her mother. Waitresses surreptitiously wiped
their foreheads with paper napkins. Janet stood at the entrance
to the marquee, listening to an ancient aunt. The shameful house
prices, the summer heat, the dog always barking in the house
next door . . . she barely heard what the old lady was telling
her. It seemed too bright today, even for a wedding. There were
no birds on the branches of the trees. The sunlight was hard
and dry, parching the garden, squinting eyes and stinging necks.
She looked across through the knots of overdressed, overheated
guests. No-one looked comfortable. Douglas was talking to her
father. Even from this distance, she knew he was explaining
something financial. She pulled a handkerchief from her sleeve
and dabbed at her throat. The aunt had asked her something.
She made a non-committal reply and forced a smile, which
seemed to work. Her dress was too tight. The bodice was digging
into her ribs. Nothing felt right today. Perhaps it was because
her parents had tried so hard to make everything perfect. He
wasn't here. She had felt sure he would come. He was always
reliable, always polite and always on time. You could set your
watch by Ralph. Maybe that was why so many people in the
neighbourhood respected him. They literally had to look up to
him, and in return he looked out for them.

But he wasn't here.

The canapés had been served and everyone was waiting to be
seated. Douglas had already settled himself beside her father.
The guests seemed unsure of themselves, as though they were
waiting for someone to tell them what to do. She felt drops of
sweat forming in the dimple of her collarbone. She turned
sharply and almost knocked the champagne glass out of his
hand. He stepped back and smiled. 'Hello, Janet.'

'Ralph. You made it. I'm so glad.' His hair used to be black
and curly, but he had shaved his head almost to the scalp. These
days she usually only saw him in a government cap. He was
wearing a terrible ill-fitting black suit. It looked like he had

bought it in the Inner City. There was a cut on the side of his face. A thin streak of blood ended just below his ear.

'I didn't think your father would want to have me here.'

'Oh, *him* – ' She glanced across the tent. 'We take no notice of him.'

'You look – '

'Radiant. That's what you're supposed to say.'

'I wasn't going to say that.'

'Then what?'

'Trapped.'

He knew her too well, but she couldn't allow him to get away with that. 'God, Ralph, even if you think it, you're not supposed to tell me.'

'I'm sure every bride feels like that for a moment. It's bound to pass. Can I ask you something?'

She shook her head. 'Oh, don't say it. Ralph. I won't dignify it with a reply.'

'But do you? Is this what you want?'

'Love him? It's not really about love, is it? I'll be fine. And how are you?'

'I have a gift for you.'

'Oh.' She glanced over to the stack of pastel-shaded boxes at the side of the tent. 'That's kind. You can put it over there with the others – '

'It's not something you can put somewhere, Janet. It's not a toaster, it wasn't on the list.'

A teaspoon sounded on the side of a wineglass. Her father was standing at the head table and calling for quiet. She had dreaded his speech. He was wearing an Arrow collar and a grey cravat, like a cartoonist's idea of a capitalist. Her mother appeared at her side and squeezed her arm as the music dwindled away. She smiled warmly at Ralph, reached over and gripped his hand with a white glove.

Raymond cleared his throat. 'Ladies and gentlemen, if I may have your attention.' Hushing sussurated through the garden. The Union Jack bunting hung limply in the dead heat. Janet studied the assembled guests and wondered what they looked like from the top of Ralph's watchtower, huddled together like the residents of some besieged town waiting for supplies to break through. 'Thank you. On this very special occasion of my lovely daughter's marriage – ' Some relatives turned to acknowledge her with puppyish eyes – 'I think about the things we're still lucky enough to have, the institution of marriage, and how unfashionable it has become these days. But we have always had our institutions. They are what make us who we are.' Douglas nodded sagely, looking into the middle distance. 'By marrying Douglas today, Janet is continuing our way of life.' Raymond looked down at his stomach and straightened his waistcoat. 'I like to think of us as the bearers of a great torch, a torch that keeps the flame of civilisation alight – '

'Oh God, I knew he'd be embarrassing.' Janet looked down at her shoes.

'There must always be a bearer, to light the way of others . . .'

The wind lifted slightly, and in the distance there came a faint sound, shouts and banging. Perhaps they had been there for a while, beneath the chatter of the guests, but now they were growing louder.

'Janet is helping to hold that torch aloft, to start another generation like the ones that went before hers – '

The shouting grew denser, louder. A car alarm began to howl, then another. At the rear of the garden, a few heads were starting to turn in consternation.

'It's for you, Janet. It's for all of us, but most of all it's for you.'

She looked at Ralph again, puzzled. There was something different about him, more focused and relaxed, less wary than usual. Something missing, too. She looked at his shirt, and the chain he always had to wear around his neck night and day. There was nothing hanging from it. 'Your card, where's your keycard?' she asked.

'Look at the sky. An end to the heat.' He pointed beyond the rooftops to low hard-edged clouds. A summer storm was building. The smashing, crashing and shouting grew in volume. Raymond had lost his thread, and was turning to look. Everyone was looking in the direction of the noise. More car horns sounded, to be joined by the low whooping of property security alarms. The cries and chants grew louder, closer. There came the sound of splintering wood, like a fence being pulled down. In the entire congregation, only Ralph seemed unconcerned.

'What's happening?' she asked anxiously. Others were looking to him. He was the guard, their protector, he was expected to know.

'I did it for you, Janet.'

'The card, it's never allowed to leave the chain around your neck. Who did you give it to?'

He reached over to a rose bush, snapped a crimson bloom from its stem and handed it to her. 'You're finally free to do what you like.'

'My God.'

The congregation had begun to scream. He watched Janet tearing at the bodice of the dress, mother-of-pearl buttons bouncing onto the perfect lawn, then she was pulling off her high heels and tugging the grips from her hair, then walking away through the whooping mob that suddenly overran the garden, then breaking into a run, until she was almost lost from his sight.

As more rowdy, laughing invaders swarmed onto the lawn, smashing down the fences, he had one last glimpse of her raised hand, still clutching the rose. Satisfied, he turned to face the boundless pandemonium of the crowd.

*Well, this is certainly the odd story out. Two things occurred;
the* Independent On Sunday *suggested I write a light piece
for summer because I had written them a gloomy winter one
they had liked, and I discovered P.G. Wodehouse. It was a
sunny day, and I was seated at the edge of Lake Como in
a setting unchanged since the 1930s; kids were swimming at
a lido, sports cars charged past, beautiful ladies in large hats
were walking their dogs, and I was laughing out loud at a
book I had avoided for years because I was sure I would detest
it. The writing appeared to be effortless because the tone was
so sure. I thought it would be interesting to at least attempt
something with a lighter touch.*

# SOMETHING FOR YOUR MONKEY

'A star is the closest thing you can get to a human being without quite being one.' That was what Helena Parole told me the day I first met her. She was seated in a too-tight white linen suit at her alabaster leather desk, with the spring sunshine throwing slats of light across her make-up, spraying plumes of cigarette smoke into the air. Smoke loitered in the coils of her coppery nylon hair, and softened her hard, heavily painted eyes from black spearheads into something vaguely corresponding to windows of the soul. Somebody once uncharitably pointed out her resemblance to a drag queen impersonating Jayne Mansfield in *The Girl Can't Help It*, but I don't recall her like that. Helena was womanly. Firm-jawed and full-busted. She had presence. She was interesting to men and women alike, for different reasons.

'I only mention it as a warning, dear,' she explained, tapping opalescent nails on the desktop. Her fingers were tapered and the nails came to sharp points, like bayonets. 'You can never afford to relax your guard around them, or they'll be on you like vampires. They don't want your blood, just your attention.'

'Is that so bad?' I asked.

'They want all of it, all the time. They suck the energy from you so fiercely that an hour in their presence is like eight hours' hard labour, and you get home at night too tired to take your knickers off.'

She returned her attention to my credentials, but after reading a few lines pushed the slim clip of papers aside. 'Your curriculum vitae isn't terribly interesting, is it? Working with the deaf, caring for crippled children. I suppose the discipline could come in useful; I understand that the handicapped can be quite selfish. But it does tend to suggest you care about people, and caring is a liability in this profession. What on earth brought you here?'

'A crisis of confidence,' I replied truthfully. 'I don't care about people as much as I thought I did. And I heard the money's good.'

'That's more like it.' She pulled open a drawer and found a pair of extraordinary tinted glasses with diamante wings, which she donned only to peer over the tops of the lenses in appraisal. 'As far as I can see, your face is your biggest advantage. Very fresh. Unspoiled. So many people look *used* these days. Nice speaking voice. I always think you can hear good breeding – though well-bred so often means in-bred, doesn't it, but that's the English for you, the upper classes simply need to get out more. You seem open and friendly. Are you?'

'I like to think so,' I replied.

'Do you upset easily?'

'Not at all.'

'You're rather short for twenty-six.'

'I'm five foot ten.'

'Make a fist.'

I made a fist.

'Oh yes. Nice strong arms. That'll come in useful.'

'I thought it was a desk job.'

'No, dear.' She gave a rather sinister, throaty chuckle. 'Not at all. You need to be physically strong.'

'I don't understand.'

'Try carrying Laurence Olivier's luggage up five flights of stairs at three in the morning and you'll see what I mean. And never admit you don't understand. It makes you sound too human.'

'I see,' I said. 'Is there anything else you want to know?'

She leaned around the desk and studied my legs. 'You have very small feet. Are you homosexual?'

'I don't see that's any business of yours,' I replied, mortified.

'I suppose you're right. It would certainly make things easier if you were. I can't afford to have someone dashing home to the little woman at half-past five, I'd much rather have you out after midnight looking for guardsmen. We're broadminded here. Where you choose to put about your generative organs is entirely your affair, provided you don't get arrested for doing it in a well-lit thoroughfare.' She examined the lipstick ring on the end of her cigarette. 'This job does not keep normal hours.'

'So I was given to understand.'

'Of course, I forgot you'd already been briefed. So you know what we do.'

'You look after famous people.'

'In a nutshell. We act as liaison officers between celebrities, the press and the public. Since the war, this particular branch of the motion picture industry has spawned a new breed of employee. You have to be a bouncer, a nursemaid, a jailer, a drill sergeant and a den mother to people who aren't used to hearing the word no, and have never been contradicted in their lives. Looking after a celebrity is rather like being at the court of Elizabeth the First, only with more make-up and swearing. You have to watch out for traps and be terribly, terribly diplomatic.'

She scraped back her chair and rose with her hand out-stretched. She was a good six inches taller than me, but most of it came from her heels. Her tanned breasts jutted from the top of her suit like Christmas balloons on Boxing Day.

'Do you want to know why I'm going to hire you? I'm going to hire you because you know nothing of these people other than what you read in the papers. Sometimes it pays to employ an unjaundiced eye. What should I call you?'

'My friends call me Billy.'

'Oh, I shall remember that. It reminds me of Billy Butlin, the camp man. Rather appropriate in your case, I should think. You can start Monday at nine.'

'Thank you, Mrs Parole.'

'Parole,' she corrected. 'Three syllables, the accent on the third. My last husband's name. But you must call me Helena. Buy yourself some decent clothes, dear. Make sure you have a current passport. And always keep little packets of paper handkerchiefs about yourself. You'll get through a lot of them. Welcome aboard.'

And that was how I got the job at Albion Public Relations.

Now, in order to be completely honest about this, I will have to change some names. Stars operate under special laws that protect them while damaging everybody else, so I have to be careful. And Albion, like every other company, had its own house rules governing the indiscretions of its employees. Of course, now it has collapsed in a blaze of dreadful publicity, I don't work there anymore. Nobody does. The offices have been taken over by a distributor of Scandinavian naturist films. And Helena . . . well, who knows where she is after the court-case that virtually every human being in England followed in the newspapers through a long hot summer . . . but old habits die hard, and I wouldn't be comfortable about identifying culprits. So the names have been changed, but not to protect the innocent. In this story, there are no innocents.

The thing you must understand about Albion is that it wasn't a glamorous company filled with smoked-glass walls and expensive modern paintings. Rather, it was an unassuming suite of offices on a third floor with an ancient trellis lift, overlooking the Charing Cross Road. You could have mistaken it for the address of a notary public. There were two reasons for this. First, it was important for the company to protect itself from unnecessary attention by appearing nondescript and unas- suming. Second, the reputation of Albion was based on its handling of 'difficult' celebrities, stars whose behaviour had given them a certain level of notoriety, so there was no point in leaving nice breakable *objets d'art* lying around the place. Indeed, Albion was the last stop for a handful of celebrities who could no longer find anyone else to look after them. These were the few who had driven their agents to alcoholism and their families to suicide, and who still did not understand that they were doing anything wrong. These were people so appallingly behaved that . . . But I'm getting ahead of myself. Let's go back to my first working day at Albion.

It was a cool, misty Monday morning at the start of spring in the year 1958 when I alighted from a bus in Charing Cross Road to begin my duties at the company. My first task as Helena Parole's assistant commenced when my new boss thrust her great lacquered doll's head through the cubby-hole that connected her parchment-white office with my cluttered dark corner.

'Pick up the other line, will you, Billy?' she called. 'It's Mal Dando. Listen to him, hear what he wants, then tell him he can't have it. And make sure you record the call. Press the button on the base of the phone. Actors lie so often without realising it that sometimes you have to play their own conversations back to them.'

I stared at my telephone's blinking red light with horror. Mal Dando had once been one of the biggest film stars in the world. (Mal Dando is not his real name, it's not even an anagram, so don't try to work it out. I changed his name even though he's dead now because stars are rather like the undead; they can reach out to strangle you from beyond the grave.) He was still extremely famous. I had never spoken to anyone famous in my life, unless you counted the greengrocer in my mother's village who had been convicted for interfering with a Brown Owl eleven years earlier.

I pressed the RECORD button and gingerly raised the receiver.

'Is Helena there?' I recognised the voice at once. Seven-eighths of the cinema-going world recognised the voice. Dando had recently finished shooting a gangster film called *Finnegan's Way* in Los Angeles, and had just checked into Claridges on the first leg of his European publicity tour. This wasn't insider knowledge; I had read about it in the *Daily Sketch*.

'She's on the other line.'

'Who the hell are you?'

'I'm her new assistant.'

'Do you have a name?'

'Billy.'

'Well, listen, Billy, would you please do me a favour?'

'Of course.'

'Take your thumb out of your ass and put Helena on the line.'

I stared at the telephone as if bitten. I had never before experienced this kind of rudeness, and frankly saw no need to put up with it now. I slowly brought the receiver back to my face. 'Anything you wish to say to her you can say to me,' I said coldly.

'Listen, you little fruit, you have about five seconds to put that bitch on the line before I have you kicked out on the street. Then you'll have to find somewhere else to drink tea from Monday to Friday until some rich old man buys your ass.'

'I'm putting you on hold,' I said firmly.

'Don't even think about – '

I dropped the receiver and pressed HOLD. Then I dug into my pocket, found a handkerchief and wiped my brow. Helena's advice was already proving useful. I remembered something else she had told me at the interview: that, despite all their bluster and arrogance, our clients needed us more than we needed them. After all, if we fired them, where else could they go? If they had come to Albion, it usually meant that they had been thrown out of every other public relations firm in the city. In those days, London was not really geared to handling the peculiar problems of the motion picture industry.

I crept into Helena's office and waited while she spoke on her private line, but a single sharp look from her told me to deal with the situation myself. So I returned to my desk and stared at the waiting call. Its light blinked back. I raised the receiver again and reconnected.

'She's still busy,' I told the seething silence. 'You can tell me what you need – '

'I'll tell you what I need, you little – '

'If you're abusive I'll hang up.'

'If you hang up I'll have your ass fired.'

I wondered why everything was bottoms with Americans. 'If you fire me, you'll be carrying your own luggage tonight.'

I heard a snort of bad grace.

'I can have her call you as soon as she's free. And I can make sure that she gets a message before then.'

'Okay, you can start by telling her that this morning's press conference is off. I am not sitting next to a director who, only two days ago, told me that I have the emotional agility of a towel-rail. If Helena remembers, and I think she does because it was on the front page of every newspaper in the country, we engaged in a fist-fight that resulted in his loss of blood and my loss of respect for a man who should not be allowed to direct cows up a plank, let alone a half a million dollar motion picture. I cannot sit next to him. I find it very hard to respect anyone I have bitten. And I am not going to pal up to him just to please a bunch of journalists who couldn't find a story if you rolled it up and wedged it down their ass cracks.'

I winced at his language, but struggled on. 'I think I have a solution to the problem. I'll arrange to have your chair moved out to the front of the stage. After all, you are the star of the film. You should be seated ahead of everyone else. And in a nicer chair. A better chair. A bigger chair.'

He thought for a moment. 'That might work. Okay, I'll forgive you for your rude demeanor earlier. Let's just put it down to your natural nervousness. After all, it's not every day you get to talk to a Hollywood legend.'

'That could be true,' I admitted. 'I have to tell you, Mr Dando, you're my second favourite movie star in the entire world.'

'Oh really?' He thought about this. 'Who's your first?'

'*Everybody else.*'

I replaced the receiver.

I knew then that I wasn't being paid enough to deal with these people. But I also knew I could do the job. I am, by nature, a stubborn man. People like Mal Dando, I decided, might regard themselves as unstoppable forces, but in me they had finally met an immovable object.

I asked Helena about Mr Dando, and she explained that behind the genial family-man image was an impossibly demanding actor and womaniser of the paid-escort variety, with a prodigious alcohol intake and a bad attitude toward the press. He was the kind of problem client she was used to handling, and she did it with her own patented blend of sinister charm, blackmail and subterfuge, controlling his public behaviour to the point where she was able to turn a potentially disastrous situation involving an underage girl in a Carlton Hotel suite at the last Cannes Film Festival to her advantage, escaping in a French military helicopter and leaving a trail of furious journalists in her wake.

'Behind the bluster they're big babies, and sometimes they need to be smacked. Mal tells me he's insecure,' she explained. 'It's a popular word around here. It's a word celebrities use when they've done something bad.'

I tried to guess how old Helena was. From the way she applied her make-up (too thick) and chose her clothes (too tight) I imagined late thirties, but I couldn't for the life of me understand the look she was going for. It wasn't until later that I found out just how old she was. There was something about her eyes that was ageless. Sometimes she looked like a sexy version of my mother, mixed with something of Margaret Leighton, although on certain mornings after film premières she looked more like Marc Fleming, the resident female impersonator at the Black Cap in Camden Town. I asked her what we should do if Dando still decided to walk out of the press conference.

'What do you mean?' she asked, genuinely puzzled.

'How do we excuse his behaviour?'

'We don't have to. He'll be there.'

'But he said – '

'Oh, that was all rubbish, darling. You honestly think he'd miss his chance to have the attention of all those journalists representing every major showbusiness journal in the Western hemisphere entirely focused on him? *Please*.' She fitted a fresh cigarette into her ivory holder and lit it. 'Most stars tell you they want the press to respect their privacy. Mal never says that. As far as I'm concerned, his absence of a denial tells me that he'd crawl two hundred miles over broken glass just for the opportunity of narrowing his eyes at some swoony old boiler from a parish magazine. I'm far more worried about Bettina.'

'Bettina La Chiesa? You know her?'

'Know her? Darling, she's one of our clients.'

'I had no idea.'

'Very few people do.'

It made no sense. Bettina La Chiesa was the world's most public virgin, a beautiful Italian model who was about to become the new face of *Vogue*. She was seventeen years old, had a seventeen-inch waist, and had just been offered the biggest contract of all time to promote make-up. She surely had no need of an end-of-the-line company like Albion.

'But why are you representing her?'

Helena thoughtfully regarded the pall of smoke that hung over her desk like a raincloud.

'It's all rather complicated. She has . . . an image problem.'

'I find that hard to believe.'

'For a start, she's not Italian.'

'I read that she was born in Rome.'

'She's from South London. Her real name is Betty Church.'

'You amaze me.'

'Nor is she dating Mal Dando.'

Bettina La Chiesa's name had been romantically linked to Dando's even though there was a considerable age difference. She had categorically denied any involvement with the rugged star, but magazines were always running photographs of them frolicking together in expensive country hotels.

'I thought they were engaged.'

'That was something I came up with to take some of the heat off them.'

'What kind of heat?'

'Did you know that Bettina is employed by the Roman Catholic Coalition of America to appear at national conventions preaching the evils of sex before marriage?'

'No, I didn't.'

'Tell me, what do you think of her?'

'I've never seen her in person, of course, but she appears to be very beautiful,' I answered. 'She has nice eyes and an alluring smile, and does not appear to wear make-up of any sort.'

'She doesn't need to, she had her eyelids tattooed. What else?'

'I remember reading that she advocates taking baths in goats' milk.'

'Ah, the famous complexion. When you've got young skin you can scrub it with Vim and a Brillo Pad without inflicting any damage. Watching a star prepare to meet her public is like having your car cleaned before you sell it: The end result has all its defects hidden away and pleasantly surprises you. In actuality her head's far too large and her body's too thin. When I first met her she was wearing a black and white Cecil Beaton suit and looked like a Belisha Beacon. Okay, what do you know about Mal Dando?'

'He's been married three times. Now divorced. And about to marry Bettina – '

'No, he's not. Just before his new film went into production, Mal checked himself into a private clinic.'

'His drink problem?'

'Therapy. But it was connected with drink. His binges had resulted in such upsetting episodes that he could no longer bear the thought of human physical contact. The therapists wrapped him in a yak-skin and put him through a lot of stick-and-eskimo-drum howling, then wired him up to some kind of electric shock device. The treatment cost him a fortune. When the doctors finally released him into the outside world again, he overcame his fears, walked on to the film set and immediately became enamoured of someone in the crew.'

'That's good, isn't it? That means the therapy worked.'

'It worked all right. But the boy he's fallen in love with is not only underage, he's an illegal Mexican who was employed to hold nails for the carpenters.'

'Heavens. Is that why you manufactured Dando's romance with Bettina La Chiesa?'

'Not exactly. I did that because she has a problem of her own.'

My head was starting to swim with these revelations. 'Perhaps you'd better tell me.'

'Okay.' Helena sucked hard on her cigarette. 'The world's most public virgin has an eight-year-old illegitimate son.'

'How could that be possible? She's only – you mean she lied about her age?'

'She's twenty-three. She's had all the fat sucked out of her face and four of her back teeth removed. She's as bitter as only a woman with absolutely no body fat can be. It's Audrey Hepburn's fault. Bettina wants to look gamine but she only has to catch a glimpse of an ice cream to put on pounds, so her trainers starve her and make her undergo colonic irrigation. But they can't keep her like that forever. They'll leave her alone for five minutes one day and she'll gorge herself sick on room service potatoes. I've seen it before. By the time she's thirty she'll look like someone drew a face on a balloon. Does all this surprise you?'

I sighed. 'In a way, no.'

The press conference for *Finnegan's Way* took place on one of the sound stages at Shepperton studios. The journalists and their photographers had been herded into separate corrals around a spotlit stage on which stood a table draped in a red cloth. Four chairs and four glasses of water stood ready for the star guests, who were the producer, the director, Mal Dando, and a small child who also featured in the film. Dando's chair was much larger than the other three, and looked more like a throne. Actually, it was a throne. I had pinched it from the set of *The Loves Of Nero*, filming next door.

Helena stayed in the background, but it was clear from the outset that she was in control of the entire operation. At her signal, the guests strolled onto the stage, the last being Dando himself, who kept one nonchalant hand in the pocket of his suit as if to suggest that this was just another opportunity for him to have a casual chat with half of the world's journalists. Helena's helpers had provided everyone in the auditorium with a set of guidelines explaining what could and could not be asked of the star.

The first few questions were so stupefyingly inane I found it hard to believe that human beings could be bothered to ask them. Nations were recovering from a world war, democracies were in danger of collapse, children were dying of starvation, and Italy wanted to know if Mal Dando had found it difficult wearing a wig for the role. Dando considered each question carefully and gave a clear, grave answer. Any jitters he had experienced earlier were gone, and in their place was a great calmness.

'It's the first thing a good director teaches an actor,' Helena whispered to me. 'To be the hero of a motion picture you need to present an immobile centre. All sophisticated heroes have still interiors. If they rushed about panicking, you wouldn't respect them.'

The film was something to do with a gang of crooks – led by Dando playing 'Finnegan' – pulling a big heist. Part of me became very angry with what I saw that day – and yet another part was attracted to the spectacle, for a reason that I only identified long after. Despite my earlier conversation with Dando, I found myself being drawn in by his easy charm. Later that day Helena took me backstage and introduced me to him.

He was smaller and older than he looked on the screen, somewhere in his early fifties. His hair was dyed an unearthly grey-banishing tint the colour of dead leaves, and he was wearing make-up in a shade that reminded me of chip-shop batter. The overall effect was rather like a colour negative of an ordinary person. His lips were drawn in a permanent half-smile across his bleached teeth. When he spoke, nothing moved very much. For a second I thought he was being operated by a ventriloquist.

'Face lift,' Helena explained. 'I don't suppose he can close his mouth without opening his bowels. There's more china in his jaw than there is in the Wedgwood window at Oxford Circus.'

Dando shook my hand and crinkled his eyes pleasantly, but looked right through me. I felt like turning around and trying to see what it was on the wall behind that interested him. He gave no sign of remembering our phonecall. Moments later a photographer asked him to pose for some pictures, and he drew away in the direction of the camera like a cat stalking a crippled moth.

'Well, what did you think of him?' Helena asked me.

'He didn't initiate any of the conversation,' I observed.

'Of course not. He's a star. He doesn't have to. That's what we're there for. We provide the basic motor skills that keep the shark moving through the water. He's not interested in us. He can't see us in his line of vision.'

'But doesn't that sort of thing affect him?'

'Naturally. Everyone notices it except him. It's that indefinable star quality the public calls magic and we call rudeness. He'll start talking when he wants something. Meanwhile the best thing we can do is make him feel warm and cosy and sleepy and protected. It's like dogs and radiators.'

I was reminded of his phonecall earlier in the day. 'What did he want, by the way?'

'Do you know, I'm still not sure.' Helena dug round for her cigarettes and lit one as she hailed a cab. 'Either it was some basic need that he subsequently fulfilled and forgot . . .'

'Or?' I prompted.

'Or it's trouble.'

On Tuesday, Helena's second diagnosis proved correct.

'He's gone,' whispered the mortified desk clerk who had been acting as a paid informant for Helena. He had summoned us to Claridges the moment he had realised his mistake. At a quarter past six in the morning, the lobby was even more gracefully calm than usual. Helena was wearing a gown covered in chartreuse rhinestones and had a fox-fur at her neck. She had obviously not been home.

'What do you mean, he's gone?' she asked slowly and dangerously.

The desk clerk touched his waxy moustache into place, as though at any moment she might lean across his desk and try to rip it off. 'Mr Dando bribed the bellboy to let him out.' Helena had paid a considerable amount of money to have Dando locked in his suite overnight.

'Are his valises still in the room?'

'Oh, yes. He took only the clothes he was standing in.'

'Then how do you know he's not just gone for a walk?'

'He left at half-past five this morning. The night porter had to unlock the front door for him because he came back for his hat.'

'Damn. He only wears that hat when he doesn't want to be recognised. Did he say where he was going?'

'Not a dickie bird.'

'It was your job to keep him here, and to let me know if he tried to get out.' Helena angrily rooted around for her lighter. 'He's chasing after his little friend. Slipped out like a thief in the night. I'm sure I could sue the therapist for turning him into a pansy. He's due on a plane at ten. If he fails to show up in Paris there'll be an international incident.'

'How do you mean?' I asked.

'Because, my dear, the French Ministry of Defence lent us their helicopter to escape from Cannes. The Air Marshal's children are big fans of his. As a token of gratitude, I arranged for them to meet their hero at Orly airport when he arrives. But now, Dando won't be on the flight, the Ministry of Defence will be snubbed and they'll be sure to make clear their displeasure by embarrassing our foreign office chaps at the Geneva conference.'

'And all this because Mal Dando has fallen in love?'

'With a young boy. An underage illegal immigrant Mexican boy.'

'How underage?'

'What does it matter?' Helena exploded. 'Isn't it enough that he has? He's sixteen or thereabouts. Mexicans mature earlier. These shoes are killing me.'

'First we must locate the object of Mr Dando's affection,' I suggested. 'Is he still in America?'

'I don't know.'

'You said he's an illegal immigrant, so he could hardly be smuggled into this country, could he?'

'I suppose not.'

'Then I suggest we check the flights to New York. If the boy isn't coming to Dando, Dando must be going to him.'

'You may have a point. You.' She slapped her hand on the reception desk, startling the desk clerk into alertness. 'For God's sake wake up. Do you have a telephone I can use?' But we drew a blank with the airlines. If Dando was registered, he had to be using an assumed name, and that would mean acquiring a false passport. Helena was convinced he hadn't the agility of thought for such a plot. I had another idea.

'Could there be a go-between?' I asked. 'Someone who knows them both, someone Mr Dando can trust?'

'He keeps the same driver wherever he goes.'

'Then let's try him.'

We called the limousine company, and by a stroke of luck discovered that Stanley, Dando's chauffeur, was passing through the West End, so the controller asked him to call at Claridges.

'Did you take Mal Dando to Heathrow Airport this morning?' snapped Helena. She stuck her great head through the passenger window of the gleaming black Wolseley. 'Has he been in here? If he told you not to say anything don't worry, I look after him and we have no secrets, do you understand? No secrets at all.' She sniffed the air. 'Someone's been eating chips. And drinking brandy. Dando drinks brandy when he's tense. Either that or it's you. Do you drink on the job? I hope not, it could get you fired. Come on, out with it.'

Stanley the driver was hunched guiltily at the wheel. I don't think he was used to being interrogated by a woman. This was years before Beatles' fans besieged cars. There was still some decorum to be found in the relationship between stars and their admirers.

'I was hungry, so I bought some chips on the way back from the airport,' Stanley admitted.

'Damn, so Dando was on a flight to New York.'

'No, Ma'am. He was going to Spain.'

'Spain!'

'Yes, Ma'am. San something.'

'That's no help at all.'

'San Sebble, Sibble, Senobia –' Stanley struggled.

'San Sebastian?' I suggested. 'It's on Mr Dando's itinerary because of the film festival they hold there.'

'That's the one,' said Stanley. 'Reminded me of the saint, it did, the one with the arrows.'

'Did Mr Dando say if he was meeting anyone there?'

'No, Ma'am.'

A fresh thought struck me. 'Wait, are you sure the boy is Mexican?'

'What else could he be with a name like Miguel? Oh my God.'

We booked the next flight to Bilbao, which, as luck would have it, was just a toothbrush-and-comb's-packing-time away. It was a beautiful day in San Sebastian, which I learned was a coastal resort in the green heart of Basque territory, an elegant seaside town with a sandy double bay, a clocktower and an old port, and a funicular railway rising to a clifftop funfair. A few hundred yards out into the sea stood a small, perfect island, with bobbing white boats and an old inn. Along the promenade and past the opera house, which stood on the bank of the river that divided the town, strolled smart Spanish couples, taking the air. There were few bare heads, no knobbly knees and no unruly children. It was a bit like Hastings, shifted much further south and devoid of the English.

'I simply don't know how we are to be expected to find Dando here,' Helena complained, shoving her luggage at a hotel porter. 'Take, take.'

'The obvious place to look first is in the festival hotel,' I replied. 'Besides, it appears to be rather a small town, and there's just one front to stroll along. Sooner or later everyone must bump into everyone else.'

'I wish I had your confidence,' Helena sighed. 'You remind me of my first husband, Alberto. I'll never forgive him for falling out of that aeroplane.' Then she seemed to perk up, and brought her hand down smartly on the reception desk's bell. She was obviously quite used to rousing sleepy hotels. 'I say, you there,' she bellowed at the desk clerk, who had been taking a siesta and was trying to button his collar on the run, 'I want a beach-front room with a bath, and I expect the water to be piping hot. Front room. Ensuite bath. Is this sinking in? Do you speak English?'

I decided to unpack later and take the sea air.

'And don't you think you can sneak out on me,' said Helena, pulling an enormous white hat back from the porter, 'I'm coming with you.' So I marched off along the promenade in my baggy cream trousers and my elegantly striped blazer, with Helena stalking along at my side, her red Hermes scarf fluttering in the warm afternoon air. There were still a few sunbathers on the sands, and couples lingered in the cafés, watching the world slowly turn.

'You realise, of course, that Albion won't be paid unless Dando completes his publicity tour. And that means negotiating the perils of the entire spring film circuit, going on to Cannes, Berlin, Venice and lord knows where else. The only point in our favour is that Bettina La Chiesa is here.'

'Why does that help us?' I asked.

Helena clutched at the brim of her hat as a particularly strong breeze assailed us. 'Don't you see, if we can engineer some fresh development in their so-called offscreen romance we may yet deflect the publicity hounds and save the day.'

'I see. And where is Bettina's child now?'

'What do you want to know that for?'

'Well goodness, it surely has a bearing on the matter at hand.'

'Oh, I agree that the press mustn't know about her little monster, but there's not much chance of them finding out from here. I've got Victor stashed away in my Mayfair apartment with ample supplies of cocoa and digestive biscuits, and there he'll stay until his mother signs with *Vogue* and renews her contract with us. He's playing Ludo with my second husband's nurse, a woman with whom few males are prepared to tangle, although a couple tried at the secure facility where she was last employed and lived to rue the day, and I trust that she'll tie the child up if he starts to misbehave, something he is prone to do at every available opportunity. The beast is quite impossible, utterly unruly and highly vocal. I've had to have my windows nailed shut. Not only does he have a disagreeable nature, but he's quite the most misshapen little thing you ever saw. Apparently he was dropped on his head when he was born. Took the midwife by surprise, I shouldn't wonder.'

'Are you not fond of children?' I asked.

'Not fond? Not when the little buggers grow up to be men who spend half their lives in front of the mirror brilliantining their hair and the other half sneaking off behind your back to have cheap flings with floozies who sell programmes at the Palladium, no.'

I let the subject drop.

'The main thing now,' I said, 'is to find Mr Dando and his friend before the press get at him.'

In the distance, a band was playing 'Only A Rose', and I was just starting to enjoy the sensation of sun on my face when Helena nudged me hard in the ribs. 'Oh my God,' she hissed, 'you spoke too soon. It's Glen Jacobs. Quick, take me across the road as fast as you can, don't let him see us and try to look casual.'

Walking toward us was a slightly gone-to-seed but still handsome gentleman in a white suit. With his pencil moustache, cigarette holder and confident stride there was something of the older Clark Gable about him.

'Faster, faster.' We hastily crossed the road, and were hooted by a passing Mercedes Benz. 'Is he looking?' Helena peeped out from beneath the brim of her hat.

'I'm rather afraid – '

'What is it? What?'

'He's spotted you and is heading this way.'

'Damn and blast. If he gets a sniff of why we're here, we're finished.'

'Who is he?'

'A reporter.'

'He doesn't look like a gentleman of the press.'

'He's no gentleman, my dear, he's an American. And worse.'

'Hey, Helena,' boomed a healthy Texan voice, 'what are you doing here?'

'Why Glen, Glen Jacobs, *quelle surprise!* We were just taking the air.'

'Just when this year's film festival is getting its first scent of gossip? Surely you couldn't be holding out on me, could you?' Glen flashed a devastating smile.

'I'm sure I have no idea what you mean,' flustered Helena. I had never seen her like this before. I decided it was time to step in.

'I'm Mrs Parole's personal assistant,' I explained, holding out my hand in a gesture of welcoming friendship.

'Another sissy, Helena? Don't you ever tire of them?'

'That is no way to speak to me,' I retorted, 'I could sue you for defamation.'

'I'd like to see you try,' he grinned cheerfully.

'Gentlemen, please! This will get us nowhere!'

'So tell me, is Helena still selling innocent souls to the devil in order to control the public behaviour of her unruly stars?' asked Glen.

'I don't know what you mean.'

'Come now, we all know why she's here. The cat's out of the bag. Mal Dando has switched from batsman to bowler. He's changed ends at half-time. He's put another skip in the hop, skip and jump.'

'Really, Glen, I think you can drop the sporting metaphors.'

'You know exactly what I mean, Helena. He's running around town with a little Spic on his arm. There's no romance with Bettina and never was. I'm on my way to the bureau now to file the story.'

'Wait.' Helena grabbed his arm, digging in her crimson nails. 'How do you know this?'

'How do I know?' He shouted a laugh. 'The guy is sitting in the private salon of the restaurant behind the Opera House dining *à deux*, that's how I know. He's having the house speciality. I slipped the waiter a fin.'

'I don't believe it.'

'Then go see for yourself. Some kind of fish served in octopus ink. Dando's career will be over by tomorrow, and we'll sell a lot of papers in Poughkeepsie.'

'We don't need to see for ourselves,' I told the Texan. 'Mr Dando is simply following my advice.'

'Oh, sure. You told him to turn pansy in order to publicise his new movie.'

'Not quite, but you're on the right track.' I caught Helena's gaze and held it. 'I acted on my own accord. I haven't yet told Helena about this. And I'm not prepared to say anything more at the moment. Go and file your story.'

'Wait, wait.' It was Glen's turn to look flustered. 'What are you saying?'

'I'm saying nothing,' I reiterated. 'The boy's full name is Miguel Arragossa. Be sure that you spell it correctly.'

The reporter was used to Helena withholding the truth from him, but my intervention was unexpected. I could see him thinking. It was obvious that we'd had no time to confer, so I couldn't be making up a story on the spot, could I?

Well, the truth was I could, and I was. But I had a plan.

'Let me get this right. You want me to go ahead and spill the beans on Dando?'

'Feel free. We need all the publicity we can get. After all, it's still a fairly taboo subject, even in European cinema. I think Dirk Bogarde may one day have a stab at it for Rank, but he'll be ahead of his time when he does . . .'

'You're telling me that Mal Dando is gonna play a queer?'

'No, I'm saying that he is to star in a thought-provoking French film about gender, race and sexuality.'

'And he's conducting a little advance research? Pull the other leg, buddy.' Glen tipped his hat to Helena. 'Tell your boy it was a nice try but I'm not buying. See you on the funny pages.'

'I have evidence,' I blurted. 'On tape. We record our telephone calls. It's strictly business. Mal Dando insulted me. He called me a fruit.'

'A little fruit,' added Helena.

'Why would he do that if he'd really become one himself?' I asked.

'You tell me.'

I cleared my throat. 'I see we shall have to let you in on our secret.'

'What secret?' asked Glen.

'Yes,' agreed Helena, amazed. 'What secret?'

'Mal Dando is going to announce his engagement to Bettina La Chiesa at a press conference here tomorrow night.' If Helena hadn't disapproved so strongly of ladies smoking in the street and had been taking a puff on her ivory cigarette holder right now, this was the moment when she would have swallowed it.

'You want me to believe that he's getting engaged, and that he's only hanging out with this Miguel because he's gonna star in a queer French movie?' Glen's jaw was growing slacker by the second.

'Basically, yes.'

'What the boy is saying – ' interrupted Helena, panicked.

'I can hear what the boy is saying, I just don't know whether or not to believe it,' said Glen.

I decided to brazen it out. 'You can ask him. Get it from the star himself. Right after the public announcement tomorrow night. Or you can go ahead and file your story rightaway.'

'He's right, Glen,' added Helena. 'It all depends on how much egg you're prepared to let Robert Mackay make you wipe off your face tomorrow.' Mackay was Glen's boss, a frustrated thespian who used any excuse to dramatically threaten his star reporter with the sack. If Glen failed to provide Mackay's readers with a scandal that was both juicy and true, after being flown out to San Sebastian all expenses paid, he would be for the high-jump. Helena honoured me with a secret smile, and we took our leave of the stunned journalist.

'My dear, you really have hurled yourself in at the deep end,' warned Helena as we were walking briskly back to our hotel. 'But your instincts are correct. Glen lives in fear of his boss. Robert Mackay is an annoyingly shrewd Scotsman, a larger-than-life sort of chap who used to tread the boards himself and never quite got over the smell of the greasepaint. He once boasted that he knew the text of every play by heart. But he had to abandon the halls after it was discovered that he had grown rather too enamoured with the dressing-up aspect of performance. Took to borrowing his wife's clothes, if memory serves. Of course it was all hushed up. I keep the details of such indiscretions in my little black book. You never know when they'll come in useful.'

'I'm not sure you should do that,' I ventured doubtfully. 'It doesn't sound very ethical.'

'My little black book is kept strictly for the purposes of blackmail. Ethics doesn't enter into it. I trust you can get us out of this situation, Billy. You realise that the future of Albion is at stake.'

'I just bought us some time. We have to act fast. Get to Dando first, and convince him to lie.'

'But why would he do that?'

'I have an idea. Tell me more about Glen Jacobs.'

'Well, I've known him for years. He suspects that he and all the rest of the entertainment journalists are being shamelessly manipulated, and he's very persistent. He'd dearly love to expose the whole PR machine to the general public.'

'But if he wrecks it, he'll be out of a job.'

'I know, isn't it simply killing? You have to understand that one half of him wants to be a crusading reporter, and the other half knows exactly which side his bread is buttered. The public thinks entertainment reporters are on to a cushy number, but they're not. Poor Glen rushes about in search of tittle-tattle, bribing and cajoling, forever being shoved aside and ignored. It's demeaning. Men so easily lose their self-respect. They wouldn't last five minutes as women. And Glen is one of the last men in the business with integrity. He would never file a story he believed to be false, poor baby.'

'Poor baby? Just how well do you know him, Helena?'

'Oh,' she said airily, 'quite well. We used to step out together, if that's what you mean, but work came between us.'

'And your reluctance to be completely honest with him pushed you apart.'

'Something like that.' She bristled. 'Quite the little detective, aren't you? Robert Mackay has become one of the most successful tabloid editors in America, and is pushing Glen to expose my company. I suspect that Glen soft-pedals his stories out of respect for our shared past, but I can't trade on those memories forever, not with his boss hovering in the wings. I knew that one day my luck would run out.'

'I couldn't help but notice how you look at him. You're still in love with him.'

'And what if I am?' She searched her handbag for a cigarette. 'It's over and that is that. Now what the hell are we going to do to stop this entire house of cards from falling down on our heads?'

'First we have to talk to Bettina.'

'Bettina? She can't help us. Glen will spread the word all over town, and everyone will be expecting Mal Dando to stand up and announce his engagement.'

'Nevertheless,' I insisted, 'it's Miss La Chiesa who holds the key to our salvation.'

'If we make it to the Cannes Film Festival in one piece, I'll buy you a lobster dinner at the Hotel Du Cap.' She thought for a moment. 'Or at least, the Carlton.'

'Why did Mr Dando call me a fruit, do you suppose?'

'When he's angry he just grabs words from the air. Believe me, you got off pretty lightly.'

'I took exception.'

'I know you did.'

'I may demand an apology.'

'A word of advice.'

'Yes?'

'Don't overdo it, dear. Remember Oscar Wilde.'

We found Bettina in her suite at the Grand, being made up for a photographic session. A pair of tiny old ladies were pinching the back of her silver dress together with dozens of clothespegs in order to stretch the material tightly across her facade. The dressing room was filled to the point of vulgarity with roses, but the model herself was far more beautiful than Helena had led me to believe.

'Darling Helena!' she screamed, kissing the air six inches from my employer's face in a move designed to prevent the make-up of both women from being smudged, 'how absolutely marvellous to see you.' She dismissed the old ladies with a fan of the fingers. 'Tell me,' she lowered her voice, 'how is my dear little Victor? Not too trying on your nerves?'

'Precious one, how thoughtful of you to ask, he's absolutely adorable, simply having the time of his life, as quiet as a mouse and no trouble at all. This, by the way, is my new assistant, Billy. He'd like to have a confidential word with you. You can trust him implicitly.' Helena turned the floor over to me.

'Miss La Chiesa,' I began nervously.

'Call me Bettina.' She modestly lowered her eyes.

'Bettina, I have to speak to you on a rather delicate matter. It concerns Mr Dando.'

'Yes, he's in a bit of a pickle, isn't he?' sighed Bettina. I detected a twinge of South London in her accent, Peckham possibly, although a dialect coach had clearly attempted to bury it beneath a Mayfair veneer.

'You know about his – indiscretion?'

'Dear boy, he tells me everything. I've had him on the telephone day and night. Pathetically lovesick. Can you imagine?'

'The point is, Bettina, darling,' Helena interrupted, 'it could end Mal's career at any moment.'

'He's had a jolly good run.' She valiantly attempted to concentrate on us, but couldn't resist catching herself in the mirror, and began bashing a huge powder puff about her face.

'May I remind you that if he goes, we all go?'

'I hardly think so. *Vogue* are signing me for a fortune. It's all I've ever wanted.'

'How would you like to make a film?' I asked her.

'I've been offered a dozen films.'

'Let's be honest, darling,' Helena pointed out, 'you've failed a dozen screen tests.'

'They said Fred Astaire couldn't dance.'

'No, my sweet, they said he could dance a bit. Nobody has suggested for a moment that you can act a bit.'

'I had a couple of key dialogue scenes in that costume drama with George Sanders,' La Chiesa pouted.

'Hmm, I remember. "Looked as scrumptious as a box of marzipan, and brought the same emetic quality to her lines." I think that was the verdict reached by Donald Zec in the *Mirror*.'

I wasn't sure that Helena was helping the situation by reminding Bettina of her inadequacies as a performer, so I attempted to take the reins of the conversation. 'Miss La Chiesa. I think the point Mrs Parole is trying to make here is that you are the only person who can help save Mr Dando's career.'

'Perhaps he doesn't want to be saved,' scowled Bettina. 'He

only calls me to complain about his involvement with this ghastly youth.'

'What do you mean?'

'Well, I'm not supposed to say.' She threw the powder puff aside and stared glumly at her face in the mirror. 'It's too awful.'

'You mean there's something we don't know?' asked Helena, clearly staggered by the idea that somebody, somewhere might be withholding information from her.

'He's being blackmailed. This Miguel is the son of a local union boss in San Sebastian. When the boy's father discovered what was going on between them, he threatened to kill Mal. But his anger was overcome by greed. He realised that a famous Hollywood star had placed himself in a compromising position, and now he's milking the situation for all it's worth. He's asked Mal for a simply enormous amount of money, and of course Mal doesn't have any because he gambles it all away, so he's been asking me . . .'

'I think I can resolve this,' I told Bettina. 'We need you to join Mr Dando at his press conference tomorrow night.'

'But why?'

'He's going to announce his engagement to the world.'

'He's not getting married!'

'No, but he's going to announce that he is, and you're to be his bride.' Helena stuck a fresh cigarette in her ivory holder. 'You will back him up, won't you, dear?'

'Me? Why on earth should I?'

I coughed discreetly into my fist. 'You've yet to sign your contract with *Vogue* . . .' I pointed out.

'I fail to see what that has to do with this.'

'Don't you see,' continued Helena, catching my drift, 'if Dando's career comes crashing down tomorrow night, Albion won't be paid, and I'll be forced to sell my flat and move back to my mother's in Worthing.'

'Then who'll look after poor Victor while I fulfil my *Vogue* contract?'

'If the cat gets out of the bag about Victor,' I pointed out, 'there won't be a *Vogue* contract.'

'We're all in this together,' said Helena conspiratorially. She patted Bettina's hand. 'You look as if you could do with a glass of sherry. Billy, pour Bettina a livener, will you? On second thoughts, pour us all one.'

After this, we made our way to Mal Dando's suite. The maid told us that the star was resting, but Helena was having none of it. 'This is a matter of the utmost urgency,' she explained, but the maid refused to stand aside.

'Who's making all that damned noise?' called Dando.

'Terrible news, Mr Dando,' I replied over the maid's shoulder. 'The test screening results on *Finnegan's Way* are back.'

Dando sent the maid away at once and ushered us in. He was occupying the Presidential Suite, which appeared to be constructed entirely of marble, onyx and bronze, rather like a Roman bathhouse. The floor was very slippery, and Helena had to fight to remain upright in her stilettos. 'So minerally,' she sniffed, looking around. 'It could certainly benefit from a few cushions.'

Dando disappeared into the bathroom for a moment and reappeared wearing his hair, which I had not realised was detached from his head in times of privacy. 'The numbers are in, you say? How are they?'

'Awful, Mr Dando. The New York public hates it. We just received a cablegram.'

'Jesus. I was afraid of this. I knew all along the movie was a dog. Nobody spends 700 dollars training a parrot to talk. That damned director was creaming money off the payroll. What the hell am I gonna say at the press conference?'

'I have an idea. We deflect attention from *Finnegan's Way* by making a big announcement. The kind of announcement that overshadows everything else.'

'What kind of announcement would draw away that amount of attention?'

I explained what Dando would have to do.

'You're not seriously suggesting I marry Bettina?' he asked, taken aback.

'No, of course not, it's merely an announcement. One of two, actually.'

'What's the other one?'

'That you're going to do a film together. A French art film. We'll broker the deal in Cannes. It will give you credibility and put your career back on track.'

Even he could see the wisdom of this. 'Ah, it'll never work. I've seen Bettina's tests. She has the acting ability of an Easter Island statue. I've seen more spontaneous displays of emotion in a bucket.'

'You know what French films are like. They're about sex, not acting. All she'll have to do is look gorgeous. And maybe take her clothes off.'

'Bettina? She'll never do that.'

'Oh, under the right circumstances she might.' I thought of little Victor, stashed away in Mayfair. 'Then afterwards, once the film comes out and it's a big continental hit, we'll announce that the two of you have parted over "creative differences". Actors do it all the time, right Helena?'

'You're absolutely correct,' Helena agreed.

'But what do I tell Miguel?'

'You must tell him nothing. For two reasons; first, because it will stop his father from pursuing you, and second, because if he really cares about you he will understand.'

'There's only one small problem,' I pointed out.

'And what's that?' they both asked.

'We're going to have to convince the press that you can speak French.'

To my surprise, Dando shrugged gamely. 'How difficult can that be? It's just learning lines, right? It's what I do for a living.'

And so the press conference took place. Mal Dando announced his intention to marry, the crowd went wild, Miguel was dragged away by his incensed father, Bettina signed her contract, and – so long as nobody spotted that I had lied about the studio cablegram informing us of *Finnegan's Way*'s supposedly poor test results – everyone was happy. Except for Helena.

'What's wrong?' I asked her as we seated ourselves in a sunlit corner of the promenade café. 'We saved Albion, didn't we?'

'You saved us, Billy.' She smoothed out the creases in her frock. On this crisp blue morning she had chosen to wear a red dress with diagonal stripes that did wonders for her figure but gave her the appearance of a barber's pole. 'Everyone was convinced except Glen. I've just heard that he still intends to file his original story.'

'Then we're sunk after all.'

'There's more. While we've been here sorting this out, Jane Broderick has arrived in London.' Jane Broderick had been one of the greatest English movie stars of the forties, and was staging her comeback playing a fading Southern belle in a Tennessee Williams revival due to open soon at the Arts Theatre.

'I'm supposed to take care of Janet for the duration of her run. If she shows signs of cracking, her agent will use us as an excuse to have her deal cancelled.'

'I don't understand. Why should she show signs of cracking?'

'My dear, she's an alcoholic, only just recovered from a nervous breakdown. The eyes of the theatre world will be upon her. The pressure will be immense.'

'Gracious, so many people seem to have nervous breakdowns in this profession.'

'They have to, dear. It's the only way they can get people to think they're human. We must return to London at once.'

And so, the whole thing started all over again.

Upon our arrival in London we took a taxi to the Savoy, and bullied Miss Broderick's secretary into letting us search her suite while she was at rehearsals. We removed every bottle we could find. We looked for anything that might contain gin. We found evidence scattered everywhere; in hip flasks, perfume atomisers, teapots, a pair of Clarice Cliff vases, a hot water bottle and in a silver polish tin hanging on a piece of garter elastic inside the toilet cistern.

'We shall have to do this every day,' warned Helena. 'Alcoholics are devious creatures. They hide refreshments inside girdles and hatboxes. They lower them out of windows on bits of string. But I think Janet may have met her match in you.'

Every morning I diligently hunted through Miss Broderick's suite with the proverbial fine-tooth comb, removing every temptation from her sight. But it seems I was not diligent enough. When the press night finally arrived I searched every inch of her dressing room for booze, and found none. But something much more important was missing; the star of the show. It wasn't until I pushed the toilet door open and saw her shoes sticking out that I realised she was unconscious. The air reeked of gin.

'Quick, give me a hand,' I instructed Helena. 'Help me get her to a chair.'

'She doesn't need a chair, she needs a hospital gurney. Something with straps.'

Miss Broderick had proven too smart for me. She managed to avoid the hazards of hidden bottles by persuading one of the backstage lads to buy her a pint of Gordons before curtain up, and had thrown it back in one draught. The show had to go on, of course, but it was a little difficult with the audience already starting to take their seats and the star out cold on the floor of her toilet.

'Perhaps I should slap her.'

'Slap her?' Helena replied. 'I'd like to knock her teeth out.'

Sending on the understudy was no good; Helena and I needed to find someone who could pass for La Broderick. We were about to admit defeat when I had a crazy idea.

'Who, in your circle of acquaintance,' I asked, 'could be persuaded to play the part at such short notice?'

Helena shrugged helplessly.

'What about Robert Mackay? From what you've told me they're about the same size and age, and you admitted he knows the role by heart. It sounds as though he's been waiting all his life for an opportunity like this.'

'My God, Billy, what a twisted mind you have,' Helena cried, 'but you know, it might just work.' She galumphed out and burst breathlessly back into the dressing room with a look of triumph on her face. 'He's entirely up for it. The part calls for so much thick make-up, no-one will spot the difference.'

'I think the cast might notice,' I pointed out.

'Darling, they're actors. Nobody cares what they think. The only people who count are out there, beyond the footlights. Mackay has a penchant for impersonation. He knows all of Janet's mannerisms. We'll delay the curtain by a few minutes, that's all. Press nights always start late.' She sat down heavily at the dressing table and checked herself in her mirror. 'My God, I'm getting too old for this rushing around. Do you know how old I am, Billy? Forty-seven. I was born three years before the Great War. I'm an *Edwardian*, for Heaven's sake.'

I was about to protest, but she held up her hand. 'Don't incriminate yourself with a reply. I know. With each passing year I become increasingly ridiculous. This is an absurdly childish and undignified way to earn a living. And it'll get worse, mark my words. The world is fast becoming a place only fit for children. I used to have a warm heart once. Now I have the emotional fragility of a crocodile. It's the only way a woman can take on males and survive.'

Helena may have been right. But for a while the world – at least our world – got better. Robert Mackay performed the role to perfection (although he took to the costume changes with perhaps too much relish), and a deal was struck. Helena agreed that Mackay's little predilection would never be exposed on the condition that Glen was made to drop his story. It seemed that we finally had the upper hand over our three wayward stars, while all around us muckraking journalists, directors, agents and actors speculated about the truth.

It was the end of an era. The end of flying by the skin of our teeth, and the start of real press manipulation. The fun was over. Gradually my time at Albion revealed a new perspective, and I came to realise that all of these petty scandals, this ridiculous need to know, was less trivial than I'd thought. Perhaps it is a sense of connection that helps keep us human, that propels us through the daily round and stops us from feeling quite so alone. Of what do our lives consist but inconsequential moments knotted together?

Albion endured. But although we were safe for the time being, we sensed that our days were numbered. Albion's cover was eventually blown from a ludicrously unlikely quarter.

It was the evening of Helena's birthday and we were attending a celebratory dinner at Rugantino's restaurant in Soho. Janet Broderick was coming out of her brief but successful run at the end of the week, Mal Dando was there with Bettina La Chiesa and her son Victor. Glen Jacobs and Robert Mackay were also in attendance.

I admit it. I had grown cocky. I had the whole thing figured like this; Mackay had spiked his star reporter's story in order to keep secret the fact that he occasionally took over from Janet Mackay when she became 'overwrought', Bettina played along with Mal because she wanted her son's existence kept secret for another six months, until she had fulfilled her *Vogue* contract, and Helena was keeping everything secret from Glen because the two of them had become an item once more. I was passing pug-faced little Victor off as my sister's son because I wanted to keep my job. It was a plate-spinning act, but by this time I could have topped the Hippodrome bill performing twice nightly. It would all have worked, too, if we hadn't been served by an overexcited and definitely drunk Spanish waiter.

The wretched man was just placing a serving dish of peas on the table before us when he did a double-take. 'Mr Mackay?' he asked, pointing at Glen's boss. 'You remember me? You signed my programme the other night after your magnificent performance. I did not recognise you in gentlemen's clothes. And this must be the lovely lady whose place you took.' He set a large whisky before Janet. 'The drink you asked for, no alcohol. Neat.' He gave a broad wink. Suddenly he spotted Mal Dando, and the double-take became a treble. 'Mr Dando! An honour to have you in our restaurant! Such a wonderful actor!

Miguel, your little playmate, he is my second cousin. He tells me about the generous letters you send him all the time. And you are with your lovely friend, Miss La Chiesa. Madame, how well I remember the dinner you had here for your twenty-first birthday. Two years you have not been back! So, can I get you anything else?' He looked around the table and saw Victor, sitting at the end in his striped vest and red shorts. 'Perhaps,' he beamed, 'something for your monkey?'

The horrified silence that followed was finally shattered by Helena's throaty laughter, which grew and grew to engulf us all, and it is that sound which follows me down through the decades.

*I always loved late night B-movies on TV, the stupid run-for-your-lives-there's-a-monster-loose ones, but also noir cheapies like* Kiss Me Deadly *and* Nightmare Alley. *The networks rarely run black and white fillers now, which is a shame. I thought the collection wouldn't be complete without a bit of noir. The trick, I feel sure, is to find something both fatalistic and redemptive. I wanted to avoid the usual detectives and seductresses, but there's one thing you can't do without in such tales: a hotel room.*

# LIVING PROOF

His first mistake, he supposed, was having himself listed in the Yellow Pages. The directory was useful for finding restaurants and upholsterers, not writers. But by that time, Gary Davenport had run out of ideas. He needed to find work quickly, and he could think of no other way. His contacts were no longer of any use, and his favours were all used up.

Gary had no more illusions about himself. He knew that he would never write the great novel he had once planned; he simply wasn't up to it. His prose was pedestrian, and his concepts were unoriginal. He had trouble conjuring characters and dialogue from thin air. Fact, not fiction, brought out the best in him.

He had once been a brilliant investigative journalist, right until the call for his skills had dried up. Back then, the Sunday newspapers had been filled with great popular journalism, highlighting corruption and exposing national scandals. He remembered them all; the Thalidomide births, the Poulson affair, Jeremy Thorpe hiring a hitman to kill his lover, the exposure of Sir Anthony Blunt, Wilson and the MI5 smears; those were good times to be a newspaperman. All the respected broadsheets had employed him at one time or another.

But eighties commercialism had put paid to his hard-hitting, account-draining style. Few of the quality journals were prepared to bankroll long-term investigations any more. They wanted fast circulation results. Reporters were no longer required to spend three years covering provincial court cases, and the exposure of subtle truths had been largely replaced by vacuous feature writing. Traditional investigators had lost their assignments to young style gurus, the hyphenates who daily bartered their night-life notoriety into column inches.

For a while he had tried to keep up. He developed a stream-lined prose technique, faster, more aggressive, simpler to digest. He stopped checking his stories with two sources when one would do. Then he stopped checking them at all, and began manufacturing his own news. It seemed to be the way that journalism was going, and Gary followed the herd. But fol-lowing it was not enough. The tabloids knew that nobody bothered to read retractions, and paid well for sensational snip-pets. Soon he was falsifying so much that he couldn't separate fact from fiction. He was finally caught out after filing a trans-parently fake story about a music celebrity who had proved extremely litigious. The newspaper was sued, the Press Com-mission upheld complaints against him and the music celebrity punched him in the face.

He wasted the fallow years after that, drinking too much, taking on the kind of work that he would have once laughed about. When even his loyal and much-abused girlfriend gave up on him, Gary finally came to his senses, cleaned his act up a little and racked his brains to find a comfortable earner. His journalistic reputation was shot to hell, so he became a biogra-pher for hire.

The idea wasn't as odd as it sounded. There was plenty of work to be had; ancient lords facing the end of hereditary peerage, ageing celebrities trying to recall their moments of youthful fame, wealthy industrialists and haughty society women who thought the world was interested in their lives, the new leisured classes, whose overdressed wives had time on their hands, they all wanted a nice leather-bound tome filled with personal history. It was a vanity enterprise, the modern equiva-lent of having your portrait painted, but it took less work, and the money was damned good.

Gary had an arrangement with a printing house in Holland

that charged a small fortune to produce the volumes, and in a good year he could write ten or twelve of them, provided the background material he required was readily available. This year hadn't been so good, though, and he was grateful to receive the call. The woman on the telephone gave little indication of what she wanted, and simply explained that she had found his number in the Yellow Pages. However, she had hinted that the commission – should it be granted – would be a substantial one.

It was raining hard when he arrived at the address he had scribbled on the inside cover of his A–Z. A pair of modern steel gates had to be opened via an intercom before he could make his way up the elegant curve of the drive. The grounds were immaculate, old and wide, and reminded him of the gardens attached to Chiswick House. A plain chapel of portland stone stood in a consecrated area behind a curtain of oaks. It was hard to imagine that such a place as this could exist only a few miles from the centre of London. The house revealed through the sycamores at the head of the drive was sedately Palladian, white stone backed with deep yellow brick, a spectacular stage-set fronting a less flamboyant block of rooms.

Gary parked his battered Fiat in a bay of recently-raked gravel; it was by far the cheapest of the six automobiles arranged there. The trees and the rain removed the stink of the traffic, leaving the air fresh and countrified. He was surrounded with verdant greens, rich browns, solid white stone. To buy this kind of peace in the city took serious wealth. It smelled of money here.

The door was opened by a handsome oriental man. He was tall and square shouldered, faintly haggard, with dark crescents under his eyes. His hair, fine and black, lifted slightly from the sides of his head, as if he had just risen, even though it was four o'clock in the afternoon. Gary's immediate thought was that this had to be the butler, an idea he quickly revised.

'You're right on time. My secretary told me to expect you. My name is Mr Sui-Ho, but please call me Lau. Do come in. I hope you are not too wet. Is there ever a day in this country without rain?' The accent had been acquired within a good public school, with no trace of the docked word-endings that often marked the oriental use of English. 'Let's see if we can get you some tea. Or would you prefer something stronger?'

'Tea will be fine,' Gary replied, a little too quickly. They moved into a tall, ornate reception room. Mr Sui-Ho indicated an armchair as he spoke softly into a tiny cordless intercom, then clicked it off.

'Good,' he said, seating himself opposite Gary and smiling warmly. 'I wonder if you'd like to give me a little of your own background first.'

Gary found himself unaccountably nervous and eager to impress. He withdrew a plastic file filled with references from his briefcase and passed it across for Mr Sui-Ho to peruse, hoping that he would not notice the gap in dates that marked his fall from grace. He waited, aware of the calm and silence that was reaching him through the house.

After reading the top two pages, Mr Sui-Ho placed the file on his knee. 'I'm sure this is all in order. Tell me, Mr Davenport, what are you most proud of achieving?'

It was an unexpected question. Gary began haltingly, then spoke in growing detail of his past commissions, finally producing a set of embossed volumes, finished works presented to satisfied customers. As he spoke, he studied his potential client. Something about Mr Sui-Ho inspired quiet confidence and maturity. There was an inner stillness to him. He had nothing to prove, no reason to show off. It made a refreshing change from the usual types Gary encountered. He was suddenly embarrassed by the gaudy books stacked on the arm of the opposite chair.

Mr Sui-Ho politely waited until he had finished his sales pitch before speaking. He lightly thumbed through the leather volume in his hands and set it aside with a look of faint distaste. 'These biographies are – ' he was clearly seeking not to offend ' – ideal, no doubt, for many of your clients, Mr Davenport, but I require something a little less hagiographic. Forgive me for saying so, but your excellent journalistic credentials present you as a writer who is capable of far more than mere rehashes of mundane family events.'

'That is, generally speaking, all that my clients require, Mr Sui-Ho.'

'Lau, please. If you find me too blunt, you must accept my apologies. Although I was latterly raised in the somewhat out-dated manner of an English gentleman, in some ways I regret that I do not think like one. That skill, perhaps, will come in time.' The irresistible smile flashed again. 'What I require from you, Mr Davenport, is no glossy repackaging of my life, but an honest and truthful document. Your press clippings would appear to indicate your ability to maintain a clinical detachment from your subject, when the subject demands such an approach. The tone of these books – I appreciate that it is not your fault, but all these radiant brides, smiling babies, proud grandfathers, they are not the stuff of fine writing. You cannot, of course, be expected to criticise your patrons.' He tapped a book cover with a manicured nail, as if sensing that the elaborately gold-edged covers were there to compensate for the banal prose.

'I would be the first to agree with you – Lau – but the client is paying the bill, and usually requires something – how can I put this? Something that his grown-up children will be able to read with pride.'

Tea arrived on a trolley, and was discreetly served by a small middle-aged woman who could have been Gary's mother.

'I appreciate that point, but let me tell you a little of myself. I was born and raised in Northern Thailand, although my parents were of Chinese extraction. They had made Chaing Mai their home because my father had business interests in the province. However, a series of financial disasters reduced his social standing, our family grew poor, and my father became sick. My brothers and sisters had no desire to go into a family business, but as the oldest, I was determined to restore my family's financial health. I faced up to my responsibilities and worked very hard – people in Thailand find no shame in working hard – but more importantly, I learned how to speak English, and how to make the right connections. I was bright. I was fast. I had a natural aptitude for business. These are merely facts – I have no interest in false modesty.' He gave a slight smile. 'Do you know Thailand, Mr Gary? In the cities people know how to make money, but what use is this talent when the East has undergone such a dramatic economic collapse? I too saw ways of making money, in the world of imports and exports. At first it was very difficult. People are suspicious of outsiders, and anxious to protect their businesses. This, of course, is to be expected. At first I was over-zealous, obsessive. I pursued my goal with a fervour that denied me any kind of private life. I even broke off my engagement to a very beautiful girl, in order that I might concentrate on my business. It was a decision I have had plenty of time to regret.'

Mr Sui-Ho took a sip of tea, and watched the rain on the windows for a moment.

'But I achieved my aim in life. I own this agreeable house, and four more in other cities. My story is, I think, sufficiently unusual to maintain your interest. I am, as yet, still unmarried at the age of thirty-five, but I am soon to alter this situation. For years I put the future of my family before my own happiness, but my sacrifices are now at an end. Soon it will be time to start a family of my own. There are no areas of my life into which you may not delve. I require honesty and clarity, not – ' he glanced down at the sample volumes which lay between them, 'not local colour. The volume I require is a simple truthful account of my life. Accuracy is all.' He sat back and finished his tea. His amber eyes remained sharply focused as he waited for an answer.

'I would be honoured to undertake this commission,' Gary replied truthfully. 'I'm sure that I can provide you with a memorable and appropriate biography.'

'I am pleased to hear that, Mr Davenport. Naturally I shall equip you with the means to perform your task. I will not demand final approval of your manuscript. All the documentation I or my secretary can provide will be made available to you. Her name is Emma Tamabu, and you can contact her here.' He passed him a cream card listing three phone lines, a mobile number and an e-mail address. 'If you require any additional information you have merely to ask either of us. There is only one proviso.'

Here it comes, thought Gary gloomily, the fly in the ointment, I knew it was too good to be true.

'I require this book to be ready for typesetting within two months. The reason is simple. I have just announced my forth-coming marriage, and would like to present the volume to my bride's family on the day of our betrothal. The lady in question is titled, and we are to be married in St Mary Undercroft, within the Houses of Parliament. A special day, I think, for a lowly boy from the provinces. A well-respected American publishing house is already interested in the story of my life. If your biog-raphy proves to be of sufficiently high quality, it may well receive publication around the world.'

Gary gave an inward sigh of relief. He could manage an eight-week schedule. Mr Sui-Ho was only thirty-five. How much could he have packed into his life so far?

'Naturally, I am prepared to pay extra for the imposition of this time limit. Let us say . . .' Unclipping the top of his Mont Blanc fountain pen, he laboriously wrote a figure on a slip of paper, clearly priding himself on his penmanship. Gary's eyes nearly fell out when he read the amount. 'This first instalment will, I trust, compensate you for any late nights incurred in the production of the volume.'

The interview was over.

He drove back through the rain with a folder containing a list of contact numbers on the passenger seat beside him, and realised that for the first time in years he was nervous about undertaking a commission. This was no string of births, deaths and marriages to be knotted together with clichés. A real biog-raphy was required, something that would stand the scrutiny of editors at a major publishing house. The stakes were high. He could not afford to screw up. He decided to set himself a few house rules. No alcohol. No corner-cutting. No lies, excuses or omissions, just concentration on the task ahead. And no falling back into his bad old ways. Hell, he could behave himself for two months. How much self-discipline did that take?

He parked the car and ran up to his flat. He wondered what Mr Sui-Ho would think if he could have seen the piles of dirty plates in the sink, the towers of unread magazines and unwashed laundry in the bedroom. Looking at the squalor around him, he realised that he was too old to live this poorly. First he scrounged a couple of cardboard boxes from the corner shop and began removing the trash from the lounge. Then he cleared a work-space in the bedroom where he could collate material, and while his newfound zeal was still upon him, changed the sheets and opened the windows, even though he had to take a chisel to the frames he had lazily painted over years before. It took him two trips to get all the bottles to the recycling bank. He dumped his dirty clothes in the laundromat. He vacuumed the carpets, and as a final touch, bought a white dahlia in a china pot from the local florist. For the last few years he had not trusted himself to keep plants alive.

Gary slept badly without a drink, but was so pleased to wake up with a clear head in a fresh-smelling environment that he set to work immediately. His computer was a model long out of date, and the keyboard was sticky with booze, so he scrubbed it down with the moist paper tissues he had saved from Kentucky Fried Chicken boxes. He had seated himself at his desk and was considering his first move when the doorbell rang.

The first thing he saw when he opened the front door was a shiny black disc. The disc tilted to reveal a slim face beneath it. The woman's features were a mixture of African and European, the best of both. Her full lips were glossed crimson, her eyes large and disconcertingly blue. She was small and shapely, in a rather robust, old-fashioned manner that he found extremely attractive. She wore a white linen suit with razor-edge pleats, and was holding a box wrapped in brown paper.

'Mr Davenport?'

'That's me.'

'I'm Mr Sui-Ho's assistant.' She held out a small gloved hand. 'Emma Tamabu.' He could not remember the last time he had seen a woman wearing gloves for the sake of fashion. In an old movie, perhaps. 'Mr Sui-Ho asked me to deliver something to you. There are top copies of documents here that he did not wish to trust to a courier.' There was a soft burr to her accent, possibly American.

'Please, come in.' He made a silent prayer of thanks that he had made an effort to clear up the apartment. Ms Tamabu stepped across the threshold and looked around at the yellowing walls. If she was repulsed by what she saw, she hid it well. 'I've also been instructed to give you this.' She reached into her jacket, withdrew a pair of slim white envelopes and held them before him. Gary knew the first one contained cash the moment he touched it. He lifted the envelope flap and saw the corner of a fifty pound note. The second contained flight coupons, two first-class round trips to Thailand.

'I'm to accompany you to Bangkok, at your convenience,' Ms Tamabu explained. 'Mr Sui-Ho thought it would be easier if you were travelling with someone who knew the territory.'

'That's very thoughtful of him. Can I get you something to drink?' he offered, trying to remember whether the milk in the fridge was within its expiry date.

'I won't stay, thank you. I have other appointments. Mr Sui-Ho is a hard worker, and expects the same from his staff.' Ms Tamabu smiled graciously and set the package down on the hall table.

'How long have you been with him?'

'Six years now. I joined his company when I was twenty-one. He's a wonderful person, Mr Davenport, the kindest man I've ever met. But he can be exacting.'

'Successful men usually are,' said Gary.

She took a step closer. 'Mr Sui-Ho wanted me to assure you

that if there's anything you need – anything at all – you should be sure to call me anytime, day or night. I really won't mind.'

'Well, that's very kind of you.'

She turned in the doorway. The shadow of her hat-brim obscured her extraordinary eyes.

'Remember what I said. If there's anything I can do for you, just call and I'll be there.'

After she had gone, he wondered if she had been making a pass at him. It had been a while since he'd found himself within range of an attractive woman. He resolved to have a shave and get himself a decent haircut. Some new clothes might be a good idea too, especially if he was planning to interview Mr Sui-Ho's colleagues. He would have to change his manner. Be less sycophantic, more independent. As he told himself, it had been a long while.

The package provided him with a starter-kit of factual information about the life of his subject. Inside was an outline of the tycoon's career to date, his family background, his business interests and hobbies, details of his fascination with motor-racing, names and addresses of the charities he funded and the foundations he supported. It came as no surprise that he was extraordinarily well-connected. There was a prospectus for the group of companies he controlled in Britain, Thailand and Malaysia, ranging from cloth imports to shipping. Photographs of him shaking hands with various prime ministers, a stack of magazine clippings, one showing a group of businessmen being presented to the President of the United States. There was a list of family contacts, with annotations to the effect that most would be a waste of time to interview as they did not speak English. There was a separate list of investors, company directors and various captains of commerce, with their private telephone numbers provided on a special side-sheet. Mr Sui-Ho had given him the bones of his rags-to-riches story; it was up to him to flesh out the tale. Gary switched on his computer and began the immediate construction of a time-line, beginning with his patron's birth and ending at the start of this month, which he decided would act as his cut-off date. Then he picked up the phone and began dialling.

He had expected to spend the first few days playing phone-tag with secretaries, voicemail lines and answering machines, but to his surprise a number of the contacts Mr Sui-Ho had provided were immediately available for comment, and proved so amenable that Gary began to suspect they had been briefed in advance. If his patron was as organised as he appeared to be, he had probably asked his secretary to call them.

By the end of the following week he had finished the outline of the stranger's life. He had done it many times before, but this time was different; there was a new diligence in his research, a determination to produce a work of genuine interest. He had grown so used to skimming careers and smoothing them off with clichés that the exercise proved demanding. He was forced to recall skills he had all but lost. He felt sure that the end result would be worth it. At the close of the first month he looked over the partially fleshed-out structure with a rediscovered sense of pride.

As no-one in Mr Sui-Ho's immediate family spoke English, the story of their most successful son's early years was the hardest part to cover by phonecalls alone, so Ms Tamabu had thoughtfully provided an itinerary for their trip. She arranged interviews with friends and relatives, and they agreed to fill in details of the headstrong young boy who had once promised to make his parents proud before his twentieth birthday.

Gary arrived in Bangkok and kept to his schedule, dutifully meeting with everyone on the list. These friends and associates told him how the young Lau had set up his first company on the day he had left school, how he had employed the boys in his class to work on trust alone and build futures for themselves, how he had encouraged his father to switch from the trafficking of traditional farming implements to the supply of electronic component casing for the West from the Chinese mainland. Mr Sui-Ho had accomplished this by teaming himself with an older, more experienced business partner, a Brazilian named Enrico Characo.

Characo had acumen and financial fluidity. He could charm money from a beggar, but had an irrational aversion to aviation and some kind of problem with his passport that appeared to restrict his movements in the international market, so he used his energetic young partner to fly the world and seal the deals. Their partnership was symbiotic, and perfectly suited them. The business continued to expand, the assets accumulated, and the money kept rolling in. Gary listened, and made notes, and fleshed out the early sections of his time-line with details.

Then he reached a point in the story of the partnership where a break occurred. Two years ago it seemed that there had been some kind of a falling-out, amicable enough, but it sundered the arrangement between Characo and Sui-Ho, and the duo had gone their separate ways. The raft of businesses in which they were involved was diverse enough to survive the split without repercussions for the shareholders. There were no details of Characo's present whereabouts on the list.

'I'd like to know what happened.' Gary was about to pour himself a glass of iced Evian, but the waiter got there before him. 'Characo went his own way, and now nobody knows where he is. He's not at any of the addresses that have been supplied to me. There are no forwarding numbers for him. He doesn't seem to collect his e-mails and his voicemail has a message on it that's eight months out of date. Did you know him?'

Emma Tamabu turned the stem of her wineglass and looked across the dimly lit restaurant of the Oriental Hotel to the river railing, where a phalanx of white-jacketed waiters were monitoring the tables, waiting to take orders. 'I suppose so, as much as anyone did.'

'What was he like?'

'The opposite to his partner in many ways. Lau calculates his risks, weighs up the odds, lets the market find its own level. He doesn't believe in forcing matters.'

'And Characo wasn't like that?'

'Not at all. He was . . . not careless exactly, but he could be reckless. Dangerous as an opponent.' She released her glass and looked up at the lights blinking in the trees.

'Dangerous? That's a strong word to describe someone you worked with.'

'I saw how he conducted business. You don't screw around with the Chinese, Mr Davenport. You play a hard straight game and they treat you with respect.'

'What was Characo like on a social level?'

'I never saw him socially.'

'Never?'

'We mostly communicated through faxes and telephones.'

'You were based in London?'

'I came out for the board meetings, mergers, new ventures. As I said, Characo didn't like to fly.'

'And he doesn't keep in touch with his old partner? I find that odd.' Gary pulled his shirtsleeves away from his arms. He had suggested that they eat outside at the river restaurant, but the heat was uncomfortable even at this late hour. On the next table a group of heavy-set businessmen from Chicago were earnestly discussing the problems of the Eastern money market. Emma looked at home here, like a convention representative unwinding after a hard day.

'Do you have any idea how I can get in touch with him now?'

'I have some places you can start looking, but you'll have to do the rest. Sometimes Characo doesn't want to be found. Good businessmen are like that. They only let you see what they want you to see.'

He watched a longboat slipping against the cross-currents of the river, its pilot balancing at the rudder. The underpowered engine was whining with the strain of its load. 'I used to be good at locating missing persons. I'm not so sure about managing it here. The return ticket's open, right? I'll need a few days.'

'Is finding him that important?'

'He was a part of your employer's life, but he's not covered on the list. That makes him important.' He left the thought in the air.

'What?'

'Nothing. Sometimes the gaps are more revealing than the facts.'

'Lau showed me some clippings. Articles by you. He says you used to be a famous investigative journalist. A natural. Instinctive.'

Gary was surprised to hear that Mr Sui-Ho knew about his past, but it figured; the man was thorough. 'I was good, too. It was the papers that grew bad around me.'

'Things change fast. The first time I came here this hotel was half the size it is now. To remain successful these days you have to be able to adapt quickly.'

'Is that why Mr Sui-Ho ended his relationship with Characo? Forgive me, but that was your boss's role, wasn't it? Playing Jekyll to his partner's Hyde? Somebody had to do the dirty work out here, and Characo seems suited for the role. Did the work get a little too dirty? Is that why Mr Sui-Ho ended the alliance?'

'I don't think you're asking the right person, Mr Davenport.'

'Then who should I ask?'

She lit a cigarette and blew aside smoke. 'You're the investigator. You figure it out.'

It was like following the trace pattern of a Chinese rocket, he thought; you could see where it had gone, you knew that there had been an explosion, but you couldn't see what had happened to the debris. Characo had clashed with the Thai authorities about warranties granted for silk exportation, an obstructive Chinese company had been forced into liquidation, its owners had disappeared, and Characo had vanished soon after. After wasting days in various offices of official records, Gary felt the trail blurring. They travelled up to Chaing-Mai, but his instincts told him he was going in the wrong direction. On one unbearably hot night the air conditioning in Emma's room broke down, and she came to his room for ice. Somehow, he wasn't quite sure how, she ended up sleeping in his bed. The hotel engineers couldn't find anything wrong with her air conditioning unit. Still, she stayed in his room for the rest of the trip. His vanity wanted to believe that she found him attractive, but he felt sure that the circumstances alone had pushed this distant business-woman toward him, and that they would part as soon as his task was completed.

One meeting triggered a distant alarm in his head. An hour spent in a gloomy, airless room in the manufacturing district yielded a police report issued against Characo at the time of his split with Mr Sui-Ho. One of the two owners of a rival export office had been fished out of the Taeng River with a bashed-in face and no hands. There was nothing to link Characo directly with the death, but he had been pulled in for interviews on two occasions. It was perhaps inevitable that Mr Sui-Ho and his partner should come up against criminal activity in their busi-ness, but there were no indications to suggest that they had personally become involved in anything dishonest. The com-pany's files were opened for him to inspect, and – as far as he could tell – appeared to be in order. What bothered him was something that wasn't there. A final-quarter gap in the financial reports coincidentally covering the period during which Characo went missing.

He sat in his icy room back at the Oriental and watched the log-barges riding the river from his picture-window. Emma rang his doorbell just as he was preparing for bed. She returned to her own suite before he was awake the next morning, leaving a note informing him that she had several appointments to attend before returning to London, so he ordered breakfast in his room and sat with the paperwork from Chaing-Mai spread out on the writing desk, mulling matters over.

Characo had kept private apartments all over the world, but there were two separate addresses in Bangkok, one here in Silom Road, the other in a far less salubrious area on the outskirts of the city. Why had he kept two homes? Emma informed him that her employer's partner had not married, so it wasn't a matter of keeping a wife and a mistress in separate properties. He decided to visit both addresses himself.

The first was a few hundred yards from the hotel, an anonymous apartment in a white concrete block now inhabited by a minuscule Thai woman who gabbled at him in alarm. When he explained that he did not understand her, she closed the door and reopened it to reveal a tall, strong son who spoke English.

'My mother say Mr Characo no live here anymore. He move out year ago.'

'Would you mind asking your mother to describe him?'

Mother and son spoke quietly for a minute or two. 'She say she only see him once, when he rent flat.'

'Never again after that?'

'She say no.'

In the distance, the golden spires of a temple glimmered in the polluted air.

Gary stepped back from the building after the door closed and thought for a minute. Before setting out for the second address, he tried calling Emma, but found her mobile switched off. The other apartment was a half-hour ride across the city by tuk-tuk. It was situated deep inside a red-clay apartment block with balconies scarred by wooden slats, crates and chicken wire. There was no answer to his knock, so he went to locate the concierge.

'You come for keys to flat?' asked the elderly concierge, who answered the door with a distressed-looking chicken wriggling in one bony hand. 'Rent all paid up, no-one come for keys.' The chicken screamed and clawed. For a moment it looked as if it might overpower its captor.

Gary asked if he could take the keys, but was rebuffed. An inexplicable confusion arose between him and the concierge as they spoke, and the old man finally went back to his kitchen with a sigh of annoyance. Gary retired to a bench in a small dusty park opposite the apartment building, and wiped his sweating neck with his handkerchief. Something bothered him, a sensation hard to define. His concentration dissipated into the heavy air. He felt the weight of failure breathing on him. Without all the information he needed to build a full picture, he would not succeed. Even if it was something he did not use in the finished memoir, he needed to discover it. If not for Mr Sui-Ho, then for himself.

He returned to the concierge's flat once more and rang the bell. This time the old man answered without his chicken. Blood stained the nails of his hands. Gary gave a smile of assurance and closed the concierge's palm over a pile of moist notes. The old man pocketed the baht and smiled back.

The apartment door was on the fifth floor, and fitted with two locks. He tried the keys, twisting them around, then pushed open the door. Inside, the electricity was off and the blinds were drawn. The air was stale and dead. It eddied lazily around him as he fumbled his way to the windows that overlooked the building's central courtyard.

The flat had clearly been used as an office; the only furniture that remained in either of the two rooms was a desk and a pair of grey metal filing cabinets that stood unlocked and empty.

But it couldn't have been the main office for Characo's partnership with Mr Sui-Ho. Even for a backroom accounts set-up it felt too small, too hidden away at the wrong end of town. This had been a sideline arrangement for Characo, something he didn't want connected with his more reputable businesses; Gary had seen such places before. The shelves had been carefully emptied, and so had the desk drawers. There was no paperwork lying about, just a few paperclips and some empty envelopes. He checked the filing cabinets again and found a third, smaller and older, set back behind the other two. Two of its three drawers were open and empty. The bottom one was either locked or jammed. He took a penknife from his pocket and tried to prise the lock, but it would not open. Finally he kicked the front panel in with the heel of his boot.

Something inside stank. A plastic bag, blue with mildew, sat on a stained pile of papers. His first thought was that a secretary had forgotten her lunch, but something about the bag's shape bothered him. It looked as though it was filled with pale, bony crabs.

He pulled the papers free from beneath the bag and examined them. Nothing interesting here, just consignment sheets for a delivery of furniture and some receipts for registered mail. But there was another carbon, stuck to the docket that was attached to the plastic bag. Holding his hand over his nose, Gary moved closer and saw that it was part of the missing last-quarter accounts, signed by Characo himself. Reaching forward, he gingerly raised the bag between the thumb and forefinger of his right hand.

The contents of the bag shifted and slipped out.

Gary kept the night-light on above his seat, much to the annoyance of the passenger behind him. The stained accounts were pressed flat in the file that lay beside his food-tray. Even with the plane's air-conditioning working it gave off a faint rancid odour. He raised the window cover slightly, but all he could see was the flashing red light on the wing, black below, stars above. He thought about finishing the book. He had everything he needed now, but the dilemma facing him had finally taken a tangible form. It was not a physical problem – the construction of the remaining chapters would be easy enough – but a matter of ethics. He had not expected to encounter something like this so late in his career.

He did not rest on the flight; the thought of the book's final text pushed aside the possibility of sleep. As a once-respected journalist, he knew all about omission of the truth; it was the politest form of lying. He considered driving to Mr Sui-Ho's residence straight from the airport, but knew that fatigue could cloud his judgement. It was important to be lucid; he needed to present his case clearly. He arrived at Heathrow dead on his feet, only to be searched by a wilfully slow customs officer. The wait was enough for him to defer his decision.

The white dahlia in his apartment was still thriving. He

brewed himself some strong coffee and typed up a page of notes, then slept for several hours. Daylight was fading when he awoke. He restarted the computer and sat down before it.

The justified type sat neatly across the screen in blocks. The sections, chapters and subheads were arranged in files that, when opened, revealed the life of an ambitious young man driven by fear of failure. But the success story was flawed; its hero wanted acceptance too badly. Mr Sui-Ho's ideals were based on a false image of European sophistication; it created a weakness in him that a more ruthless man might exploit. A man like Enrico Characo.

This was the element that Gary had not dared to include in his previous biographies; an overt criticism of his subject. His mind was made up; perhaps it had never been in doubt. Mr Sui-Ho had specifically requested an honest documentary. He would finish the book without consultation or compromise.

Rain was once more sifting through the sycamore trees on the day he returned to Mr Sui-Ho's house. From the drive, the front rooms looked dark and deserted, but Emma Tamabu greeted him when he rang the doorbell. There had been little contact between them in the intervening time. He wondered if she had thought about him at all. He had tried calling her, but she was always out on business appointments.

'Gary, come in, he's expecting you. He's on a call to New York.' She took his wet coat and hung it up to dry, noting the package he held under his arm. 'I presume that's the famous book.'

'I promised I'd bring another one with me.' Gary hefted the volume in his hand. He had sent the first copy to Mr Sui-Ho two days earlier, and wanted to gauge his reaction. 'I hope he's pleased. Of course, it's too late to change anything now.'

'I'm looking forward to reading it. He hasn't let me near his copy.' She smiled. 'Don't look so worried. He's in a very good mood. I'll arrange for some tea.' She left him alone in the hall, and the sound of rain falling on the skylight slowly replaced her footsteps. Gary walked across the chequered tiles and examined a gloomy painting of some horses. The house smelled of damp and disuse. He could hear water pouring from a damaged gutter beyond the main staircase. The doors to the reception room opened behind him.

'Mr Davenport, how nice to see you. Please come in.' His benefactor looked tired. The crescents beneath his eyes were even darker than usual. Gary seated himself in the armchair opposite Mr Sui-Ho's desk. The volume he had sent ahead lay between them. He was glad he had toned down the embossing on the title.

'I imagine you're anxious for a reaction to the book.' Mr Sui-Ho seated himself and rested a manicured hand on the cover, touching the title with his fingertips, as though reading it in braille. Gary shifted uncomfortably. He began to feel nervous.

'First, the title, "Living Proof", an embodiment of your central thesis; that one man can stand as a symbol of capitalism, good and bad. I think it's very clever.' Mr Sui-Ho lifted the cover and examined the chapter headings. 'You've certainly earned your money. You've been very thorough. I'm pleased about that. Most importantly, you have introduced a surprising element of honesty into my story. Surprising even to me.'

An image from the abandoned apartment in Bangkok flashed back into Gary's mind; the contents of the plastic bag slipping out into the drawer. A pair of raggedly severed hands, rotten and squishy with mildew, threaded with maggots like grains of brown rice.

Mr Sui-Ho closed the book and looked directly into Gary's eyes. He spoke slowly and clearly, separating each word. 'Tell me how you knew.'

'It was something Emma said. About having to play tough with the Chinese to gain their respect. You couldn't afford to be seen doing it yourself; you were moving in new circles, becoming a westernised gentleman. You needed an alter ego, someone to do the dirty work. Characo served that purpose. Then he vanished. At first, I thought you'd had him killed, but that seemed too crass. Then I realised you invented him. You made two mistakes. The first was keeping the hands of your rival.'

'I needed something that could be used as a warning to others after Characo was gone.'

'The second was penmanship. All those telltale flourishes. To keep a second identity, you really need to develop a second signature.'

To his surprise, Mr Sui-Ho softly laughed. 'Oh, you're good. My faith in you was justified.' He opened his chequebook and began to write. 'You do see now why I commissioned you?' He tore out the cheque and fanned it dry. 'I am marrying a daughter of the state. There will be media attention. I simply had to know if my past could be discovered.'

Gary folded the cheque in half and placed it inside his jacket pocket, anxious to leave. Mr Sui-Ho rose and shook his hand solemnly. 'Thank you, Mr Davenport. You have acquitted yourself with honour.' As he glanced back at the book, his voice was low and sincere. 'I wonder, did you realise that title would apply to you as well?'

'That,' Gary admitted, 'was the one thing I hadn't thought of.' The deal concluded, he collected his coat and they walked to the front door together.

'So,' said Mr Sui-Ho, opening it to the melancholy vista beyond. 'I would like to give you some time to enjoy your money. It is only fair. Shall we say six weeks before we close the final chapter?'

As Gary sat in his car, watching the sheets of rain obscure the chapel beside the drive, he felt no fear now, only a sense of relief. And something else; a perverse pride in the knowledge that he had restored his integrity, even though it meant surrendering his life.

He wondered now if Emma had been trying to warn him over dinner on that sweltering Bangkok night. 'Good businessmen,' she had said, 'only let you see what they want you to see.'

Six weeks of living well, and then – he felt sure he could rely on Mr Sui-Ho to provide him with a discreet and hopefully painless exit. Gary permitted himself a brief moment of regret, but it faded into a smile long before he arrived at the finest restaurant in town.

*I turned on my TV late one night hoping I might find a crazy old B-movie showing, only to be faced with a perky young woman bouncing an enormous black rubber willy on her knees. Sex fills the schedules, and suddenly, after decades of being one of the most sexually furtive countries in the world, we've adopted a weird wholesome attitude to the subject, and chat-show guests are passing edible knickers and nipple clamps about as though they're trying to price antiques. Says something about us as a nation, I think.*

# SEX MONKEYS

For every person who is cautious about having sex, there are dozens who aren't. For many people it's not such a big deal and it has very little to do with love, because love is the thing that's supposed to affect the shape of your life, not sex.

But it doesn't really work that way at all.

After months of lolling about doing nothing, Chance Temper was finally sent to earn a trade by his exasperated father, an embittered Catholic who wanted him to get out of the house and start bringing home the coal, as he put it, so he agreed to bankroll his son for an IT course on the condition that he stayed home and studied every weeknight, and also stopped seeing the girl over the road who sent up Chance's dad behind his back every time she came over. The alternative was being chucked out on the streets of Camden Town, which already had more people outdoors than in and would probably implode from the strain if just one more person sat on the beer-sticky pavement beside the Barclays cashpoint making people feel guilty for using their Connect cards.

Of course Chance ignored the rules, going out and meeting up with Betty after the old man was asleep. Betty was doing graphic design at St Martin's, and had some strange ideas. One of them was going to a fetish club in King's Cross on Thursday nights, where they usually stayed until the smell of hot rubber began to get a little retchy, and Betty, who liked to have sex in public places, wanted to fuck in the archway behind the club. She also liked Chance to wear a rather smart chromium-plated cock-ring when they did it, but after a while the damned thing pinched his balls and he had to take it off.

Everything becomes normal eventually, even the steel vice that encircled Chance's genitals during their lovemaking. He always disengaged it afterwards and tucked it in his trouser pocket. One night he got a little drunk, and forgot about it. Dropping Betty back at her bedsit, he crept into his father's house at four-thirty, just as it was starting to get light. He entered his bedroom and started undressing, not bothering to empty out his combats, and as he drunkenly hopped about and whipped his trousers off, something shot out of the open window and hit a car with a deafening clang. The noise was enough to wake his father (who slept downstairs) and set the dog howling. The old man went out of the house, rootled around in his Nissan and came up to Chance's room with something in his hand.

'What the hell,' he asked, 'is this?'

A truthful answer was not always the most welcome one with Chance's father, and he didn't feel comfortable admitting that it was a cock-ring finished in high-grade polished chrome, so he made up some preposterous lie about it being an engine washer that had fallen off a passing plane. Chance thought he had got away with it. He thought his father might even admire the workmanship, but no such luck. Chance's dad made him write out a cheque to have the dent hammered out of his bonnet, threw his son out on the street, then phoned British Airways' complaints department so often that they sent a couple of policemen around to turn his lounge over.

Chance had been enjoying his IT course and wanted to finish it, so he needed a flexitime job to cover his tuition fees. He now needed to find somewhere to sleep. Betty was freaked when he turned up on her doorstep the next evening asking if he could inhabit her couch, but agreed to let him stay for a couple of nights until he could sort himself out. Unfortunately, her land-lord saw them and, convinced that they were living together, doubled the rent.

Betty couldn't afford to lose the flat because the lease was in her sister's name, and as Chance was broke she decided to raise some cash by advertising her services as a dominatrix in callboxes along the Bayswater Road. She had been drawn to this sexual lifestyle ever since falling in love with her GP and then bumping into him in a leather bar in Vauxhall. He had briefly persuaded her to train as a therapist, but after a grim winter spent teaching Christmas shopping to agoraphobics, she switched to riding crops.

A few nights after Chance threw himself upon her mercy, Betty took on a young Asian marketing manager named Sanjeev who was getting married in a few weeks' time and wanted to try something exotic before settling down to a lifetime of upsetting his wife's parents.

Betty introduced Sanjeev to some rubber fetishism which was mild for her but pretty extreme to him, and Sanjeev found to his surprise that, far from being able to rule out the stretch and snap of the glossy elastic vest in which his *maîtresse* had encased him as an interesting one-off, he was completely captivated by the tang and texture of her dunlop *décolletage*, so much so that, after his session, he asked if he could buy the vest and wear it home beneath his Marks & Spencer workshirt.

Betty was happy to grant him this small wish for the additional price of eighty pounds, which was sixty more than she paid for such items, being entitled to a discount at the store called 'Violation' in Old Street where she was now purchasing the tools of her trade. She also forgot to caution Sanjeev about the constriction danger involved in the wearing of such items, and how to counteract it.

Sanjeev arrived back at his flat in Stoke Newington at eleven forty-five, intoxicated and empowered by the squeaky surface he could feel between his buttons (intoxicated too by the five pints of lager he had consumed before plucking up the courage to visit Betty). He drew the blinds in his bedroom and removed his shirt, his breath growing fast and shallow as he admired his strange new physique in the mirror. After a while the novelty began to wear off as the hangover set in, and Sanjeev attempted to undress. He vaguely recalled the lustrous Betty tugging on the tight rubber top, and would have remembered her warning about the need to apply liberal doses of talcum, had she remembered to give it. But Betty was thinking about Chance's continued presence on her settee, signified most mornings by the discovery of his socks in the microwave, and forgot to deliver her customary caution.

Consequently, Sanjeev managed to pull the vest halfway over his ears before it stuck tight, leaving his mouth and nostrils covered in airless rubber, and his arms trapped above his head, so that he looked like someone drowning in an oily lake. After stumbling around the room for two or three minutes he managed to connect the jamb of the open bedroom door with his ribs, and stumbled out on the landing. He could not call for help. He could not see. He could not breathe. Heliotrope starbursts exploded before his eyes, and he went over the landing banisters like a seesawing plank dropped into the hold of a ship, plummeting three floors down to the tiled lobby floor. The fall compacted his wrists, his vertebrae and fractured his skull, denting it like a punctured football, although mercifully this happened so quickly that he felt little more than confusion and anger at the probability of his body being discovered in such an embarrassing mode of dress.

When Sanjeev's bride found out what had happened, she blamed herself for refusing to indulge in premarital sex, and embarked on a string of disastrous short-term relationships that mortified her parents, who grew tired of hearing from supposedly well-meaning relatives that their daughter was now an English slut, and decided to sell their respectable Brick Lane leather outlet so that they could return to Bombay without her.

Chance's father was an accountant, and by one of those odd coincidences that people insist never happen in real life, his biggest single client was the Brick Lane leather outlet, so that when it changed ownership and the buyers decided to reinvent the business as an internet company, he suddenly found himself out of work. Soon he was drinking hard again, just as he used to when Chance's mother was still on the scene, and found solace in the arms of an older woman named Joy, a schoolteacher who, as luck would have it, had a voracious alcoholic appetite of her own, so he sold his now lonely house, opened an account with Joy's local branch of Threshers and the pair settled into hazy, argumentative bliss on the wrong side of Peckham.

Joy had lived an unhappy life, having spent twenty-two years married to a man who was at best inappropriate and at worst abusive. Consequently, Joy was quite joyless until meeting Chance's father, and didn't really change much then, but years of dreadful sex with a husband she loathed were at least at an end, so she dyed her hair, shed a few pounds and went at it hammer and tongs with Chance's shocked dad. In order to indulge in this newly discovered pleasure, it was, however, necessary to make certain purchases to ensure that her partner could manage to perform with several large whiskies inside him. One of these was a spray called Raging Stallion, which she took to carrying in her handbag, because Chance's father often met her from work, and they would zip off to the ladies' loos at the back of the school for a sip from his hipflask and a quick stocking-ripper in one of the cubicles. This less than dilatory behaviour was pretty hypocritical coming from Chance's dad, who usually treated women like airport runways, circling above them for ages before coming in for a landing.

It was unfortunate that the frenzy of their passion as Chance's dad attempted his final approach caused Joy to drop her handbag, because when she gathered up her belongings in a state of shaky post-coital tension she missed the spray-can, which had rolled under one of the sinks. She also lost her doorkeys down the toilet, along with the heel of one shoe and the remains of her dignity. When Chance's Dad asked her to repeat the experience a few weeks later, she ditched him in a fit of self-loathing and became a really argumentative lesbian. It would be nice to imagine that this relationship fulfilled her in a way that had been denied to her all her life, but the woman she fell in love with was a mental patient on day release from the Maudesley.

Soon after they met she stabbed Joy to death in Kennington park because, she later told the police, she 'felt sorry for her'.

Joy's can of Raging Stallion was discovered by a girl called Jeffy whose kleptomaniac tendencies encouraged her to keep all manner of found items in a huge shoulder-bag. Jeffy kept everything she could lay her hands on in the profound belief that one day she would own everything she needed to have a happy life. Her boyfriends tended to drift off after squeezing their way to her bedroom through mounds of pilfered knick-knacks, so she never grew close enough to anyone to explain the reason for her eclectic taste. She eventually began dating a woman-hating designer called Bimmer who worked for *The Face* and who encouraged her to go down on him whenever they were driving on motorways at night, which was how she came to use the Raging Stallion. Jeffy failed to read the instructions on the canister and, assuming that it was intended as an oral aphrodisiac, squirted him in the mouth as he yawned. Her action caught Bimmer by surprise, especially as most of the liquid went into his eyes, and he shot his lovingly restored Sunbeam Alpine off an exit ramp of the M2 at a little over fifty miles an hour. The car upended in someone's back garden, causing Bimmer to fly through the Sunbeam's windscreen and grow wretchedly etiolated in the tangled embrace of a wild rose bush. The rose, of course, is the traditional symbol for silence. Jeffy spent the next eighteen months with her neck in a brace, after which she discovered that she could no longer have sexual relations without thinking of death, nor could she get into a car without being violently sick.

So disturbed was Jeffy by these psychological problems that she joined an anarchist group based in a rebellious part of Berkshire whose criteria for staying together were mutual truculence and confusion. The following May Day she was cruelly blinded by a missile tossed by one of her friends at a rally in Trafalgar Square. Concluding, understandably, that fate was against her, she determined to do the job properly and took an overdose of sleeping pills, upon which she promptly passed, unmourned, into the velvet thankfulness of oblivion.

Chance Temper's IT course paid off after he set up a fetishwear web-portal and found himself making a fortune from companies who wanted him to market incontinence pants via the internet. One of these companies was the Brick Lane outlet that had formerly belonged to Sanjeev's bride's parents, and which would never have come to him had he not pulled off his trousers with such vigour several months earlier.

Oddly enough, the girl Chance eventually married had been up in her bedroom ordering backlaced leather thongs from one of his fetishwear sites when Bimmer's car landed in the exact spot she would have been standing on had she not decided to delay pruning her roses until after she had surfed the internet.

Not that Chance's marriage lasted very long, because, like the rest of the characters in this moebian tale, neither he nor his wife ever figured out what they really wanted from sex, or love, or life, or death, or themselves, or each other, or anything.

There used to be an advertisement in the backs of American comics for Sea Monkeys. According to the illustration, they sat in a water tank wearing little crowns, forming the ideal family unit; dad with pipe and slippers, mother in a frilly apron, children playing happily at their feet. But when you sent away for the product, what you received was a packet of dried brine shrimp that only ever grew to an eighth of an inch and looked nothing like the drawing. The product didn't do what it promised. So it is with the sexual drive, a wayward force that defies all attempted delineation.

But there are those who insist that life is merely a pearl-string of bright moments, and if many of those moments involve the expectation of sex, however poorly realised, we can at least say that we have lived in anticipation of something fine.

And doesn't that help to shape our lives after all?

*If I say I was annoyed by the ludicrous censorship laws in Britain, you'll get the picture. We have a film censorship body that manages to be both autonomous and answerable to the government, that obeys the demands of 'witch-hunt' campaigns mounted by tabloids merely to increase their circulation, and displays the kind of bizarre inconsistencies no fiction could do justice to. When you attempt to enforce a moral code you are bound to make a fool of yourself, as many politicians know. This story is a fictional variant on the subject.*

# EIGHTEEN AND OVER

Dear Sir,

We are pleased to inform you that the film you submitted to us recently for classification:

—'PLAGUE OF TERROR'—

has been passed for national theatrical exhibition under a certificate admitting members of the public aged 18 years and over. In order for said film to be granted a Certificate of Classification* we would like to recommend the following alterations to the content:

(*All feature films intended for theatrical exhibition require a registered Certificate Of Classification, issued by the British Board Of Classification)

Reel 1

(2 mins) Scene: Flashback: Gelbart as a small boy, sitting on sunlit lawn playing with row of plastic toy soldiers given to him by his father.

Remove scene in its entirety. A child of such an early age could easily choke on such toys, which are intended for use by older age-groups.

(6 mins) Scene: Present Day: Gelbart's army training.

Delete c.u. shot of sergeant's repeated slapping of Gelbart after disobedience – 1–3 slaps is permissible, but no more than this amount.

(16 mins) Scene: Gelbart hacks off head of rising soldier with a shovel.

Delete extreme close-up of victim's bloodshot eyes in throes of death.

Delete two-second shot showing blood pumping from stump of victim's neck.

Reel 2

(12 mins) Scene: Gelbart wakes up in army hospital bed screaming.

Delete Gelbart's direct reference to President Clinton ending in phrase ' . . . terrible nightmare'.

Delete close-up of tube being yanked from arm, spraying blood onto sheet.

Delete extreme close-up of swollen needle-marks on Gelbart's arm.

Reel 3

(3 mins) Scene: Gelbart recovers at Laura's house.

Delete shot of Gelbart's fingers entering Laura's panties, with the clearly suggested indication of digital/vaginal penetration.

Delete shot of Gelbart's hand probing Laura's buttocks.

Delete moans of Laura's pleasure on soundtrack.

Delete Gelbart squeezing Laura's nipple between thumb and forefinger.

Delete look of pleasure on Laura's face.

Delete extreme close-up suggested wetness on Laura's thigh.

Delete close-up of Laura's lips. Delete all following close-ups indicating Laura's enjoyment.

Delete newsreel shot of pretty White House interns lining up to meet President Clinton.

This scene should be re-edited to reduce look of sexual urgency on faces of protagonists, and to reduce duration of lovemaking to a more acceptable length of say, thirty seconds.

Reel 4

(7 mins) Gelbart returns to army camp.

Delete close-ups of injured men.

Delete reference to superiors as 'motherfuckers'.

Reduce length of medium shot showing drill sergeant demonstrating use of bayonet, as this action could result in copycat behaviour from impressionable viewers.

Reduce sergeant's speech from 'We are no better than the enemy' to 'Because the government wants us to'. Remove unacceptable reference to 'legitimised slaughter.'


(11 mins) 'War montage' sequence.

We are particularly concerned about reality being blurred with fiction in this montage.

Delete documentary insert of President Nixon being sworn in at his inauguration ceremony.

Delete documentary insert of American gunfire crossing night sky above Vietnamese jungle.

Delete documentary insert of Vietnam children screaming in terror.

Reduce scene of Gelbart's division receiving lecture outlining 'utter destruction of enemy', recommencing scene at commanding officer's dialogue line ' . . . can only be reasonably expected to do your duty.'


(14 mins) Flashback sequence: Gelbart's father arrives in Saigon.

Delete mid-shot of Gelbart's father's hands closing around Vietnamese boy's throat.

Delete close-up of Gelbart's father thrusting knife into boy's stomach.

Delete all shots that could be construed to suggest pleasure on face of Gelbart's father.

Suggest replacing these shots with extended sequence of tickertape parade honouring Gelbart's father as he returns home.

Reel 5
Scene: (1 min) Gelbart's father returns to 'normal life' at home.
Use of real-life images in a film of this nature is, we repeat, entirely unacceptable. Delete shot of Gelbart watching TV monitor depicting close-up of President Reagan's face during Iran–Contra hearings.

(2 mins) Laura's murder.
Delete extreme close-up of the medal Gelbart wears around his neck becoming soaked with blood as Gelbart slashes Laura's throat.

(9 mins) Gelbart undergoes traumatic collapse.
Delete entire sequences of Gelbart machine-gunning occupants of McDonald's restaurant / blowing up customers in Kentucky Fried Chicken outlet.

(13 mins) Gelbart defies authorities.
Delete Gelbart opening fire on crowd from roof of shopping mall.

(17 mins) Fantasy sequence.
Remove all crosscut shots of real life figures: Ho Chi Min, Saddam Hussein, Ronald Reagan, President Clinton, George W. Bush.
Crucially, avoid intercutting between little girl in shopping mall and crying Iraqi girl in order to avoid the suggestion that these children having anything in common with one another.

Reel 6
(3 mins) Gelbart's confrontation with armed response.
Repeat earlier shot of Gelbart firing at policeman in order to clarify Gelbart's stance on right and wrong, clearly showing that he opposes freedom and democracy.

Remove all close-ups of Gelbart's face indicating confusion, pain, anger, remorse, fear, bitterness, disappointment, betrayal.

(17 mins) Victory of law enforcement officers over renegade citizen.

Reduce shot of police sharpshooters bringing down Gelbart in a hail of bullets to one single shot from fresh-faced sniper.

Remove all shots of Gelbart's body being kicked and stamped on by police sergeant.

Remove documentary footage of Lt. William Calley on trial for his part in the My Lai massacre juxtaposed with Vietnamese man being shot in head at point blank range.

Remove shot of Iraqi children fleeing from burning desert building in terror.

Remove shot of Rodney King being beaten by LAPD officers.

Remove all shots of British monarchy standing at attention.

It is essential that the pace of this fast-cut montage be slowed down in order to prevent the absorption of subliminal imagery.

(19 mins) Pan across naked girl on poster as passer-by in foreground is shot dead.

Remove all following scenes of desire/violence/anti-patriotism/teen rebellion.

Replace slow-motion end sequence of Gelbart as an idealistic young man enlisting in the US army, paying particular attention to reduction and removal of scenes which show joyful expression on Gelbart's face as he is honoured by his town during homecoming.

(20 mins) Unnecessary symbolism.

Remove, in its entirety, sequence of small boy playing on sunlit lawn, as camera pans across toy soldiers to reveal his father's medal of honour lying in the grass.

Remove defiant look in child's eyes as he listens to recording of the president's inauguration address.

Remove any suggestion, be it visual, graphic or in voiceover, that Gelbart's spirit of violent rebellion lives on in his son, and that the boy may one day follow in his father's footsteps.

Remove all existing 'popular' music tracks with antisocial lyrics that can be heard over factual footage and replace with harmonic instrumental score from fictional scenes. [For a full detailed list of required music cuts see attached appendix A.]

The board requires that the above requirements must be met for classification, but I would like to add that I personally feel the film to be of marginal entertainment value, having no intrinsic artistic merit. In its current form it clearly possesses unpleasant, unhealthy and undesirable disruptive social tendencies.

In concluding this approval of classification, may I remind you that the changes requested are in no way open to negotiation or arbitration, and must be carried out in full before this film can again be submitted for consideration as a licensed film for theatrical exhibition.

May I also remind you that while we at the British Board Of Classification naturally respect the artistic freedom of those wishing to produce filmed entertainment for public exhibition in a reasonable and free society, common sense dictates that the continued welfare of the state can only be harmed by scenes and plotlines that wilfully offend the public by drawing conclusions from real life and presenting them in radically opinionated fictional form. It is this blurring of factual information and fictional speculation which I feel is most harmful to the common good. Images of state betrayal and an advocation of terrorism are simply not fit subjects upon which to build a fictional story. We must remind ourselves that fiction is created for the enjoyment of all members of society, and that some may have greater difficulty than others in distinguishing fact from fantasy.

I know that it is possible to present motion pictures for classification to the board that require only minimal alterations, and hope that we can soon reach a situation of mutual resolution in this matter.

I understand from your producer that you are only seventeen years old, and hope that you can find positive benefit from the classification process, so that you can eventually appreciate how the system works, and can act accordingly within it as your film-making skills mature.

> Yours sincerely,
> Mark Petersham
> Signed and dated

MEMO TO:
  M. Petersham
  British Board Of Film Classification
FROM:
  Stephen Elly
  Director, 'Plague Of Terror'

Dear Mr Petersham,

I am in receipt of your letter for the 'classification' of my film, and am interested to note that, at no point in your suggested amendments, do you or your board ask yourselves what exactly we were trying to achieve with our blend of performance, sound and imagery.

Ever since I was a tiny child I have been bombarded by the same handful of scenes on the evening news; youths throwing stones across barbed wire, police horses marching forward into crowds, sullen royals greeting troops, disgraced MPs still happily lying to the cameras, smiling presidents signing pacts with their counterparts, reports from shattered communities, interviews with ordinary people stunned into ruin and disillusionment. I'm sure you have been bombarded with these same scenes, too. Perhaps you never questioned them. Perhaps you did, and decided that such matters were better left in the hands of others. We simply decided to make sense of them in a fictional narrative. We tried to see the world through the eyes of a child who expects things to turn out right, or to at least make some kind of sense. Isn't that what everyone tries to do?

For a long while I gave organisations such as yours the benefit of the doubt. I thought you were just acting on orders from a higher authority. Now I see that you are actually the root of the problem. You are not devoid of responsibility. You exist at the very heart of our troubles. You think you are the keeper of the status quo. To me you are the debaser, the destroyer.

You suggest that because I am seventeen years old I still have a lot to learn, whereas I feel that I have learned enough. The absurd thing is, even if you passed my film, I would still not be legally old enough to see it. I have therefore decided to withdraw my film from the classification process altogether, and embark upon a very different course.

I am sending you a short video feature I made as a child entitled 'The Happy Elves' Christmas'. You will find it in the box that accompanies this letter, and I trust it will prove more to your liking.

Yours,<br>S. Elly

TELETEXT———Seven killed in West End bomb blast

Five men and two women died and dozens more were injured in an explosion that rocked the West End this afternoon. At approximately 4 p.m. a device sent to the office of the British

Board Of Film Classification was detonated in a busy office, sending bricks, glass and other debris over a hundred and fifty yards into the surrounding streets. Police believe that the bomb was hidden inside a package of videotape and hand-delivered to the board's acting chief of staff. No motive for the attack has yet been established.

TELETEXT———Prince injured in Mall blast

Prince William suffered bruising and facial cuts after a bomb exploded in Pall Mall this morning. A palace spokesman told press that the prince is expected to make a full recovery from his injuries in a few days. The blast also killed two Australian tourists. This is the fourth recent attack carried out by the man national news agencies are referring to as the 'Freedom Bomber'.

TELETEXT———London Freedom Bomber killed in police shoot-out

The so-called 'Freedom Bomber', recently identified as seventeen-year-old failed film-maker Stephen Elly, was shot dead in a shoot-out which ended the twelve-hour rooftop siege at the Ministry of Defence. Elly's demands to have sensitive documents covering Britain's involvement in overseas arms sales publicly released were not met.

NEXT MONTH AT BLOCKBUSTER
'Plague Of Terror' 98 mins (US)
The story of an unstable ex-soldier who embarks upon a savagely violent campaign to overthrow democracy, and the beautiful FBI agent who loves him. Based on a true story. Starring Matt LeBlanc and Ashley Judd. Title song by Jennifer Lopez.

*Time seems to be one of the most pervasive and universal subjects after love, and of course, like love, your relationship to it changes as you grow older. It's hard to tackle in short form; the ideas slide away. Perhaps the truth about time must remain elusive, or else we would lose a reason to be happy. There are seven dials in the story, by the way.*

# SEVEN DIALS

## 1. BLACKING OUT THE MOON

The hands are pressed tin, black and thin and fine. The face is white enamel. The second arm skims roman numerals, lightly pausing at each. The tick is created by the rise and fall of a slender brass ratchet. The clock requires winding nightly, by a large key designed to be inserted into the face and slowly turned by two hands. The front of the case is ebony, the back is of some cheaper wood. Whoever undertakes to keep the spring wound enters a contract with the clock, one of trust and faith, to keep its arms sailing, to keep its cogs and wheels free from the tarnish of stilled time. To allow it to stop is to allow it to die.

'I'll have to be getting back, Mrs B,' said Ethel, drying her hands and replacing the teatowel in its holder. 'My Alf creates merry hell if he don't get his tea on time, and I'm late as it is.'

'Do tell him it was my fault,' urged Bea. 'It was kind of you to help out.'

Ethel sniffed. 'You do what you can with all this goin' on.' She yanked her felt hat over her hair and stuck a pin through it. 'I'll be glad when everything settles back to normal.'

'Could you take these back as you go?' She handed Ethel a pair of empty bottles, cod liver oil and concentrated orange juice. 'And you'd better pick up some more soap flakes at Lynch's.' She looked over at her husband, who was half-asleep in front of the fire, his chair tipped back at a precarious angle. 'Harold, Eth's off now.'

'Oh, don't wake him up, Mrs B. He's like Alf, dead to the world when 'e's not up and about, but it's a good thing. After we lost Bert I didn't think none of us would sleep again.' Ethel's oldest son had been killed at sea. She slipped the bottles into her bicycle basket. 'I'll collect the linens from Walpoles and be back in the morning around half-past ten, I shouldn't wonder.'

'I shall be here,' Bea promised. 'I agreed to let the Services Comfort Committee have the piano, and they're coming to collect it. I've warned them it will need tuning. Mrs Keighley is donating all her sheet music.'

'I don't know what you're going to do for a sing-song now, I'm sure.'

She was about to tell Ethel that the National Gallery's lunch-hour concerts would be a preferable alternative to Harold hammering out 'Whispering Grass' on the upright, but she didn't get a chance to speak. Nor did Ethel manage to get her bicycle out of the scullery door, because there was a deafening explosion and all the crockery in the dresser was thrown forward, smashing to pieces on the scullery floor.

'What the bloody hell – ?' Harold's chair fell forward and he found himself sprawled across the table.

'Lawd, not again,' complained Ethel, quickly closing the door to the street and retreating inside. 'That's the second time this week without a blooming warning.'

A louder blast pulsed the air from the room and shattered one of the kitchen windows. Harold had been building an Anderson shelter in the garden, but it still wasn't finished, so they usually stayed in the cupboard under the stairs until the all-clear.

'Eth, you'd best stay with us for a while,' said Bea. 'That's too close for comfort.' She noticed that the cleaning lady's face was bleeding from a dozen tiny cuts. 'You've got some glass in you, love. Harold, give me a hand, don't just sit there like an article.' She grabbed a flannel from the draining board, dipped it in the washing up water and gingerly dabbed Ethel's face, removing as many splinters as she could find, but daylight was fading and she could not turn on the lamp because the blackout curtains had been blown from the main window.

'It's like the world's comin' to an end,' said Ethel sadly. Her face was a red mask, but if the process of retrieving the shards from her skin hurt, she made no complaint. The third detonation was further away, across the road, nearer to Vauxhall Bridge by the sound of it. Everyone who lived within sight of the river was in danger because the bombers used it as a flightpath into London.

Harold looked out through the collapsed window frame and saw a great mound of bricks. The house beside it looked like a cutaway model, its interior embarrassingly revealed to the world. Several slender glass vases on its lounge mantelpiece were still in place, some pictures on the remaining wall had not even been knocked crooked, and over a shattered window hung an untouched lace curtain. As always, it was the arbitrariness of it all that shocked most. This time nothing seemed to be burning and there was no smoke, but the air was dry and there were effusions of dense yellow dust. Several people were wandering in the road, lost to the shock of the blast.

'Blimey, the Keighleys' house has taken a hit. Put Eth under the stairs and get the kettle on, love. Buck her up with something. I'm going to see what I can do.'

'Be careful, Harold,' called his wife. 'I didn't hear an all-clear, I didn't hear any sirens at all.' The bombs were falling further away now, sounding like a thunderstorm in retreat. It was Tuesday the 12th of November, 1940, the ninth week of the event that became known as The Blitz, and London's populace was becoming used to the continual threat of air attack. When the sirens sounded, it formed orderly queues into the city's tube stations, or slept in public shelters. Those who stayed at home ducked into homemade Andersons, crammed themselves into cupboards and hid under the stairs. The government was trying to get everyone to sleep at ground level, but many refused to give up their beds for a patch of cold linoleum in the kitchen.

The war forced an intimacy on people that made them uncomfortable.

On an average night, over 200 tons of high explosive and over 180 incendiary devices rained down on the city. The bombardment had begun in earnest on September the 7th, and continued night after night across the country until May of the following year. In London, the old City and the East End simply ceased to exist. So many terrible things happened, so many killed, so many injured, so many made homeless, that there was no adequate human response to the devastation. Photographs of the time capture the most shocking moments; a picture of some women's shoes and a champagne bottle, taken when thirty-four people died in the Café de Paris, another of the Bank tube station after it had received a direct hit, killing more than 110 men, women and children sheltering inside. One photograph showed the devastation inflicted on a row of houses in Hendon after a single massive 2500kg bomb exploded moments before the alert could be sounded. And to some, the most shocking picture of all, a gaping hole in the eastern end of the roof of St Paul's, where a bomb had dropped through, demolishing the High Altar with such perfect precision that it became easy to believe in the ascendant power of dark forces.

Then there were the censored pictures that nobody in England saw for years, the ARP wardens cradling dead babies, the double decker bus blown clear into the air, the row of terraced houses reduced to loose bricks and matchwood, no human life left intact. All this horror was still to come.

Harold picked his way between stacks of fallen masonry, crumpled chunks of an internal lath-and-plaster wall, and an entire fireplace surround that had landed perfectly upright in the road, as if it had been placed there by the hand of God.

'Mrs Keighley,' he called, 'stay right there. I wouldn't move if I were you.' His neighbour was standing dazed on a splintered band of wood that jutted out above her cellar, all that remained of her living room floor. She was dressed in a torn green blouse and skirt, and bedroom slippers, and had been preparing some supper to eat in front of the radio, which was still playing even though it dangled from the end of a flex. A jaunty foxtrot, 'Til The Lights Of London Shine Again', came to an end as Harold inched his way out onto the creaking platform. 'Give me your hand, love,' he called softly.

'And now, Syd Lipton and the Grosvenor House Dance Band play "Blacking Out The Moon", for every – ' The radio spat an electrical pulse and went dead. All that could be heard was the soft moaning of the injured, the chink and tumble of dislodged bricks. Harold reached out his hand. 'You can do it, love. Don't look down. Just reach toward me.'

Mrs Keighley remained still, staring past him to where the wall had been. To where her husband had been sitting, waiting for his meal.

'He's not there,' Harold explained carefully. 'He's gone, love, and the house has gone.' He had passed the old man's body on the way into the house, crushed beneath a collapsed chimney stack. Nearby, a grandfather clock had landed face down on the pavement, like a felled soldier.

She noticed him for the first time, and fluttered her eyelids as though coming to her senses. For a moment he thought she might faint and fall into darkness. Then she held out her arm, just enough for him to grab at her, and haul her back from the edge. 'My name's Irene,' she murmured, and passed out in his arms.

## 2. LISTENING TO THE PAST

The timepiece stands on four adjustable pedestals, and requires rebalancing whenever it is moved. To wind the mechanism, one must open the face by lifting a clasp on its right side. The hands are elegantly tapered into the points of aces. The case fits so snugly over the workings that no dust can possibly enter. The clock was first wound on the day of Ellen's eighteenth birthday, and has never been allowed to run down even though it is no longer in her possession. Perhaps, in some strange way, it is linked to her destiny.

The funeral was running late. Congested traffic held up the cortege, and those who were not travelling in the procession had been left standing under the narrow canopy of the chapel, trying to avoid the rain. Nobody could be admitted into the building because the previous departure was running behind as well, and that service had still not finished. They were backed up like buses.

'Trust Tony to be late for his own – well, you know,' said his Aunt Hilda, wiping a patch of condensation from the car window with the back of her glove. 'He was never on time for anything in his life.'

Ellen looked around her at the aunts and uncles she barely knew. Tony had introduced her to one or two before they were married, and a few more at their wedding, but she hadn't seen them since that time, twenty-nine years ago, and now conversation between them all was hopelessly forced.

'So you and Tony didn't have children,' prompted Aunt Hilda, in a bid to break the silence that kept resettling on them like some kind of determined insect.

'No, we wanted to. We tried for a few years, but after a while I couldn't have them.' The other aunts and uncles shut up as tightly as if she had mouthed 'collapsed tubes' at them. Times might have moved on, but the duties of government wives were no concern of theirs. That was what she was, even with Tony dead. They had produced no children because they had spent their lives on the move. How many times had she watched her crockery and furniture being packed and unpacked? How many times had she written the name 'Farrell' on top of a crate bound for Canada, New Zealand, Germany, Norway? Everywhere had been the same; dead air in barely inhabited rooms, chilly receptions in government houses, muted dinner parties invariably held in the oldest buildings in the city, cocktail hours where the men discussed office politics and the wives – never women, always wives – were expected to find amusement with each other. Each posting was described to her in terms of the quality of the shopping. 'You'll love it here, wait until you see the shops.' Eventually she had stopped playing the game, stopped being so damned nice. She went drinking. She went local. Once she had thought that her father would be proud of her for travelling so much, but he wasn't, he was merely disappointed not to see her.

'Still,' sighed Aunt Hilda, plodding bravely on. 'It was a – long – marriage. By today's standards, anyhow.' For one awful moment Ellen thought she had been about to call it a happy marriage, but even these rarely-seen relatives knew better than to suggest that. Tony had not been a good husband. He had been a melancholy bully whose pessimism had hardened into a mean spirit, and while nobody was pleased to see him die, they weren't that sorry either. For most of them it was just another name to cross off the Christmas card list.

Ellen barely heard the service. Apart from compulsory attendance at weddings and funerals, her husband had entered church only three times in his own cause, christening, marriage and funeral, a classic case of hatch, match and dispatch. The vicar had nothing to say about him, and even the vague phrases he fell back on managed to be inappropriate. He had not 'shown kindness to others'. He had not led 'a decent, peaceful life' or 'treated his fellow humans with respect'. He had worked for Her Majesty, chivvying along arms deals, doing things he couldn't talk about. The vicar looked as bored with his lies as they were. Nobody seemed to remember the words to any of the hymns, even though they had been truncated to first and last verses.

Her shoes were pinching. She just wanted to be home now, to clear the last of his stuff out and expand her own life into the house. It had taken her years to realise that she did not love, or even like, her husband. It sounded absurd to make such a claim in this age, when women were meant to be the captains of their fates. When she had married Tony she had taken on the government, and had challenged it at such a personal level that the rest of his staff might as well have been in bed with them. He saw it as a vocation. She saw it as a third person who had wrecked their marriage. It came to incense her that he could not connect what he did for a living with the sight of a twelve-year-old shouldering a Kalashnikov in Lebanon, or Serbia, or Zimbabwe. Any discussion of ideals would transform itself into an argument about putting food on the table. She exhibited signs of clinical depression. She avoided contact with the outside world. She drank. She slept.

She had only lately noticed the dreams of longing, strange pillow-thoughts of dark men in dark suits, who walked through rain between old London – always London – buildings with their eyes in shadow, men who were not like her husband, not like any men she had ever met. She spent too much time in her world of dreams, and almost managed to have an affair, although it came to nothing. Alan had been a government man also, a colleague of Tony's, but the thing was all too close. She felt no guilt, only the fear of discovery, fear of losing the only world she had. She was sure she could regain control of her life if they could just be posted home. And when that had finally happened, Tony died.

The wake was held at Hilda's smart little semi somewhere off the North Circular. Minuscule sandwiches, muted tones, children rowdily misbehaving around solemn adults. Some people from his office came, the husbands still talking shop, the wives trying not to notice the smallness of the house. Aunt Hilda was pursuing an autumnal theme through her life, unwisely in Ellen's opinion. Everything the poor woman wore and every room she inhabited was decked in flower prints, browns and oranges, the colours of drying and dying, a hay-fever sufferer's nightmare. She was a large woman who ate as much food as she offered around, but at least Hilda showed signs of being alive, which was more than could be said for most of the others.

*Am I like them?* Ellen wondered. *Married for nearly thirty years to a man I came to detest, who dismissed me at every turn, who virtually stamped me into the ground until I was invisible. It wasn't even as if we'd needed to stay together for the sake of any children. Some women are born mice. As quiet as a mouse, that's me.*

*To hell with this,* she thought, *I don't even like these people. I'm going home.*

So she did.

But even though she shifted four binliners filled with his clothing out into the porch for collection by Oxfam, the house still felt as though it was his. It was in Tony's name, and he had kept up the payments by standing order, right until his heart attack. What would happen now? She didn't even know where he stored his important papers.

*Then you'll find them,* she told herself, *there's nowhere you can't look now. He's not here to tell you off.* She went upstairs to his study, the room where he went to work but sat watching the football, the room any normal family would have earmarked as a nursery. There wasn't much in it, just a couple of leather armchairs, a television and the kind of desk she imagined he had at the office. But she found a small wooden case in the bottom of the desk, and instinctively knew that the little key she had seen in the pot in the kitchen would fit its lock.

The contents of the box were a bit of a disappointment; his passport, school reports, government documentation, a swimming certificate, a long service medal belonging to his grandfather, bank details about the house, a dead wristwatch, a stack of boring-looking letters. Something concerning the Official Secrets Act that looked as if it might be mysterious and exciting, but wasn't. No illicit lover's notes, no hidden share portfolio. But there was a letter addressed with her name, not in Tony's handwriting but Harold's.

Her father had written to her, and the envelope was torn open. The front of it read: *For My Daughter Ellen.* Inside was a piece of sheet music for the piano, a forties' song called 'Blacking Out The Moon'. Tony must have been as mystified by this as she was, and had impatiently stuffed it back into the envelope, but by doing so had missed her father's note on the back of the sheet. He had written with a fountain pen in turquoise ink, and for a moment she could hear his voice in his words. She read to the bottom of the page with growing puzzlement, then read the last part again.

'I suppose I'd saved her life, but back then you did things without thinking twice. You always helped your neighbours. Me and your mother took Irene Keighley in. Her old man had been killed by the bomb, and it turned out their house wasn't insured, and she was left destitute. The government had a scheme going to rebuild houses, but she didn't want to live on the spot where her husband had died. I thought she was being silly about it. So while she stayed with us she kept hold of the land, and didn't sell it back even though she could have done with the money. She passed on when you were eight or nine, and left the deed to me. I've never had much faith in banks, so I hung onto it. I should have acted earlier, then it might have been worth something. You know you were always my favourite little girl, and I have so little to leave you, I feel ashamed – '

He had intended this letter to be given to her after his death. Tony had known and had hidden it. At least he was consistent in his behaviour.

The deed would be well over half a century old by now, and had probably been claimed by the government long ago. But the thought of it set her mind to work. Her parents had been living in Vauxhall back then, and the Keighleys had lived in the end house, diagonally opposite theirs. The whole street was under tarmac now, buried beneath the poisonous trunk road that ran along the south bank of the Thames. There couldn't be anything left at all.

She decided to go and have a look, anyway.

Ellen alighted from Vauxhall station and walked back past dirt-crusted railway arches to where their terraced house had once stood. Hardly anyone walked around here. It wasn't just the traffic noise and the exhaust fumes; the road didn't lead to anything that might prove useful or interesting. Signs of life still existed under the arches themselves, an auto-parts centre, a nightclub, various wholesalers, but the houses were all gone.

She reached the spot where number 7 had once stood. She knew it because of the plane trees; everything else had changed. She remembered the dusty front gardens, the rusting Anderson shelters, the alley running past the gardens where she used to play hopscotch. Her memories had not gilded themselves with time; there had been no palaces here, but no slums either, just families living quietly. *Bit of a jump from Vauxhall to Kuwait,* she thought, not entirely sure that she didn't prefer the former. Studying the grass-hemmed paving slabs, she was shocked to see that they had contained their lives in such a small area. This was where the front gateposts had been, and over there had been the Keighleys – she looked up at the road, then across to the opposite corner, waiting for the traffic to clear.

## 3. TAKING ON THE LAW

Her heart was thumping as she reboarded the train. She tried to shuffle her thoughts into some kind of actionable order. If the government had taken back the Keighleys' deed to their property, why hadn't they built on it? Could it be that the right of possession attached to the deed was still somehow valid? The land would be worth – how could you even begin to calculate? Had her father actually been given a physical deed to the property? The thought of trying to find out made her sick with panic. For nearly thirty years she had been a housewife, nothing more, a silent woman who dusted and cooked and swept. The very idea was too big, too far beyond her. And yet.

Take it step by step, she told herself, what have you got to lose by checking just a little further? What would you be doing with your time instead, waiting for the bank to come knocking at the door with news that Tony hadn't kept up your mortgage repayments, waiting to have your own house taken away? What would it take to find out the truth? The Keighleys were dead, her father and husband were dead. Who could it possibly hurt?

As the train bore her home, she tried to follow the idea through. If her father had been given a property deed, what on earth would he have done with it? Harold had been a clockmaker, and had kept his workshop in Seven Dials right up until he died. The space where he had once spent his days hunched over a bench was now a restaurant. His equipment had been shifted into Ellen's garden shed, where it had rusted and rotted, untouched by Tony or herself. She wondered if there were any answers lying amongst the tools and lathes.

She found nothing there but spiders and woodlice, discoloured discs of glass and orange flakes of iron. The planes and saws, the rasps and polishers had greyed with disuse, as though they had perished with him. A rain-damaged order book lay on the damp-split workbench. She had trouble ungluing it from the wood and tore the cover doing so, but took the rest indoors to study. She found it filled with scrupulously tidy lists and strange abbreviations, the cryptography of a simpler world.

Ellen searched through her wardrobe for something appropriate to wear. She hadn't given her clothes much thought in the past few years; she hadn't needed to, because government wives wore variations of each other's outfits. Tony had rarely allowed his wife to socialise beyond their circle, his refusal to share her masquerading as concern. Consequently, she had dozens of reception dresses and nothing suitable for a meeting in the city. She finally settled on a purple dress she had owned for years but had hardly ever worn. Ellen was forty-nine, and after years of acting older than her age, decided that the clock could stand still for a little while; time owed her that much.

London was looking shabby, for all its much-vaunted newness. She looked from the window of the taxi and saw graffiti scrawled into every available space, sickly plants sprouting from aged brickwork, monstrously ugly supermarkets jammed into high streets, litter, drunks, angry faces. The city's architects were obsessed with glass canopies, so that even the most sedate buildings had been made as cheap and flashy as carnival fairings. The taxi pulled up in front of a government building, but for once she would not be expected to make small talk over a carefully measured glass of champagne.

Miss Sanders at the Land Registry Office used the same kind of language she had heard around her for years, a cross between normal speech and an instructional leaflet. She outlined the laws concerning the transferral of property, and provided Ellen with an armful of unreadable government brochures.

'The Land Registry records ownership of interests in land whenever applications are made,' she explained. 'Over the years, different areas of the country became subject to compulsory registration, and the whole of England and Wales has been in a compulsory area since December 1990. Before, registration was only required when a property was sold. The triggers have altered since then. Now most changes of ownership, such as passing on after a death or as a gift, trigger the first registration.'

Ellen was about to thank the registrar and walk away when a thought occurred to her. 'If a piece of land was transferred before compulsory registration, would you know about it?'

'Probably not,' Ms Sanders admitted. 'Although there's a consequence for not notifying us in that the legal estate wouldn't pass. We have no means of forcing people to come forward. Still, the legislation enables central or local government departments to acquire land, and they can force the sale no matter who the owner is.'

'But if they don't know who it is, what happens then?'

'If the government actually admits that they've no idea who the land belongs to, we may well simply give them the title to an interest in it.'

'Then how do people protect themselves? I mean, suppose I was left something and no-one knew about it . . .'

'The Limitation Acts allow someone to acquire land not being used by the owner. The idea behind the policy is not to let people tie up valuable land and let it go stale. Normally speaking, if someone occupies a site for twelve years without complaint by the owner, then the owner can no longer claim the land back. If someone claims title to land and can't prove it, we won't give them a title merely because nobody else has claimed it. It's all in the leaflets.'

Ellen doubted she would ever be able to decode the written law. 'What if the land is still unoccupied and I find I've been given the property deed?'

'Then all you have to do is register it.'

'And suppose the government wants it?'

'They have to make public their intention to purchase the land. If the land in question is not registered by the owner within a certain time period, the transaction goes through.' Ms Sanders studied her thoughtfully. 'I take it you're talking about a specific site of interest?'

'I'm sorry?'

'You want to find out if there's a compulsory purchase order pending on a specific site?'

'Yes.'

'Then perhaps you'd like to give me the details.'

They had found it on a 1/2500 scale map together, a slim oblong beyond the blue track of the river, exactly bordering the eastern side of the MI5 building. Ms Sanders went off to make some phonecalls, and Ellen returned to the waiting room. Fifteen minutes later she was called to the front desk again.

'You're in luck if you know someone who's planning to register that particular property,' said Ms Sanders. 'There's been a legal row going on about it for years, but the government has finally placed a compulsory purchase order on the land. It's been posted for nearly three months, and the registration is still open until the 17th.' She looked at her watch. 'That gives you until noon next Saturday.'

'What if I don't have the deed or any proof that it's mine?' Ellen asked.

'Then you'd better find something,' suggested Ms Sanders, handing her a card. 'If you do, just call me on this number and I'll do the rest.' She watched Ellen leave. 'Good luck,' she added. 'I like your dress, by the way.'

So there it was. Without the deed, she had no claim. She

returned to the house and noticed that it still smelled of Tony's cigarettes, but the smell was stale and dead now. It no longer felt as if he had just walked out into the street.

That afternoon she searched the shed again, but found nothing. She was sure her father had known the whereabouts of the deed when he died; why else would he have written her a note? It was typical of him to recall it at the last possible minute, just as it had been typical of Tony to hold back a letter addressed to her and then dismiss it without proper examination. She had loved her father very much. She had seen the growing confusion in his eyes, but had spent so little time with him. Tony's endless array of sullen looks and angry faces had delayed her until it was too late. She wondered how she could rebuild her own confidence. After years of being ignored, she knew there was no time to relearn the skills she had once possessed.

In bed that night, she studied her father's order book for clocks constructed and sold to clients in the years after the Blitz. He had taken so long to produce each timepiece that no more than ten were ever sold in one year. The sales receipts for the clocks he built during the war and the period after were attached to the order entries. She didn't know what she was looking for, but remembered how her father's mind worked. She reread his letter once more. *I should have acted earlier, then it might have been worth something. You know you were always my favourite little girl.* It was as though he had left the deed in such an obvious place that he didn't feel the need to mention it.

She turned out the light and lay looking up at the ceiling, still missing the sound that had calibrated the night for so long. Harold had loved his clocks. Each one had been a work of art, but they were so time-consuming to construct that he had been forced to sell them all – except for the pair he had made Ellen and her brother, to mark their eighteenth birthdays. Presumably Simon still had his, but Tony had sold hers to his former boss in order to pay off a company loan. They had fought bitterly about it, because he had not asked her permission.

She decided to steel herself and pay a call on Simon.

'That's twice we've seen you now,' said Trisha, standing in the doorway with her arms folded, 'including the funeral. What do you want?'

'Is my brother around?'

'He's at work. You should have phoned first.' Trisha wasn't about to let her into the house without a reason.

'Well, it's not really him I want to see. Can I come in?'

Her sister-in-law grudgingly moved from the doorway. 'I was about to go out,' she said flatly. Trisha had never liked her. Ellen had married badly and moved back to an old house full of damp-smelling books, but she still seemed to think she was better than them. She had nothing to feel superior about; her husband had been no good when he was alive, and had died leaving her nothing but debts. Now here she was, coming around to see a brother she had hardly bothered with, probably preparing to ask for a loan.

Ellen felt just as uncomfortable in Trisha's tight, bright little house, a monument to the art of home stencilling that was as devoid of life as any embassy hall, and smelled of antiseptic wipes. She followed her sister-in-law into the lounge and looked around. 'I was wondering if Simon still had the clock Dad gave him for his eighteenth birthday?'

'That horrible old thing,' said Trisha, who might have been considered thoughtless were she capable of spontaneous emotion. 'I was sure it had woodworm. "You're not keeping that in here", I told him. It didn't suit the room. I wanted us to go pastel.'

'You didn't throw it away, did you?'

'No, he wouldn't let me. I put it in our Warren's room.'

'Can I see it?'

Trisha was reluctant to let her snoop about in other parts of the house. 'You've got one of your own,' she reminded her. 'I thought they were exactly the same.'

'That's just it,' said Ellen, 'I don't think they are.'

Trisha did not want to let her go up, but was intrigued. She opened the door to her son's bedroom. The usual assortment of adolescent posters covered the walls, Manchester United, Buffy the Vampire Slayer, The X-Men. On the mantelpiece at the end of the room stood Simon's clock.

'Warren had a go at painting it,' explained Trisha. Crimson drips hung from the casing like baby stalactites. The glass in the face had been cracked and not replaced. Ellen picked up the clock and turned it over. She had forgotten how heavy they were.

'Be careful with it,' warned her sister-in-law. 'What exactly are you looking for, anyway?'

'I think Dad might have put something in one of them.' She opened the back and peered inside.

'What sort of thing?'

'A memento. Something for his children.'

Trisha's eyes took on the glassy hardness of pecuniary advantage. 'You mean money?'

'Well, not exactly, no.' She had said more than she meant to say. Besides, there was nothing here. She tipped the clock to the light.

Trisha was watching her suspiciously. 'You should be careful with that, it's delicate.'

*I know how delicate they are*, thought Ellen. *I watched him work on this, night after night at the kitchen table.* There was nothing inside Simon's clock, but she had proven a theory. The panel at the rear consisted of two fine layers of wood. There was a gap between them large enough to hold a well-filled envelope.

'If you think he left you something, wouldn't he have put it in yours?' asked Trisha.

'I don't know. I don't have mine anymore.'

'Oh, don't you? Simon would never have got rid of his.'

'I didn't want to. I was very upset when I found out.'

'Where did it go?'

'Tony gave it to his boss to pay off a debt.' It was more than she had meant to say.

'Oh, well. That doesn't surprise me.' Trisha waited in the doorway. 'He was always doing dodgy deals, that one. No-one could trust him. Not to speak ill of the dead, you understand. I'd offer you coffee but I'm going out.'

'Don't bother,' smiled Ellen. 'It was nice to see you again. Say hello to Warren for me. I hope he's overcoming his eating disorder.'

Trisha's mouth fell open. 'He hasn't got an eating disorder!'

'He must have,' said Ellen, 'he's as fat as a pig.'

*I've been wanting to say that for years,* she thought, bouncing back down the path between pairs of topiary ducks.

'Simon,' Trisha hissed down the phone the second the front door was shut, 'your bitch of a sister gave that clock Harold made for her to Tony's old boss, and there's something valuable inside it. I don't know, she was probably having an affair with him. You two used to go out drinking together, you could go round there. Yes, now, when did you think I meant? You've got the car and she's on public transport. You'll be there ages before her.'

Ellen sat and thought about the clock, built in the workshop in Seven Dials, wrapped in brown paper and string, and brought home for her birthday. The party had ended, and her friends had all gone back to their homes. The four of them sat around the kitchen table. Her mother and father, and her brother Simon. Harold had stood the package in the centre of the table. All Ellen had to do was cut the string with kitchen scissors. The paper fell away. The hands of the clock stood at midnight. The time was three minutes to twelve.

'You must wait to start it,' advised her father. 'Here's the key.' As Bea counted off the seconds she slipped the great silver handle into the clockface, and slowly turned until it was fully wound.

'Twelve o'clock, precisely,' said her father, holding the telephone receiver away from his ear so that they could all hear TIM. 'Take out the key.'

Only then did the second hand start to move. Inside, the spring tightened and the mechanism came to life, the wheels spinning, the cogs turning, hammers tripping, rods rising and dropping, the beat of the clock more regular than any human heart.

## 4. FOLDING BACK THE SKY

Ellen sat in the reception area of Barrison Waite. She pretended to read a magazine, but enviously watched employees skirting a curved glass desk where two immaculately coutured women fielded phonecalls on their headsets. Both were young and black, but she had seen no other black members of staff walk by. Presumably it was enough for the company to be seen employing minorities, without having to put them in positions of higher responsibility. No woman larger than a size eight passed her. The open-plan offices beyond were built on angled slabs of cream concrete, with recessed cubicle lighting and interior support beams of scoured steel. Ellen could see from where she sat that dirt had built up in the corners of the room, where the cleaners had not bothered to run their polishers. If these were the corridors of power, they wanted hoovering.

'Mr Donaldson can't see you, but his PA is just down there,' whispered one of the girls, pointing the way. Ellen pulled down the back of her dress, feeling self-consciously suburban. Tony's former boss had a glass box of his own in a corner of the building. She presumed it was a sign of status, even though the area was slightly smaller than Warren the Pig's bedroom.

The office was bright and cold with machine-milled air. Ellen tugged the ends of her sleeves down. Donaldson's assistant was a thin crop-headed girl who had the hunted look of a bullied child. *She could be my daughter*, thought Ellen. *If she was, I'd make her eat more carbohydrates.* 'He's very tied up,' the assistant explained. 'His appointments are usually made three to four weeks ahead, so he hardly ever has a window.'

'That's all right,' said Ellen. 'You can probably help me. My husband used to work for Mr Donaldson.' She partly explained the story of the clock, but was learning to leave out certain details. 'I thought it might still be in his office.'

'I don't know, I haven't seen it, but then I haven't been here long.'

'Could you ask him?'

'He's not interruptable, but someone else might – ' She stopped an older woman who was passing with a cardboard tray full of cappuccinos. 'Janine, have you seen an old clock in Mr Donaldson's office?'

'Someone else was just asking about his clock,' said Janine.

'A tall gentleman with a narrow beard?' asked Ellen.

'Well yes, except I don't remember a beard, he was here about twenty minutes ago.'

'What did you tell him?'

'That Mr Donaldson gave it to a colleague, when he moved into his new office.' It transpired that the colleague's wife ran an antique shop, and had traded it from him just the other day. Mr Donaldson collected sixties kitsch, and had got himself a plexiglass coffee table in return. Janine had given the tall gentleman the address of the shop. As Ellen left, the dot-matrix clock at the far end of the room clicked over 1 p.m., and several people rose from their desks. As a housewife she'd had too much time to think, but here it didn't look as if much thought was needed at all. She headed gratefully into the wet street.

'Did you get to see Donaldson?' asked Trisha, wiping the inside of her sink cupboard with an antiseptic cloth. The cordless phone was wedged under her chin.

'I couldn't get there,' Simon complained. 'The bloody car's gone down on me. Electronics. Give me something you can get a socket set round any day.'

'You'd better go down there right now, Simon, or she'll be in before you.' Trisha scrubbed at a stubborn oil-mark. 'She was always your father's favourite.'

'I don't have time for this, Trisha. I'm trying to run a business.

Someone has to bring in the money to pay for your little shopping sprees.'

Trisha gripped her cloth and shoved harder against the stain. She knew she could remove it if she made herself angry enough. 'Perhaps you'd like to shop for your own dinner, then.'

'Fine by me, I'll get a curry after the pub.'

'I hope it bloody chokes you.' She punched the call off and returned her attention to the shelf unit.

It was raining hard in Bermondsey. The warehouses behind the market were closed and bolted. In a city now bristling with steel and glass, a few enclaves had remained defiantly Victorian. Water sluiced from gutters into cobbled yards where stables had been filled with bric-à-brac; old furniture and ugly brown paintings that tourists bought for the frames. Ellen had written the address down on a slip of paper, but couldn't work out how the numbers ran. She wondered which car Simon was driving now. He owned a showroom, and changed vehicles monthly. She hoped she wouldn't have to confront him. Trisha must have called his office the moment she had left.

She finally saw the number she was looking for, painted on a wide wooden door at the rear of a narrow courtyard. She peered in through the window, but the lights were out. Dim shapes formed, a rocking horse, a sofa, some ornamental garden pots. She tried the door and found it unlocked.

'Hello?' The sound of her voice was absorbed into the gloom. The floor was cobbled and still had a section of tram-track set in it. She took a step further inside. Someone was standing in the dark at the back of the room. He was motionless but he was there, she was sure of that. 'Simon?' she called, 'is that you?' Somewhere on the floor above a clock chimed the hour, a melancholy dischord. Drawing a deep breath, she walked forward into the penumbral interior.

She could see him now, not her brother but someone much taller.

'You led me here, Mrs Farrell,' he said simply. 'Perhaps you'd like to see for yourself.' He reached across and turned on a desk

244 ♦ CHRISTOPHER FOWLER

lamp. There stood the clock. She approached it and turned the timepiece over, felt between the panels at the back and pulled the envelope free with ease. She held it lightly between her hands. The last person to touch this had been her father. The envelope contained the original property deed and a letter of transfer, signed over by Mrs Irene Keighley. She held it to her nose. It smelled of old picture books.

'There were only three more days to go,' the man said, smiling pleasantly, although she could not see his eyes.

'Oh, Alan, it's you. I wasn't expecting you.' She felt suddenly tired. 'How are you settling in? How's Christine?'

'She hates it here. The weather, the tourists. Can't wait for us to be posted somewhere else. We thought it was odd of you to go to a government office for help.'

'I needed to understand how land registry worked. I should have known they'd get in touch with you.'

'We all wish you had waited, Mrs Farrell.'

'Oh, you can call me Ellen,' she said wearily. 'We know each other well enough. Why should I have waited?' She sensed the answer already.

'As you can see, the deed is still legally binding.'

'Then I suppose you can buy it from me.'

'I'm not authorised to do that.'

'What are you authorised to do?'

She thought back to what she had seen in Vauxhall, when she had looked up from the plot of land where her family house had once stood. Across the road, through the traffic, she found herself looking at the headquarters of the British Secret Service, the MI5 Building, a confection of orange brick, deep green steel and cypress trees that had, bizarrely, become a London landmark.

And right next door to it, she had seen the empty plot of land. They had built under it. It was common knowledge that MI5 had constructed bomb-proof bunkers. They had already used the ground, it just wasn't theirs legally. The answers were all under her feet. The remains of her father's home. The remains of the Keighleys' life. The shadow-world of government security.

Rain fell from a gutter like the tick of a clock, bringing her back to the tramshed.

'Can I ask you something, Ellen?'

'Please.'

'Why on earth did you marry him?'

'Ah yes, that. Ironically enough, I was going to have a baby. We both thought it would save face. I lost it, though.'

'I'm sorry.'

'Don't be. I've lost more since.' She still had the envelope in her hand. 'What happens now?'

'You give me back the deed, you sign some papers, you get an increase in your widow's pension. There isn't really any other way that ensures your safe conduct from these premises.'

'And if I don't, I become another of those things you don't talk about, I suppose.'

'Something like that. National security. It's a pretty big deal.'

'Of course.'

'I'm glad we understand each other.'

'I have another idea,' she said.

The low white villa stood in the shadow of the Savaric cliffs, near the village of Eze. Enclosed by fragrant pine trees and grapefruit bushes, it was barely visible from the road. Nobody knew her here. She was no danger to anyone. She could come and go as she pleased.

Ellen had picked a wealthy area because she knew that the rich were virtually invisible. She had not even bothered to post her name on the letterbox at the top of the garden. She sat beside the pool and watched the changeless sky. Away from the low cloud cover of London, she felt connected to the world. The sun had settled behind the mountains, and only St Jean Cap Ferrat was still in light. Some raucous crickets had started their sawing. She felt at peace.

She thought of the bombs that had fallen, and her father's

imprecise legacy. Harold would have been happy to see her so contented. The clock stood in her kitchen, calibrating each fresh new day.